W9-AXG-689

The
Listener

RACHEL BASCH

PEGASUS BOOKS
NEW YORK LONDON

THE LISTENER

Pegasus Books LLC
80 Broad Street, 5th Floor
New York, NY 10004

First Pegasus Books cloth edition March 2015

Interior design by Maria Fernandez

ISBN: 978-1-60598-688-3

10 9 8 7 6 5 4 3 2 1

Printed in the United States of America
Distributed by W. W. Norton & Company, Inc.

For my parents, Sheldon and Norma Basch,
for teaching me the value of art and ideas

1

She was a freshman, allergic to sulfa drugs and codeine. She didn't wear corrective lenses and she didn't smoke. She wasn't taking any medication. She'd checked "yes" for vitamin supplements and "no" for birth control. At the bottom of the form on the line that read "Other," she'd printed "OTHER" in big block letters.

Malcolm slid the new patient information into his notebook and looked over at the lanky girl anchored at the far end of the couch, her head bowed. "Leah's a beautiful name." He considered sharing that he had a daughter named Leah, who was fond of reminding him that he got paid as much for what he didn't say as what he did, maybe more.

The girl abruptly shoved her hands into the pockets of her down vest and leaned her head over her flip-flops. He hoped she wasn't going to throw up. It had been a particularly viral winter, and just last week one of his younger patients in the private practice he shared with his partner Gordon had nailed a brand-new set of Legos.

"You okay?"

"I don't know." Her voice traveled toward him from somewhere near her flannel-covered shins.

He walked to the cabinets beneath the bookshelves and pulled out a bottle of water for each of them. He crossed the room and placed one of the bottles at the girl's exposed feet.

"Thank you."

He slumped back into his chair and waited. "You on anything?"

The girl jerked up her head, and a flush broke out unevenly on either side of her fine thin nose. She had steep, sharp cheekbones and marine blue eyes just visible beneath lashes heavy with black mascara. Malcolm found her almost alarmingly beautiful and had to fight the urge to stare. "Occupational hazard," he would say to his daughters, who occasionally snapped their fingers inches from his face, irritated by what they called his "slack-jawed stupefaction with random people." At stoplights and checkout counters, and, of course, in his office, he tended to look too long and too hard.

"Have you taken anything today?"

"I don't do drugs." She sipped from the water and then rested it on her bony knee. "I'm just . . . nervous."

He nodded and waited. "Nervous about what?"

"This, I guess."

Malcolm ran his thumb up and down the slight hollow above his lips. It always made him a little sad when patients said that, as if psychotherapy were like dentistry—drilling into the heart, scraping at the edges of the soul. "What about being here is making you nervous?"

She shrugged, and the ends of her straight blond hair swept noisily across the shoulders of her down vest.

2

Last September, Mental Health Services had been renamed the Center for Behavioral Health, and the college had simultaneously reduced the fifty-minute hour to thirty-five minutes, so as to better meet the growing demand for counseling at the school. Twenty-plus years in private practice had taught Malcolm that silence was an essential part of the process, and with so little time in these new sessions, it was tough to wait for the two or three or five minutes of mutual silence to mass and rout the next well-hidden truth.

"What were you hoping to talk about when you made the appointment?" he asked.

The girl slid back on the sofa cushion and crossed one leg over the other, pale bare ankle to knobby knee. "It's not the usual shit you're used to hearing in here," she said.

Kids always assumed their kinks were kinkier, their sadness more intractable, their loneliness unique in its stultifying isolation, and all of it the result of an outrageous error, an egregious reneging on the promise of happiness. It's why Malcolm loved treating adolescents. At nineteen, your pain individuated you. By fifty-three, loss and failure, the inevitable accumulation of lead in the belly, was so ubiquitous as to render you indistinct.

"I'm interested in knowing what's troubling you," he said.

"There's like a lot of very . . . *regular* kids at this school," she said.

"There's probably a lot more sadness on this campus than you think."

"Hey, I'm not saying rich kids don't have their problems." She looked out the window. Behavioral Health was in the only high-rise on the Baxter campus. From this office, you could see clear across the quad to the center of Smithport and all the way out to Casco Bay. On a map of Maine, Smithport resembled nothing so much as a poorly inflated balloon animal, its four uneven peninsulas dangling limply into the bay.

Leah shook her closed water bottle from side to side as if it were a rhythm instrument. "Where's your real office?"

"My private practice? In town, in the Watson's Mill building."

"The old fire hose factory."

"Did you grow up in town?"

She gestured toward his notebook with her jaw, and he glanced down at the intake form. She'd listed her home address as Freeman Street. A townie. When she first walked in, he'd had the gauzy sense of having met her before. Most likely he'd crossed paths with her dozens of times, at the bank, the supermarket, the rec center. "You live on campus, though," he said, reading off the form.

"Rutledge, the new dorm." She shifted her long narrow body on the couch cushion and sighed, exhaling through her nose with enough force to disturb her veil of hair. "You live in Smithport?"

"Are you worried something you tell me will get out in town?"

She pushed the tight sleeve of her thermal underwear up past her elbow and then immediately tugged it down, stretching it beyond the tips of her fingers. "You're not from here, like, originally, are you?"

Malcolm had helped more than a few students sort through their simultaneous pride and loathing at being locals. In the four years that his older daughter, Susannah, had attended Baxter, she'd never worn a single item of clothing from the college store, claiming it was "completely weird" to see a silhouette of her childhood landscape on the back of a million T-shirts.

Malcolm leaned forward in the peeling leatherette chair. "What you tell me is confidential."

She snorted.

It was ludicrous to think that trust could be earned in thirty-five minutes. These shortened sessions weren't therapy, but triage. He'd already seen five kids this morning. There were days when he felt as if he were manning an in-person Samaritans' hotline.

The girl turned her left palm up in her lap and checked the watch face on the inside of her wrist.

"We're okay on time," Malcolm said.

Leah pushed her lips into a soft round pout, and Malcolm was reminded of those pitiful little girls in beauty contests. What you saw and what you felt about what you saw, impossible to reconcile.

"Is that clock right?" she asked.

He looked up at the old Westclox on the bookshelf and nodded. Leah cradled her face in her palms.

"What're you thinking?" Malcolm asked.

"That I shouldn't have come. I'm, like, wasting your time."

"Maybe you can talk about what happened the last time you trusted someone with this secret." It was a risk, but if they didn't get to it soon, he doubted she would return. He could feel her moving toward the door, out the window. Some old panic within him fluttered, the unsecured line that could come loose and then whip.

"It was another . . . counselor or whatever. It didn't go well." Leah trailed her index finger along the raised edge of the khaki sofa cushion. "They were kind of freaked by me."

"Well, then, I give you credit for trying one of us again."

"Maybe it's just stupid. Isn't the definition of insanity doing the same thing over again and expecting different results?"

Malcolm laughed. "I haven't seen that in the diagnostic manual; not yet, anyway." He saw Leah looking back at the clock. "Let's not worry about that right now, okay?"

"Do you have another patient?"

"Do you have a class?"

"No."

"How long ago did you see this other therapist?"

"Back in high school. Not Smithport High. I had a scholarship to Casco Collegiate."

"Was it a guidance counselor you talked with back then?"

"I disgusted her."

"*Disgust's* a pretty strong word."

"It's a useful word." Leah stood and walked to the bookcase against the wall. One of the other therapists who used this office collected Kachina dolls. Leah picked one out and sat down with it, turning it over, trying to move its limbs, inspecting under its ceremonial fringed skirt. She looked up at him.

"Not mine," Malcolm said. "The Etch A Sketch and the Rubik's Cube are my contribution to the décor in here. And these." He turned to the wall behind him and pointed at the large Hopper print and the framed Roz Chast cartoon, "The Party, After You Left."

She nodded without looking up at them.

"My daughters still have most of their dolls—well, one of them, my older daughter. And she's twenty-three."

"I don't have any dolls," she said flatly.

"Did you, when you were growing up?"

"Did you?" she snapped.

Malcolm loved the dogleg. The surprise in the process was the high that kept him addicted to the job. "Yes, I did, as a matter of fact."

"They must have belonged to a sister or something."

The Raggedy Andy had belonged to his father. Malcolm's grandmother would tuck the pitiful old doll beside him as she put him to bed. Who was he not to love what his father had loved? He doubted anyone under fifty knew who Raggedy Andy was anymore.

"Do you have brothers or sisters?"

She shook her head.

"When you're not here at school, you live with . . . ?"

"My mother."

"And your father?"

Leah wedged the doll into the gap between the cushions, forcing it to stand erect. "He died when I was two and a half."

"I'm sorry."

She shrugged. "He was sixty when I was born. He was a drummer, one of my mother's music professors. We have a lot of records and some eight-tracks of him playing. He was kind of a big jazz guy, I guess."

"Do you remember him?"

"I don't know."

Malcolm's daughters had been six and nine when their mother died. His younger daughter—his Leah—had recently confessed that the only certain memory she had of Laura was of disappointing her.

"How're you feeling right now?"

"Embarrassed."

"Why?" he asked, softly.

"This position, are you like considered a faculty member?"

"I'm an employee of the college."

"Do you know people on the faculty here? I mean, is that who you hang out with?"

"Are you concerned that I might know some of your professors?" She shrugged.

"It's likely that I know several of your professors, but they'll never know that I know you. If we run into each other on campus or in town, and you're with friends or your mother, I won't acknowledge you unless you greet me first. You're free to ignore me or introduce me however you like."

"You mean, I could lie?" She brightened.

"I mean, if this relationship is a private one for you, say what you need to say to maintain that privacy."

She pulled the doll from between the cushions and walked her across the tops of her legs. "Do you think there's a difference between a lie and a secret?"

"Do *you* think there's a difference between a lie and a secret?"

"Well . . . lies have a more negative thing about them than secrets. A secret's like . . . just . . . there. But a lie . . . you have to go out of your way to tell a lie."

"Secrets seem more passive, not quite so bad?" Malcolm felt his pulse shift gears, as if he were suddenly ascending a hill.

"Some secrets are necessary, right?"

"Are you asking me?"

"There's military secrets," she said.

He nodded and noted the alteration in her engagement, as if she'd latched on to something.

"Those are like secrets that actually protect people," she said.

Malcolm clasped his hands together and leaned toward her. "Who are you protecting by keeping your secret a secret?"

Leah shrugged, encircled the Kachina doll with her thumb and forefinger, and walked across the room toward the bookcase. She eased the doll back onto the shelf with a gentleness usually reserved for living things. Then, as she turned to go back to her seat, she stopped in front of the small ceramic mirror by the door. She was fascinated by something. Malcolm waited, watched as she turned one long leg inward, twisting her torso for a slightly different view of her cheekbone. She was close enough to the glass to be fogging it, engaged in a quasi-medical scan of her face. Malcolm pivoted his whole body in order to watch her watching herself, and he wondered if she'd consciously engineered this voyeuristic moment. He cleared his throat. She turned, made a move to place her hands in pants pockets that weren't there, walked back across the room, and sat down on the sofa.

"Can you tell me who you're protecting?"

"There are people I care about who could get hurt, you know?"

He leveled his gaze now at the girl. "Have you thought that maybe you're right, then, to keep this secret to yourself?"

Leah shook her head, and with her fists clenched she uncrossed her legs and shifted her body on the couch. Malcolm was reminded of a morphing action figure he used in play therapy. If you pulled on the limbs and rotated the torso, a completely different being emerged. He stared at Leah now, half-expecting this palpable anger to transform her.

"You make it sound like keeping this . . . to myself would make me feel the same as if I told it."

Her fury passed quickly, and the additional musculature she'd exhibited only moments before vanished. Despair was limp. "Do you know what you're sad about?" he asked.

"This." She tugged at her clothes and slapped her thighs, the sound of her long thin hands oddly dull against the flannel.

Malcolm set down his notebook and watched as she kicked off her sandals, then pounded barefoot across the room toward the mirror. She stood there and cupped her fingers at the edge of her forehead and tugged.

Leah's blond hair was gone, a wig tossed onto an empty chair.

Malcolm stood, instinctively, as if under threat—what kind he wasn't sure. As he moved in the direction of the mirror, Leah shook off the down vest, gripped the hem of her thermal shirt, and began to pull it over her head and her real, chin-length, black hair. Malcolm watched as Leah hid inside the folds of the shirt, face obscured, but chest revealed. A male chest. And then the shirt was on the carpet, and Malcolm was facing a half-naked boy, a freshman he'd seen for a few sessions back in the fall. *Noah*, Malcolm remembered after a moment, the kid's name riding in on a wave of regret.

Malcolm moved one step closer toward the boy, with the impulse to hug him. Instead, he stopped and said softly, "I didn't know."

The boy let out a guttural sound from somewhere at the back of his throat and lurched into Malcolm, his hands awkwardly at his sides, as if he were in restraints. Malcolm encircled him, his palms on Noah's cool bare back. Noah's heart was pounding so that Malcolm could feel it in his own chest. They stood like that while doors in the outer offices opened and closed, bells rang in the clock tower to mark the hour, someone whistled through his teeth in the quad below. Malcolm used the time and the boy in his arms to steady himself. He was not used to missing the mark in his work. He'd always been able to divine other people's pain. He was in the pain business, and he was good at it.

As Noah began to cry—a choking, strangling cry—Malcolm pinched his own wrist hair. He waited, the two of them superimposed on the ghostly third, until the crying moved into a more regular rhythm. He pulled one hand from Noah's back and reached into the pocket of his corduroy trousers for his handkerchief. He pressed it into Noah's right hand, which was still hanging limply at his side, as if he were a stroke victim or a crude hand puppet—all head and no limbs.

Malcolm guided the boy over to the couch. "You must be cold," he said, and before Noah could respond, Malcolm walked back to the abandoned costume, hesitated for a moment, then picked up the baby blue thermal shirt. He turned it so that it was no longer inside out and handed it to Noah. Reversing the shirt struck Malcolm as strangely intimate, the quotidian action of a parent. He turned from Noah while he dressed, a ludicrous attempt at privacy given the circumstances.

9

"That was very brave, what you did. Very courageous," Malcolm said, sitting down next to Noah on the couch.

Noah blew his nose and then placed his face in his hands. He ran his thumbs along the inside corners of both eyes and wiped his blackened fingers on the handkerchief.

"How're you feeling now?" Malcolm struggled to keep his gaze off his own feet.

"Numb."

Malcolm nodded.

"I told you . . ."

Malcolm turned on the couch so that he could look at Noah's face, at least at half of it. "What? What did you tell me?"

"I warned you . . . that you'd be disgusted."

"What makes you think I'm disgusted?" Sitting beside Noah, Malcolm felt large and graceless. Each time he moved, even slightly, the boy was jostled.

"How could you not be?"

"I'm going to tell you how I feel, even though it's your feelings we're focused on here. But since you've taken the risk of being so honest with me . . . I feel badly that I didn't know this was something you wanted to tell me. That must have been very difficult. I think maybe you're confused—"

"I'm not confused—"

Malcolm placed his large hand on top of Noah's pale slender one. The reddish hair on his thick knuckles glinted beneath the track lights. "Let me finish. What I was going to say was that I think you're confusing your own disgust with mine."

Noah slid his hand out from under Malcolm's and moved so that his back was resting against one arm of the sofa. Then he pulled up his bare feet to sit cross-legged and dropped the sodden handkerchief on top of his backpack.

From what Malcolm could remember, Noah had come in that first time chiefly complaining of loneliness. In the subsequent session, they'd focused, for the most part, on practical matters—things he might do to more fully engage in the communal life of the school. Malcolm had been struck by the boy's looks. He recalled thinking that Noah was beautiful, not necessarily effeminate, just perfected, like an artist's creation—fair skin, thick, wavy black hair, and deep blue eyes. At the end of that initial session, Malcolm remembered jotting in the margins of his notes, "Get him to realize his own beauty."

Noah lifted his eyes, the long black lashes still curled stiffly upward. He scanned the room, looking for a place to rest his gaze. When he settled on the shelf filled with Kachina dolls, he said, "Just don't lie to me. I mean, don't. . . . The thing about disgust is—it can't be like co-opted by PC bullshit, you know?"

"No. Not really."

Noah ran his hands through his hair, pulling it into a momentary ponytail. "Disgust is honest. I don't want you telling me what you think I want to hear. I want an honest reaction."

"I'm pretty much in the truth business, Noah."

Malcolm caught the beginning of a smile, or maybe just a twitch. He leaned into his corner of the couch and touched the tips of his fingers to the whorl at the back of his head. "How are you different when you're Leah?"

"It's how I think of myself to myself."

Malcolm nodded. He looked over at the clock and then at Noah. "We have to stop?"

"For today." Malcolm made no move to get up.

"I, like, already have another appointment scheduled. . . . Which is a bonus of having a split personality." Noah laughed a careful half laugh.

"You don't really believe—"

"No. I mean. . . . No. It's just. . . ."

"I certainly don't want you leaving here concerned about a multiple-personality disorder, because that's—"

"No. It's not that. I'm not worried about that."

"What *are* you worried about?" Malcolm might have asked the question of himself. His pulse was idling on high. He pressed the heel of his hands into the wide wale of the fabric on the thigh of his pants.

"Well, you said a lot of stuff, but you never told me what you thought, you know?"

Malcolm was confused. He leaned in on his elbows, as if to literally bridge the communication gap.

"I mean, what did you think, you know, of Leah?" Noah blushed deeply, then parted his lips to speak again. "Do you think she's beautiful?"

2

O nce inside the handicapped bathroom, Noah locked the door.
He pulled the dark blond wig from his backpack and balled
his fist into a little skull for the hair. Jiggling his wrist, he
attempted to shake out the tangles. The wig was the first thing he'd
ever charged on a credit card. So far he'd only paid $65 of the $540
it cost. He didn't want to put it away uncombed.

He flattened the brushed wig as best he could and slid it into a
two-gallon-size plastic bag. Hair behind plastic was always creepy.
His mother kept a lock of his baby hair tucked in an album of pictures
from when he was first born. The Ziploc bag with the wig looked

like something the father character on an episode of *CSI* would get handed when he showed up at the morgue.

Noah placed the bag in his backpack and pulled on a pair of socks. He traded his sandals for running shoes and took out the eye-makeup remover he carried in an unmarked squeeze bottle. He grabbed a wad of toilet paper and leaned into the mirror above the large, low handicap sink. It had taken him over thirty minutes to get Leah ready in here earlier this morning. He'd been applying his foundation when someone had knocked on the door. He'd lied, saying he'd be just a minute. The whole time he was doing his eyes, he'd worried that some guy was pissing his wheelchair. He'd wondered if he should exit the bathroom limping or drooling, one arm hanging twisted like it had been put on wrong at the factory. What was an added tic here or there when you were crossing over the double yellow to begin with?

How long had he sat on that couch with mascara streaking his face like this? Was Dowd blind, or just polite? Noah ripped the sodden toilet paper in half and swept each piece under his eyes from the inside corners to the outer, the way he'd seen the saleswomen do at the Macy's makeup counter. Dowd hadn't mentioned Leah's appearance. Noah wanted Leah to look on the outside the way he felt on the inside—winsome. He'd first read the word in seventh grade, in one of his mother's ancient novels. He wanted Dr. Dowd to find Leah winsome. He wanted to impress Dowd, to reveal not just something secret about himself, but something extraordinary.

His initial take back in October was that Dowd with his button-down shirt, wire-rim glasses, and oxblood loafers was going to prove nothing more than a cultural and societal enforcement officer. Even his graying blond hair was ramrod-straight. It refused a part and hung directly down the fall line of his forehead, making him look like a middle-aged Cub Scout. Noah had spent much of that first session stacking up reasons never to return. But then in the middle of their blah, blah, blahing, Dowd leaned forward, and it was like he was pressing the ZOOM button on top of the camera, allowing Noah to fill the whole frame. "What's it like for you, right now, talking to me about all this?" Dowd had asked. And everything in the room quieted. The fog of continuous existence lifted. And Noah thought for a second that maybe Dowd knew, that anyone so attentive might also have emotional x-ray vision, and that even if he didn't know, he'd be genuinely interested in finding out.

Exiting the Behavioral Health Building, Noah added to the mess of sneaker treads on the snow-dusted walkway. It was lunchtime, but he couldn't see going to the dining hall. Waiting in line at the grill there made him feel like an unwitting participant in a social experiment gone horribly wrong. He stopped at the kiosk in front of the chapel and slid his backpack from his shoulders. He slipped his partly numb right hand down beyond the plastic bag with the wig, the sandals, the Ziplocs filled with makeup, and felt around for his gloves. He unzipped the side pockets of his down vest and searched himself. There were a couple of snow-dampened flyers for spring-break trips to Cozumel and Belize. He'd be spending break at the too-blue, two-bedroom bungalow his mother had bought when she'd gotten the job teaching music at Baxter fifteen years ago. For every flyer about a philosophy lecture or an amazing way for college students to earn money NOW, there were three bright orange notices announcing meetings of the Genderqueer Club. Noah zipped up his backpack and slung it over one shoulder. Who was the fiend with the staple gun who papered over opportunities to get smart or get rich with invitations to a club that had no committed members?

For all the planning this morning had necessitated, Noah had not planned on crying. Walking through the waiting room and into Dowd's office, he'd experienced a rush of adrenaline that almost made him sick. He'd rehearsed the big reveal, the how and when of it, but he hadn't thought beyond that show-stopping number. He had not imagined that half-dressed and completely exposed, the nesting dolls in full view, he'd be embraced by Dowd without hesitation. Nothing like it had ever happened to him before. His head had landed in the center of Dowd's chest, as if all along that's where he'd belonged.

Noah jumped when the chapel bell rang twelve-thirty, and two girls laughed as they passed by.

"Fuck you," he said, audibly, stunned that he'd said anything, much less out loud, possibly as loud as the chapel bells. The blood rushed to his face, where he doubted it could all be contained.

"Exxxcuuuuse me." Tory Liggett, who was in the ensemble of *Les Mis* with him, stopped and faced him. She was bosomy and blond. Her friend, equally bosomy but blonder, continued to walk for a few paces.

A tall, well-fed guy trailing a few feet behind the girls looked up from his phone and over at Noah. He pushed back the hood of his forest green Baxter College Sailing Team sweatshirt. "Really? What'd you just say to them?"

Noah recognized the kid from having waited on him at Homefires, where he worked all summer and on and off during the school year. Skipper, here, was one of the guys Noah had ratted out to the owner for boosting an entire flat of boutique-size Heinz ketchup bottles.

"Did you just curse at my friends?" The guy began to move in Noah's direction, leading with his cleft chin.

Noah looked from the approaching boy to the stationary girls, his mind flooding so quickly with all that might go wrong that some part of it simply floated free and he found himself studying them—the MAC lipstick (Crème de la Femme?), the straight-ironed hair, the diamond studs, their purses (those soft bags with the paisley designs).

"I know you," the boy said, as if this were the primary reason they were all gathered together as the snow turned to sleet.

Noah inhaled, searching his own formless, quilted being for something solid. It was hard to stand up for yourself when you didn't know who your self was.

"He's a fucking freshman." Tory slid two manicured fingers along the shaft of her streaked blond hair.

"He's in *Les Mis*." The friend was congratulating herself on having made the connection. "He's a—"

"Tranny." The guy was working his thumb and forefingers like pincers aimed in the direction of Noah's chest. "Come on." He mimed a nipple tweak. "Before it asks to borrow a dress for Saturday night."

Noah told himself to turn and walk. It was as if he had been waiting for them to dismiss him. Jesus, why had he even stopped to begin with? What the fuck was wrong with him? As he headed away from the chapel, he heard their laughter mixed with the freezing rain pinging against his down vest, a riotous orchestra of stinging bites.

He had twenty minutes until Sociology, enough time to get a sandwich or a protein bar, but now he couldn't eat. This happened a lot. Everything happened a lot, everything except for feeling normal, calm, some sort of okay. If Dowd couldn't help him . . . expecting that anyone might help him was probably delusional. That's what Paul said. He'd been friends with Paul all through elementary and high school. Paul was gay, in-your-face gay, as if his whole personality could be summed up by saying "I'm gay." And all the time Paul was after him to come out, the whole business like some varsity team on which Noah was being offered a place.

Noah pulled open the double doors to the student center and moved with the mass of wet wool and sodden down, toward the post office. He dialed the combination to open his mail box and pulled out a yellow slip. Maybe the best thing about college was being able to send away for things and receive them in the privacy of your own post office box. As he waited at the service window, he stared at the open metal shelves stacked with padded envelopes and cartons from Apple and Verizon, L.L. Bean, Nordstrom.

"Hey!" He heard the voice at the same time he felt long thin fingers drape over his shoulders and tap his collarbone.

"Hey." He turned to face his mother, then looked back quickly to see if the postal clerk behind the counter had found his package.

"I was hoping I might run into you. I got this visiting mandolin player. It's my turn. I went all last semester without babysitting a musician. So anyway, he's coming to the house for dinner tonight, and then we're going to Monroe's."

Noah turned slightly from his mother and very insignificantly shook his head at the clerk, who was walking toward the beaten-up little mail window with a shrunken, coffin-shaped box.

"I'm making a chicken tagine and maybe—"

"This thing's been giving us the creeps for two days." The clerk thrust the box through the window. Noah nodded, turned his attention to his mother, and then reached his arm behind him, feeling for the window and the little pine box he knew contained a pair of Dead to Rights black mules, size eleven. He flexed his fingers, searching for a corner of the box while never breaking eye contact with his mother. "Are you . . . going to make . . . "—Noah grappled with the package behind him—"chocolate mousse for this guy too?"

"What is that? It looks expensive—the packaging." His mother tucked her wavy black hair behind her ears and elongated her already swan-like neck. A friend of his mother's had once drawn a caricature of her, riffing on the body of a guitar. It was mostly neck. For a while, it had hung in the bathroom.

"No, no, it's just like a marketing thing. It's a . . . a water bottle. I needed a new Nalgene."

She nodded. "Where're you headed now?"

"Kirby."

She nodded again and reached into the pocket of her long, faded down coat. "Want some gum?"

"No, thanks." Back when Noah was little and that coat was bright red and too big for him, he liked to wear it to take out the trash, or to measure the snow, or to look at the stars.

"I'll walk that way," she said, as if he'd asked her.

He pivoted on one foot and scooped the sarcophagus shoebox up under one arm. "I should probably go to my room first and drop this off." He moved away from the mail window and started toward the door to the outside.

His mother followed, tucking her hair into her Gorbachev hat and retying her scarf. "Stick it in my office, if you want, so you don't have to go all the way across campus. I promise I won't use it. Is there really only a water bottle in there? What a waste of . . . everything—though it is kind of cool." She tilted her head to get a better look at the box welded to his side.

He could feel sweat begin to permeate at least one of the two genders' worth of underwear he had on. The thing was, he knew she wouldn't look in the box if he left it with her.

"You could bring a friend if you want. Uncle Billy's coming."

"There's an incentive."

"The first set at Monroe's is at nine, okay? So, we're going to eat like at six."

Noah hated Monroe's. No, that wasn't really true. He hated the fact that his mother was so uncharacteristically embracing of the place. No, that really wasn't it either. It was just the hold the place had on her and she on it. Everyone there thought Carmen Shipley was a goddess. He really didn't like watching her perform. Paul said it was because he was jealous. Not only was she talented, but she could get up in front of people and actually wear a dress. And even if Noah had the balls to do that, Paul said he'd never look as good as Carmen. But the truth was, he looked damn good in some of her clothes. And he wasn't jealous of her playing. He had no interest in classical guitar. It was just that after watching her perform, people always thought they knew something about her, something private and true, when really it was all a trick. And Noah thought the trick especially mean.

"I know you don't love Monroe's," she said, fishing in her pocket for the empty gum wrapper.

He smiled. She often guessed what he was thinking—well, some of it, anyway. He waited until she'd carefully folded the silver wrapper around the chewed gum, and he leaned in and kissed her a bit wetly, like an unthinking kid, on her cool cheek.

"Love you," she whispered. "See you tonight," she said, more loudly.

As they separated, a guy—maybe a professor, maybe someone from administration or the state mental hospital—came out of nowhere and slapped her on the back. "Cara!" he yelled. "How's it going?"

She laughed and tugged on the scarf she'd knotted at the front of her throat, and then she was too far away for Noah to hear what she said, but he watched them walk, moving away from him, shoulders bumping.

There was a time, around second grade and up until fifth or sixth, when he'd hoped for a new father. He didn't know anyone then who had only one parent, and he thought his mother should fix that, get them regular and normal, like everyone else. She had never dated when he was younger, not that he was aware of, anyway. She went out at night plenty, but always to a gig, and sometimes she traveled for a few days to perform or to attend a conference. Once, when he was in middle school and his Uncle Billy was supposedly taking care of him, Billy had asked Noah if he thought his mother ever got any. That was Billy, completely tactless, but, according to his mother, with a heart of gold.

Noah pushed the tight cuff of his long underwear up over his watch and considered his options. It was as if the contents of the box under his arm were alive. He could hear the shoes rubbing against each other. He was desperate to have a look at them, to run his fingers along their slender heels, and of course to see how his foot, his gait, his carriage, his whole self might be altered by them. But he didn't want to miss Sociology. "Oh, so you're a rule-keeper," Dr. Dowd had said to him when he mentioned back in the fall that he'd never cut a class. He could run into the men's room in Kirby and hunker down in one of the stalls for a minute and open the package. But then he'd have to carry the box into class in the lecture hall, an amphitheater that never failed to trigger images of lions chowing on Christians. There was no way to fit the box into his backpack. So he'd have to clutch it, with all the packing tape stripped, completely capable of spilling its contents, *likely* to spill its contents.

Okay, chill, just chill, he told himself.

Noah stopped at the soda machine in the lobby of Kirby and fed it some coins and a sweaty single. Did anyone's double identity ever kill them? Directly, not through drugs or choking on your own vomit or all the dark stuff most people thought of when they thought of drag queens, like stained sheets and needles and. . . . He tried to iron the dollar on the thigh of his flannel pants. Everyone knew that secrets caused anxiety and anxiety caused heart attacks. What if some day, soon even, someone would have to call his mother to tell her he'd been found dead—not ill or dying, just dead. His mother wanted him to meditate. She told him it was like having a home base to which you could always return. Soul work, she called it, and she did it every day, putting a sign on her bedroom door, at least when he was around. The Snapple came banging down the machine and Noah placed the shoebox on the floor between his feet and reached in for the cold bottle. Fuck, this sucked.

"Oh my god, Dead to Rights. You ordered Dead to Rights shoes. I hate you." Amanda, he didn't know her last name but she was in his Victorian Lit class, had dropped her backpack and was unzipping her coat, as if the interaction with these shoes was about to get intimate.

"God, I'm going to be late for Soc."

"No, you're not. Let me see. I didn't even know they made guys' shoes." She pulled off her gloves with her teeth and bent down toward the box.

"Yeah," he said. "They're not. They don't. I don't think so. I don't know. These are for my mother. For some reason, I don't know, they got sent to my box—some mix-up."

"Your mother's really going to wear them?" Amanda didn't bother to look up at him, for which he was thankful. Instead, she slipped into a crouch beside the box, as if it were a puppy.

Noah shrugged and smiled.

"Your mother's cool, isn't she? I've heard that." Amanda finished removing her coat and tossed it on the floor. "Christ, it's hot in here."

The lobby of Kirby was suddenly thick with students shaking off melted snow. Now he really was going to be late. No way would he be able to have a look inside the box before class. "See you later," he said abruptly even as he was turning away from the girl. Jesus, he so sucked.

Noah slipped into the only available seat, which was in a row uncomfortably close to the front of the room. He pulled out his notebook and began to write automatically, transcribing what the professor was saying without really hearing him. The reading assignment had been from *Uniforms: Why We Are What We Wear*, and Noah had read the excerpt somewhat frantically, hoping to find something of himself, his behavior mentioned in its pages. He'd gotten to the end of the two chapters with a perfect view of what hadn't been included and only a vague sense as to what had. He'd promised himself he would stop doing that, tearing through books looking for some kind of psychological DNA match. He'd spent the summer between tenth and eleventh grade borrowing books through inter-library loan, none of which he could enter on his summer reading list. He was like a chop shop mechanic, stripping perfectly coherent books for the one or two bits that fit with his own missing parts. Reading that way was unfair to the books. And besides, there was always the internet—blogs, chat rooms, bulletin boards in which he merely bore witness, remaining mute, reading through other people's stories, the enumeration of their obsessions, their passions, their interminable, misunderstood pain. It was like scanning a Red Cross list after a disaster in search of your own name.

The lights had been dimmed so that they could see a bunch of slides. He apologized to the girl next to him when he bumped her trying to kick off his right sneaker beneath the table top. While looking up at a slide of a soldier in full dress, he carefully placed his sneakerless foot on top of the Dead to Rights shoebox, anything to stop his racing pulse.

In those sessions back in the fall, Noah had only told Dowd that he thought Baxter was the wrong place for him. Even though he had friends, he was lonely, unaccountably lonely. Dowd hadn't asked him if he were a virgin, which he was, still. He hadn't asked him if he were gay, which Noah couldn't be sure of. Instead, Dowd asked him who he was, who he wanted to be. And when Noah couldn't answer, Dowd said that growth was about becoming more and more yourself, and nothing was more difficult than being your true self. And he said he really looked forward to getting to know Noah's true self.

The PowerPoint went off and the lights came on, and the information Noah had been suppressing gushed beyond the confines of the usual pathways. What had he done this morning? What was he thinking, showing up in Dowd's office dressed like Leah? He'd actually exposed Leah to the receptionist in Behavioral Health. Anyone getting on or off the elevator in the crazy kids' waiting room might have seen him. It was no different from taking a crap in public, really, if you thought about it, which he didn't want to. He was certain it was possible to die of shame, annihilated from the inside out. What he'd done was irrevocable. What made him think he could trust Dowd? Dowd, with his regulation-code life. Right now Dowd was most likely trying to pawn him off on some psychiatrist, someone who would want to medicate him, or hospitalize him. Whatever affection Dowd had shown for him, and Noah thought it was real, had been real—he'd chosen to detonate, because he couldn't fucking keep a secret.

"Here." The girl to his right, the one he'd bumped because he just had to feel the pulse of his new shoes through his socks, was shaking a stack of handouts in front of his face.

"Oh, sorry."

"You're someplace else." She slid the papers toward him. "Hope it's better than this hole."

Noah smiled. He took the top sheet, the rubric for the midterm paper, and passed the rest to his left. "Not really," he said.

"That's too bad."

Noah saw that they were wearing the same down vest, but hers was black. Everything she had on, sweatpants and sweatshirt, was black. She might as well have been working stage crew. The only dash of color was her red hair, which she'd tried, unsuccessfully, to hide by stuffing it into the hood of her sweatshirt. She was what his mother would call "a big girl." She had a plush face that reminded him of a Cabbage Patch doll—a little overstuffed in spots, but welcoming.

"The buzzing halogens of the mind." She tugged on the drawstrings of her sweatshirt hood.

For a minute he had the impulse to touch her, or something that belonged to her. He patted her spiral notebook. "I know."

"You don't usually sit here."

"No. I like to sit on the side, but I was late." Noah worked his foot back into his sneaker. Everyone was standing up, zipping, shoving, snapping, coughing. He reached beneath his seat and retrieved his box.

"You a freshman?"

Noah nodded.

"Sophomore."

He nodded again. He tried to think of what would naturally come next. "You live on campus?"

"Rutledge," she said.

"No way. I've never seen you. I live there, fifth floor."

"No one sees me. I'm always working. I have like seventeen shitty jobs. Being a student is my sideline."

He followed her up the shallow carpeted steps, where kids sometimes sat when there was a guest lecturer and the room got too crowded.

"Where do you work?" He grabbed the door from a kid who'd been in his Comp class last fall. The boy gave a nod.

"I work in the kitchen at the Grille Room, at the Sci Li, sometimes in the reserve room at Baldwin, and in the winter I have a snow removal service."

"You have a plow?"

"No, I do walkways, some driveways—for old guys, retired professors."

"Like with a shovel?" Noah followed her as they exited Kirby.

She shrugged. "Someone's got to. Thirty dollars for the driveways on Cardinal Place. I can do two an hour. Not bad."

He clutched his shoebox, which was wet now from the snow that had melted off his sneakers during class. "I work down in town at Homefires."

She nodded. "Real job."

"I work there all summer, too, so. . . ."

Noah was following the girl now out toward the fieldhouse, a place he had no reason to be going. He pushed back the sleeve of his long underwear and tried to look at his watch. The pine box smelled wet. He hoped the shoes were wrapped in plastic. They had to be. You couldn't go sending shoes around the world, in worldwide weather, without taking precautions.

"I wish I could lose the work-study thing. The money sucks." She rubbed the heel of her hand against her much-pierced left ear. "They think they're doing you a favor—but I'd be much better off just getting my own job. Can't wait tables, though."

They were both still walking, which was making it even harder for him to read his watch. Just as Noah widened the angle of his right elbow, the one responsible for holding the box against his ribcage, the big girl reached over with her broad knuckles and rapped once. "Cool-looking box," she said. The box shot down through the tunnel of his arm, slammed onto the wet pavement, and split open.

The upper part of the shoe was done in a pebbled, ebony leather, and the heels looked to be brushed nickel or steel. They hadn't been wrapped in plastic, but they had been surrounded by plastic air pillows that now lay on the wet walkway like malfunctioning parachutes.

"Special occasion," the girl said, taking a step back.

Noah didn't have the stomach to look up at her, at this person whose name was still unknown to him. He could feel his pulse, and it wasn't a good feeling, all that throbbing in the calves, the neck, the temple. His father had died of a stroke. He "stroked out," his mother sometimes said, as if the act of dying was, in fact, active. Maybe he'd had a secret too.

The girl knelt, her knees filling the space allotted by her sweatpants. They were knees you could stand on, sit on, certainly bounce on. She lifted one shoe, gently holding it at the toe and under the infinitesimal point of the heel. "Can you really walk in these?"

Noah crouched beside her and reached for the other shoe. Fingering the heel as if it were the stem of a wineglass, he pulled the shoe briefly under his nose, then slid it into his backpack.

They were beyond the central hub of the campus, and the few students who walked by seemed oblivious to his humiliation.

The girl stood and audibly sniffed the shoe. "It's real, huh? Real leather. Gotta love that smell."

Noah nodded.

Before handing him the shoe, she pinched it by its skinny heel and lightly touched the pointy toe to her soft, pink cheek. "I'm Alex," she said. "No joke. It's like they knew."

Noah reached over and took the shoe from her, barely unzipping the backpack again, to tuck it inside. The blood pounding inside his head was so noisy, he could hardly hear her. "Excuse me?"

"Your name?" she asked.

"Oh, sorry. Noah. Sorry . . . I thought you said . . . something else. Sorry."

"I did."

Noah cautiously placed the backpack over one shoulder. He didn't look up at her, but instead at the sad pine coffin lying deconstructed on the slushy path.

"I mean, you name a kid like when they're minutes old. How could they have known how right they'd be?"

Noah took a step toward the shattered box. He could never litter, never just leave it there. That would be wrong, plus his name was on the damn thing.

"I mean . . . well, actually, you probably have to look at me, which lots of people don't really like doing . . . to know what I mean. You'd have to. . . ."

A secretary from the music department biked down the path, forcing Noah and Alex onto the grass. Noah knelt and picked up the neatly split wood with his gloves. When he straightened, he noticed that Alex was standing still, as if giving him a chance to take her in. He felt again what he'd felt in the lecture hall, an overwhelming desire to touch her. It was like going to the beach. When you arrived, you had to sink into the sand, roll in it to believe you were finally, really there. It didn't seem possible to know this girl without laying his hands on her. He pulled off one glove and began to reach up. "Never mind," she said abruptly. "God, I didn't mean to get weird on you."

Noah blushed, embarrassed at his aborted move, hand in midair. He knocked away the lame hand with the one holding the remains of the shoebox. "Talk about weird, huh?" He tried to smile.

"Sorry I made you drop them. It was a really cool box. You probably wanted to save it. I'm not going to—"

He shook his head.

"I mean, I don't believe in outing people, you know?"

He nodded. "I should go," he said, as the chapel bells rang. "I don't think you really can out someone, anyway." He needed to get this last bit in under the wire, before she turned. "I mean, someone else. If I don't know who I am, I mean, how could you out me?"

Her face widened, causing her cheeks to reconfigure themselves into two highly polished orbs, more heat than flesh.

"I know," she said, gripping the sleeve of his coat with force and pulling on it excitedly. "God!" She punched him, not that lightly, in the arm. "I should go. See you in class."

Noah nodded, holding up his empty hand to wave. And right before she turned, she grabbed it, hard, and squeezed twice.

3

Malcolm didn't like the indoor pool at the Baxter Rec Center, but moving his body through water was one of the only ways to clear his mind of everyone else's stories, at least until May when he could put the Rhodes back in the water. On nights like tonight when it felt unforgiving to cross an icy parking lot and strip down to nearly nothing before diving into underheated, chemically treated water, he liked to think of his body as a boat. He could steer it, speed it up or slow it down, slice through the water or drift.

His father's father had begun taking him sailing when he was seven. His grandparents had retired by then to Smithport, to their farm perched above an inlet, the property sloping down to an old boathouse and a series of docks. One of Malcolm's earliest memories was of being carried in his father's arms from the brilliant light of a hot summer afternoon into the dark, salty cool of the boathouse, an indoor space where the outdoors could swell up at any moment, the wake of a boat way out eventually making itself known, soaking the weathered floorboards, causing a great creaking and rattling within. Malcolm had loved the orderliness of everything having to do with sailing and maintaining boats. Excess line was coiled in the gunnels and about the cleats at the end of the dock. Unused sails were folded, like the flag, in a series of triangles and stored in the sail loft. And the orange life vests his grandmother called Mae Wests hung in ascending size on a pegboard inside the boathouse. Malcolm's grandfather, a psychiatrist, had undergone his medical training in the 1920s, and he had a tendency to address Malcolm on the boat the way a kindly but all-knowing surgeon would speak to his scrub nurse. "Everything in its place, and a place for everything," a favorite saying of his grandfather's, was occasionally extended to include people as well.

Malcolm did a flip turn, pushed off from the end of the pool, and allowed himself to glide part way down the lane. It had been a long time since an encounter with a patient had rocked his confidence the way this thing with Noah Burrell had today. Malcolm was not used to feeling inadequate at the office. As he picked up the pace, pulling one elbow and then the next out of the water faster and faster, he could feel and hear his own exhaled breaths bubbling continuously behind him. He was reminded of the way the centerboard of his grandfather's old catboat used to literally hum on a beat. He swam one more lap, made a guess at what the clock on the gym wall would show, and wiped the water from his eyes. The pool closed at eight, and he needed to get in the seventy-two laps tonight.

His father had killed himself on the day that Malcolm had finally learned to swim. It was Labor Day weekend, and Malcolm's father was visiting, out on a pass from McLean's. Malcolm had been at his grandparents' for most of the summer, and he was desperate to master the dead man's float before he had to return to New York with his mother for the start of the school year. Being able to float was the prerequisite for being able to sail with his grandfather and, he hoped, his father.

He'd spent that Saturday afternoon at South Cove with the Quillens, the family next door. The shallows of the sandy beach were almost warm. With his chin barely grazing the water, he walked on his hands, elbows and wrists locked stiffly in place. Malcolm had seen his grandfather dress his father earlier that summer, tugging an undershirt down over his head, bending his father's rigid arms through one sleeve hole and then the other. Malcolm had watched the push and pull, had felt it in his own shoulders and back and chest. It hadn't been all that long since someone had last dressed him, and he knew the shame of it. Over and over Malcolm lowered his face into the water of South Cove. First two hands planted deep into the cool and shifting sand, then one, then just a finger, until the ripple effect from a wave or the wake of a boat or a splashing kid had knocked his hold on the oily bottom, and he was doing the dead man's float.

He hadn't wanted Mrs. Quillen to follow him into the house when she dropped him off at the end of the afternoon. He was in a hurry to find his grandfather and go with him down to the dock. Malcolm knew it would be harder there, scarier. But doing the dead man's float had felt just like flying. No super powers involved. It was intrinsic, as intrinsic as the belief that everything within and without could be made right.

The house was empty, hot and still. They walked through the kitchen and then out the side door to the yard. Mrs. Quillen had reached for his hand when they saw the little crowd down by the water. Too many people, he thought, were balanced on the dock.

His father's body was found that evening before it got dark, about a half mile out into the bay. His father had taken the Quillens' aluminum canoe, slicing his wrists against the sharp metal of the bow either before or after he'd paddled out beyond the inlet and into deeper water. Using a bowline, he'd attached a thirty-five-pound Danforth to his waist. And with a reef knot he'd secured himself to the canoe so that both he and the boat could be returned to their owners.

It would be two years before Malcolm would swim again. His grandmother eventually made the connection. "Some call it the 'jellyfish float,'" she said, before launching into a lesson on the Australian crawl and the life-saving power of motion.

⌒∞⌒

Malcolm stopped just inside the double doors of the rec center, patting down the pockets of his parka for his cell phone. He checked all three sections of his backpack, then walked to his car, hoping to see his phone in the cup holder. He pressed the dome light and looked in the back seat, lifting the box he'd promised to send his daughter's boyfriend. The very thoughtful Matt wanted to digitize the old audio cassettes of Laura singing as a surprise for Susannah's birthday. Certainly an engagement ring wouldn't be far behind, a prospect which gave Malcolm the vague but nagging sensation that he was approaching the edge (if not the end) of something, like moving about in the pitch black when you knew you were in the vicinity of a flight of stairs. Some slight shift in the heat or heft of the air around you signaled that your next step might not be across, but down.

Malcolm started the car and began the serpentine drive out of the campus toward his office in town, the last place he remembered having his phone.

⌒∞⌒

The front entrance of the Watson's Mill Building was locked, and as Malcolm pulled out his key, he looked around him. After dark, the place couldn't help but revert to its originally industrial, intrinsically evil nature. During the renovation of the building, the local paper had run stories from its archives about several dubious workplace accidents and the unsolved murder of a shop steward. His partner's wife, Jane,

31

wouldn't meet Gordon here at night. Her fear that their offices were haunted gave rise to no end of ribbing from her husband.

Malcolm stepped off the elevator to the sounds of a vacuum rumbling and then receding from within the optometrists' suite. He walked the long corridor to the end, to the door with the copper sailboat cutting through verdigris waves. Gordon had insisted that they go with the generic *Lincoln County Counseling Center*, and Malcolm had agreed as long as he had "artistic control" of their business cards: "We can't control the wind; we can adjust our sails."

Malcolm slid his office key into the lock and stopped. From inside, he heard a high-pitched, silvery tinkle, as if an infinitesimal percussion instrument had just been sounded. The cleaning people played the radio, but Wednesday was cleaning day. Before the door to the waiting room shut behind him, he heard it again, more loudly—a festive jingling, as if one of his young patients had holed up inside with Santa Claus or a belly dancer. He reached into the basket of picture books by the couch and picked up the biggest hardcover. His office door was closed; so was Gordon's. The tinkling ceased.

"Jesus!"

Gordon emerged from his dark office, shutting the door on a whole new round of frenzied jingling. He was naked from the waist up and barefoot. "You scared the shit out of me!"

"I scared you?" Malcolm's heart raced wildly, now that there was no good reason.

"I . . . I need to talk to you." Gordon was flushed. He looked the way he often did when they skied together. He'd get to the bottom of a mogul field and turn to Malcolm with that blood-hot face and more relish than should be allotted one man. "There's something you have to understand, that I need to—"

"You're shitting me, right?" Malcolm shook his head, a gesture Gordon had told him the last time was *pathetically self-righteous*. "What if I had scheduled a patient?"

Gordon opened his mouth; but instead of speaking, he closed it, puffed out his cheeks, and blasted a sigh.

"We need to talk about this now, tonight," Malcolm said.

Gordon nodded. Malcolm tossed *Ride a Purple Pelican* back into the basket, unlocked his office door, and grabbed his cell phone from his desk. When he returned to the waiting room, he saw Gordon standing there, the loose ends of his stiff brown belt jutting out in front of him like a beak.

"Meet me at Monroe's in thirty minutes," Malcolm said.

Gordon looked up at him as if he might cry. He pulled the belt tight and jammed the metal prong through the hole with his thumb. "Shit."

⌘

Monroe's was warm and moist with people; musicians were setting up in the back and every stool at the bar was occupied. Malcolm grabbed a menu, sat down at a small table over by the exposed brick wall, and took off his coat. He hoped the music wouldn't get too loud. The last thing he wanted was Gordon shouting about the dual use of his couch above some double bass riff.

"Hey, Dr. Dowd."

Malcolm recognized the waitress as one of the girls from the junior sailing team he'd coached before Leah reached high school. "I've never seen you with shoes on," he said, her name lost to him.

"Yeah, dry land." She smiled. "You waiting for someone?"

He nodded and turned the menu over to the back, where the wines were listed. He ordered a bottle, an Italian red, and asked for some olives and bread.

"Leah still sail?" the girl asked as she finished writing down the bin number.

"She's on the club team at school. Just about to get back in the water in another month or so."

"Wow, I wish I still raced, but between work and school. . . ."

He nodded. "It's a long life," he said. "You'll get back to it."

She shrugged and slid his menu off the table. "Be right back with the wine."

Malcolm looked at his watch and then at the door. This was like lying in wait for an errant teenager to come home after an informing phone call from another parent.

It had taken them two months to get over their rift the first time Malcolm had caught Gordon cheating. They'd been at a conference together in Santa Fe. Gordon had called Malcolm sanctimonious. Sanctimonious and envious. He'd requested a seat change on the flight home, and Malcolm had marveled at Gordon's ability to fashion himself the injured party. For over a month they'd greeted each other, when forced, with grunts and nods. Malcolm kept his white-noise machine on even when he wasn't in session. After a few weeks, they resorted to e-mail, meeting in cyberspace when they were separated by nothing more than a sheet of drywall. Then one gray Sunday afternoon, while Malcolm was carrying rocks from the trunk of his wagon to the patio wall he was trying to repair, Gordon had appeared, hands in pockets, head bowed, and admitted to being a dickhead.

"I could have behaved better, too," Malcolm had said, pulling off his work gloves. "You put me in an awkward position, though, you know? I mean, I like your wife."

"Everyone does," Gordon said, without any trace of his usual glibness. He pushed on one of the loose boulders, rocking it back and forth. "She's one of those people you gravitate toward because you want to be like them, you know. And every day is another opportunity to find you've come up short."

⁂

The girl Malcolm remembered as always shivering under her life vest placed the wine on the table and pulled a corkscrew from her faux-leather apron. She struggled to insert the tip of the opener into the cork, and twice the black-and-silver corkscrew clattered onto the table. She looked behind her at the bar and then in the direction of the kitchen to see if anyone had noticed. The music had already started, a guitar and something that looked like a mini-guitar.

"I don't work dinner that often. At lunch, people have beers or wine by the glass, you know."

"I don't want you to get in trouble, but I could. . . ."

She turned around again, surveying the busy room, and nodded.

"Okay," he said. "You stand in front of me, and I'll just keep it on the chair." Malcolm placed the bottle between his legs on the seat of the bistro chair, screwed the opener into the cork, which he could now see was soft and wet, and pulled the plug on the wine in one swift, short movement. "The first summer Leah's older sister worked at the Bayberry Inn, it was mid-August before she removed an intact cork."

"Thanks." The young woman touched his shoulder and walked away.

At the far end of the restaurant a small, burnished man and a woman with a long, graceful neck and wavy black hair were playing guitar, not in tandem, not the same notes at the same time he didn't think, but what did he know. The music sounded classical, almost like a conversation, with the occasional overlap, at first gentle, and then building in intensity. The two sat facing one another quite closely, perched on bar stools high above the rest of the room. The man braced one foot against the highest rung of the woman's stool, and the woman sat so that her long skirt was pulled taut into a hammock for her guitar. Their fingers plucked and strummed wildly now. He didn't know if it was the music or the musicians, but he felt the need to look away.

For a long time after Laura died, he couldn't listen to any music at all. Sound had been her province. She was always introducing him to some new artist, or song or arrangement. "Listen," she would say, the word a portal, a promise, her enthusiasm an art form in itself. They couldn't drive in the car without her pressing in a tape. Often when he would ask her what she was thinking, she would answer, "Nothing, just hearing."

The first time he saw her perform, a solo with the Outermost Chorale, he realized how little he'd really known her. They were both living in Provincetown. She had a winter share in a house in the East End, the windows on the harbor side crusted with dried salt by November. As the tourists receded and his hours at the marina got cut, he spent more and more time in her bedroom, ducking his head as he ran up the nearly vertical stairway with its shallow steps, wondering about the two centuries of men before him who'd raced up those uneven treads with the same manic craving.

Twenty-eight years later, he could still picture her in the purple cassock belted with mooring line that the singers each wore. As she stepped out of the chorus toward the audience and sounded those first few notes, he was forced to begin revising his every perception of her. He had thought she was a tidy package, petite, contained, navigable and knowable. But there on stage she was suddenly more compelling, deeper and darker, even taller than she'd been just hours earlier lying beside him on the Indian print spread covering her bed. Her voice poured forth from some secret place his explorations of her had not yet revealed. Having learned nothing at all in that moment about his own dim imagination, he was seized by a new kind of desire, a determination to chart the whole of her, to find his way to her very ends. Later that night in bed after the concert, he tried to explain what it was like to hear her sing. "To stand there and share all that. . . . That people, some people can actually do that. . . . It's like proof. . . ."

She took his hand in the dark and brought it to her breast, as if swearing an oath. "I'm never more myself than when I'm singing."

The first responder to her one-car crash had written Malcolm a few weeks after the accident. The state trooper said that as he'd approached the car on the wet, empty road, he'd heard music—like nuns singing in a cathedral. He wanted Malcolm to know that even as the other rescue workers arrived on the scene, no one turned off the tape. The eleven-year-old Honda had been Malcolm's, the car he drove to work, not the one they drove as a family of four. At the lot where it had ultimately been towed, he scanned the rows, focusing on the colors of the cars, not their caved-in roofs, crunched hoods, and most especially not their shattered windshields. He approached the Civic from the passenger's side and, like diving underwater, reached in once quickly for the contents of the glove compartment, walked up and down the row, then went back in for the last time to retrieve the cassette in the tape deck. The label on the cassette was in Laura's script, *Les Dix Dames Sans Merci, rehearsal October 3*. She'd been listening to her own *a capella* group.

⤜∞⤛

"Thanks," Gordon said as Malcolm poured him a glass of wine and slid it across the dark wood table.

"Why don't you . . ." Gordon's eyes darted everywhere but in the direction of Malcolm's face. "I think you should speak first."

Malcolm looked at him. "I think I should speak first too."

Gordon's head bobbed nervously.

"I'm pissed. I "

"You guys want to order?" The sad sailing girl was back at the table, and now Malcolm wished he'd gone up and asked the bartender her name so that he could introduce Gordon, so that it didn't seem so much like he was the patron and she the server, or that it had been so long since she had been a kid and he her coach.

Gordon raised his eyebrows, but not his head. "Grey Goose on the rocks and a glass of water."

"Anything to eat?"

"No."

Malcolm waited until the girl was past the next table. "Our work lives are pretty intertwined. We've got our own practice and then, since I'm over at Baxter. . . . When you take certain actions, the repercussions are not. . . . You put me in jeopardy too. I mean, what is this business but reputation? By using our space so inappropriately, you—"

"It's worse than that." Gordon looked down at the table. "I mean, what I've done, what I'm doing is even worse than you think."

Had they been back at the office in the middle of a slow afternoon engaged in the verbal equivalent of kicking the ball around, Malcolm would have said, "What makes you think you even know what I'm thinking?" But Gordon seemed suddenly incapable of guarding himself, much less sparring with his opponent. Gordon, whose ice-blue eyes worked like a psychic can opener on whomever he was talking to, covered his face with his large hairy hands, his thick silver wedding band slapping against his closed left eye.

The waitress placed Gordon's vodka on one corner of the table and slid it only slightly in his direction. Malcolm smiled at her, and she bit her lip.

"It's a patient," Gordon said.

"I'll get you that bread and the olives," the girl said.

"That's okay. I think we're all set for now." Malcolm spoke loudly, too cheerfully.

Gordon removed his hands from his face. His nose was running. "Shit." He reached for the cloth napkin and blew.

"A woman?" Malcolm asked.

"She's our age, well, a little younger. Of course, a woman. You really think I would—"

"No. I meant as opposed to a man." Malcolm grinned.

"What the fuck, this isn't funny."

"Sorry, it's just . . . I had a wild gender-bending experience this morning." Before Noah had even left the office, Malcolm thought about telling the story to Gordon. But as he finished up his private sessions for the day, interrupted by occasional flashes of the wig and the chest hair, he'd begun to feel that whatever had gone on between him and the kid, or maybe just him and himself, was between the two of them alone.

Gordon pulled his vodka closer to him and took a big drink. Malcolm watched him roll a cube around in his mouth and then crush it. "I love her. It's been . . . it's not sudden. I've . . . I've never felt this way before. Is this what it is? The thing people write poems about—because. . . ." He stopped, went to reach for his drink, and instead pressed the heel of his hand to his chest.

"You want to go outside, get some air?"

Gordon's nose was red and his eyes were a little wet, yet Malcolm could see that even in this state of duress, he appeared to be the focus of some female attention from the bar. One night when they were waiting for a table at Per Bacco, Jane had told Malcolm it was ninety percent about the hair. Her theory was that it was the combo of that boyishly curly hair, no matter it was going gray, atop the broad shoulders and beefy chest. It was the boy/man thing women fell for. She knew that Gordon's female patients—adolescent girls, young women, old women—frequently fell in love with him, or at least thought they did. "If I only saw him in a controlled environment fifty minutes a week, I'd probably lose it for him, too. Anyone can be perfect for an hour." Malcolm had long ago realized that Gordon's female patients were a somewhat homogeneous, self-selected group. People who were drawn to a therapist like Gordon, whose sexuality was right out there, were people who needed to work through that particular issue. More than once, Malcolm had told Gordon, while discussing a patient, that Gordon's own phallic-narcissism could be an excellent therapeutic tool.

"What were you treating her for?"

"Well, initially, adjustment disorder, grief reaction."

"You're not still treating her, right?"

"Christ almighty, only two minutes ago it was all—'I'm here for you'—and now. . . . That judgment thing, you fucking need to work on that."

Malcolm pushed away from the table. The male guitarist was singing. Malcolm knew even less about languages than he did about music, but he guessed the lyrics were Portuguese. People were talking, laughing, some loudly. It struck Malcolm as nearly unbearably painful that someone should be offering up such a heartfelt gift to so unconscious a crowd.

"Sorry," Gordon said, spitting a cube back into his rocks glass.

Malcolm pulled the foil off the neck of the wine bottle. He'd already drunk half of it. "Is she married?"

"No."

"Kids?"

"No." Gordon shifted in his chair and leaned into the table, his chin nearly touching the oil lamp in the center. "I need you to listen

to me, and not talk, just for a few minutes. I need to tell you something, Malcolm. I can't tell anyone else, and I can't bear not to talk
about it anymore."

Malcolm breathed in and waited.

"It's not an affair." Gordon hooked the heel of his hiking boot onto
the rung of the chair. "This connection . . . it's like it pre-existed our
meeting. Sleeping with that woman in Santa Fe—that was my trying
to send Charlotte—like in croquet, you know—you hit one ball to
beat back another one." He tore a corner of his cocktail napkin.

"Jane must sense something." Though, of course, Malcolm hadn't
known his own wife had a secret life, hadn't seen it coming, as people
liked to say—not any of it.

"I caught *you* off guard," Gordon said.

"Myopia's on special today. Two for one." He was fond of telling
patients that people committed to maintaining secrets were capable
of doing so with a mastery often unparalleled in other aspects of their
lives. If someone didn't want you to know something, you couldn't
blame yourself for being in the dark. But neither Noah nor Gordon
had made heroic efforts to keep him blindfolded. In fact, it seemed,
they'd been forced to chase him down and rip the scales from his eyes.
"I wasn't looking for it, you know."

"It's always about denial on some level—"

"If that's true—what about your own?"

"What?" Gordon reached into his drink and plucked out the lime,
which he placed on the ripped napkin.

"You kill me." Malcolm shook his head. "First of all, she could
turn around and sue your ass off. Ever think about that?"

Gordon looked up at him, as if searching for something, rifling
through files. "Of everyone I know, I thought you'd understand,
make the effort to understand. I thought that at least you had the
capacity for it."

Malcolm could feel his anger, taut across his clavicle like a wire
string. He looked around at all the glass in the place. The floor-
to-ceiling windows, the antique mirror behind the bar, the pilsner

glasses and wine goblets, the brandy snifters. He unspooled a fantasy of rampaging through this room with his nine iron. He tried to wear himself out with the image—the noise, the crunch of broken glass underfoot. After a long while, he said, "Tell me what you want me to understand."

Gordon pulled his shirt away from the tops of one shoulder, then the other, as if it were too small, as if he might burst the seams of his own clothing with this emergent self. "It's just that, God, this amazing thing is happening, something I didn't even know existed, something that made what I thought was my life—the world, even—open up into a place so much larger, infinitely larger, infinitely more. . . ."

Malcolm wanted to lay waste to this euphoria, to tell Gordon this kind of high was all about cathexis without real love. Instead, he just said "You're happy, really happy."

"For the first fucking time in my life." Gordon looked up at him and the tears just started falling, copious and noisy. "Jesus." He grabbed the cocktail napkin from under Malcolm's wine glass and scrubbed his face. "I used to look at you and think . . ." he stopped and reached for the glass of wine Malcolm had poured him when he first sat down. "You were like sadness incarnate, you know—when I first met you when you moved up here. Then, as time went by . . . there you were—kids and work and kids and work and nothing else, and I stopped feeling sorry for you. You stopped scaring me."

Malcolm's anger, which had threatened to overpower reason only moments before, was replaced by a sense of dislocation, as if the way back from this place would not be along the same route he'd traveled to arrive. He tried to remember when he'd seen Gordon vulnerable, not defeated, but untended.

"You were a *widower*. The word's always spooked me. I mean, just listen to it. It's a ghoulish, haunting word. But after a while, I realized you were probably happier than I was. I'm sure that sounds callous. . . ." Gordon clamped down on his molars, as if to stop himself from continuing.

"You weren't happy with Jane?"

"It was like I was dead."

"Depressed?" Malcolm couldn't really remember a time when Gordon had seemed depressed—not ever.

"No. Dead."

Malcolm nodded, the sounds of the guitar at the end of the room only emphasizing how meager words could be. "Did it have to be sexual?"

Gordon sighed, his massive chest inflating and deflating visibly. "I struggled with that for over a year. But the thing of it is, it wasn't a physical attraction. It didn't start that way, at all. It was something completely different—this gravitational force, this feeling that I knew her, that when I spoke, I never had to explain." He rubbed the glass salt and pepper shakers between his palms, rolling them as if they were dice. "She . . . she sits on the couch, and even though she's coming to me for help, even at first . . . it was never like that. It wasn't like she was asking for anything, really." Gordon stopped, shook his head, and looked up at Malcolm, looked into his eyes as if begging for something. "I'm telling you true stuff here. Don't diagnose it. Please."

Susannah had said something similar to him over the phone recently. "Being cynical, even skeptical, Dad, doesn't make you smarter." What he couldn't tell her, what he couldn't tell Gordon, was: *Be careful.* You can't even begin to fathom what it is you don't know about this person who professes to love you, whom you love. And one day, what you don't know can rise up out of nowhere and take your whole life away. "When are you going to tell Jane?"

"Soon."

∽∾

Malcolm let his body slide down in the stiff chair, closing his eyes occasionally to better hear the guitar. Only the woman was playing now, the music so resonant that Malcolm felt the chords being plucked from deep within his own recesses.

He'd ordered coffee once Gordon had left, but he barely had the energy to lift it to his lips. Gordon had stood to go after Jane had called his cell phone. "Monroe's," he'd said, pressing the phone to his cheek. "Malcolm. Yeah, I'll tell him. Okay." Then he'd put on his coat and pushed open the doors to the outside, appearing some seconds later on the other side of the steamed-up window as he made his way down Spring Street.

In addition to the prohibition about using the office, Malcolm would have to add that he didn't want to be Gordon's alibi. Bad enough to know this and keep it from Jane, but to be an active part of the deception was unacceptable.

It was Jane who Susannah had called at work one afternoon in eighth grade, and Jane who'd arrived at the house forty minutes later with a canvas tote filled with feminine hygiene products. It was Jane who took Susannah to New York for the weekend when her high school boyfriend dumped her. And it was Jane who scrolled through her computer's history one night after Leah, then fourteen, had been babysitting for the boys. "'Life after Death.' 'Angels Among Us.' 'Messages From the Other Side.' You need to talk to her, Malcolm."

"You missing Mom especially these days?" he asked a few nights later as they were folding laundry and watching the Celtics. From the beginning, he'd told the girls that their mother's car accident had been caused by a number of perfectly aligned, unfortunate factors. It had been raining hard all that late October day, and the winding road on which she was traveling was newly paved, the oils in the tar rising to the surface. There were two other accidents that night farther west on 208. Laura had likely been driving above the speed limit. She'd been late leaving the house, late for the rehearsal she was conducting.

"Not everyone leaves a note." Leah looked down into the basket of clothes.

"What do you mean?"

She shrugged, then pulled out one of Malcolm's undershirts.

"What are you wondering?"

"Did your father leave a note?"

"There was a birthday card." Malcolm's birthday was in November. The card with the envelope addressed to him had been tucked into the upstairs hall mirror that Labor Day Weekend. The front of the card pictured a cowboy on a bucking bronco, his lariat forming a bright red 6. Inside, in faint letters, his father had penciled "Love, Daddy."

"Mom didn't commit suicide," he said.

"Is it inherited?" Leah looked straight ahead at the television.

Malcolm's grandfather had told Malcolm once that he thought Malcolm's father had worked hard every day he was alive not to kill himself. "Mom died in an accident, LeeLee. She wasn't mentally ill. That's not something you need to be worried about, okay?"

"It's not that," Leah said.

He pulled a pair of his blue jeans from the basket and snapped the pants in the air before beginning to fold them. The featured fear was that he'd copy his father, and maybe she would too. But perhaps she was asking him then about the flip side of the legacy—in which you, the survivor, were tagged and targeted for repeat tragedy. He made a crease in the pants and folded them into thirds. When he looked up, she was gone.

⌒∞⌒

Malcolm paid the bill with the fifty that Gordon had left. Infidelity had made him generous. The lot behind the restaurant remained unplowed after the day's piddling snow, and as Malcolm approached the driver's-side door, he clicked the soles of his boots together to loosen the packed slush. He pulled off his glove with his teeth and dug around in his pants pocket for his car keys. It would take about twenty minutes to drive home. Then he'd have to let out Merlin and get him back in, go through the mail, phone messages. He should have left when Gordon did—or before.

Just as he put his key in the lock, he heard a female voice say "shit," softly, almost tenderly, as if offering a condolence. A woman in a long down coat poked her head from the other side of the car.

Malcolm nodded. Ending her phone conversation, the woman walked around the front of the car, and when she did the sodium lights fell in such a way that even beneath the camouflage of her hat and scarf, he could see she was the guitarist from inside the bar.

"The music was . . . incredible. I don't think I ever heard guitar like that before."

"Oh, that's Eduardo, the mandolin player. He's visiting here from Brazil. Yeah. Isn't he something else?"

Malcolm nodded. "You too." The words came out in an obscuring puff of air.

She thanked him and shifted her gaze to the rear entrance of Monroe's. He'd barely been able to see her face from where he'd been sitting with Gordon. But now he noticed the dramatic slope of her cheekbones and her large almond-shaped eyes. Standing out here on the frozen tundra of the municipal lot with her jet black hair peeking out from beneath a Russian-style hat, she looked exotic. He was almost surprised that she was speaking to him in English.

"I'm really glad you enjoyed it. Most people don't stay for both sets."

"Yeah," he said stupidly. "I wish I could have spent more time listening to you instead of to the friend I was with."

"Gordon, yeah, well, Gordon's a good talker, huh?"

"You know him?"

She smiled and then nodded, but offered nothing else for a while, as if considering. "Friend of a . . . friend."

Just like Gordon to be so self-absorbed that he never even noticed he knew the guitarist. "Yeah, Gordon and I are partners—at work, in a work. . . ."

She laughed. "I understood what you meant. So, that means you're a shrink too. Oh—" She put her hand to her mouth. "You probably hate that term."

He waved her away with the glove he was holding. "Yeah, I'm a psychologist."

"A friend of mine's a dermatologist, and as soon as people find that out, they're always asking her to look at their moles."

Her lips were broad plain and rolling hill. When her mouth opened on "dermatologist," Malcolm got caught up in tracking her tongue as it touched the roof of her mouth, the back of her teeth. Her face was a relief map of dramatic high-steppe country, somewhere little New England boys with reticent, thin lips dreamed of going. God. He laughed, sucking cold wet air into his throat so that he sputtered. "With psychologists, the consult is always about someone else."

Her phone rang and she jumped a little, as if it were sending out a charge.

Malcolm nodded toward the phone and gave a little wave.

She smiled, her face rearranging itself, as if mountains could be moved. He got in his car, managing to successfully back out of his spot, all the while staring at the woman in the puffy red coat and the black fur hat.

4

Noah skulked in the men's room until it was time for his appointment. He hated the waiting room, everyone doing the same thing, trying to check out who else was there without being caught at it. This bathroom outside Behavioral Health was his green room. "Five minutes, Mr. Burrell." He aped before the mirror—prodigy, stoner, siren—and knocked his French homework into the sink.

The guy Noah had seen with Dr. Dowd last week at Monroe's had been crying. Their chairs had been pulled up close enough that Noah imagined their knees must have been touching beneath the table. No, not Dowd. Nothing about him pointed to it. Yet they had embraced, and the other guy, all buff, had definitely come unglued.

Noah picked at a bristly hair between his eyebrows, crowding the mirror to verify that it was what it felt like. Maybe he just wanted Dr. Dowd to be gay. If Dowd were gay, he'd be less likely to judge him. No, that wasn't true. Fags were just as likely to be judgmental as anyone else.

He walked over to the hand drier and held his French homework underneath. He loved French—the language, not the class. He heard the doors of the mental health offices open, the soft unclicking of latches, metal sucking metal. He checked his watch, shouldered his backpack, and looked in the mirror once more. He was wearing the rolled-collar sweater his aunt had given him for Christmas. When he'd tried it on for her, she'd said he looked just like the model in the catalogue. Looking at himself now, he felt what he'd felt then: That it was just one more costume.

⸎

Noah took a seat on the couch and watched as Dowd sat down in his chair, centering his tie down the middle of his shirt. When he'd greeted Noah at the door, he'd thrust out his hand. He hadn't done that last week, not to Leah, but his previous appointments with Dowd had both begun and ended with that old-school handshake.

"How are you?" Dr. Dowd asked, as if he really meant it.

Noah cracked his neck first to the left and then to the right. "Okay, I guess."

Dowd smiled.

"I've thought a lot about . . . about last time." Noah looked down at his boots, at the weave in the beige carpeting.

"Me too."

"I thought maybe you'd be pissed at me, and maybe you are. I mean, maybe I should have just tried to tell you."

"I'm not pissed. In fact, I'm the opposite of pissed." Dowd paused and smiled at him. "I'm grateful that you shared . . . that side of yourself with me."

"It's not a side." Noah was perspiring under the sweater. God, it always got so fucking hot in here.

Dowd looked at him eagerly, eyebrows raised just the way a dog might prick up its ears.

"It's not separate."

Dowd was writing now, fast and nodding. Noah looked at a plant in the far corner of the room and hoped it was real. He had worried, for about half a day in tenth grade—when this loser English teacher had made them read *Sybil*—that he had a split personality. But there wasn't enough of him for two whole personas. He was more like the fat guy on an airplane, big rolls of being spilling over the armrest and into the seat beside him. He had no interest in getting any smaller, only in removing that fucking armrest and freeing up the middle seat.

"I saw you at Monroe's last week."

Dowd looked up. "Was it strange to see me outside this context?"

Noah wondered if Dr. Dowd ever got drunk, just absolutely wasted. Something about him seemed so excessively moderate, like he'd never do anything in the extreme. He had tried, unsuccessfully, to imagine Dowd coming.

"What were you thinking about, just then?"

Noah felt his chest flush, the heat pushing up past the stupid collar of his sweater and onto his face. He cupped his ears, hot enough to warm his hands, little campfires on either side of his head. How fucking pathetic. He pretended to look out the window as if he cared about the steely sky and the bare branches. He could feel Dowd staring at him, trying to get him to say something, something meaningful or transparent or shocking. "When people look at me, all they see is this." He ran his fingertips the length of his body in what he knew was a slightly lewd gesture.

Dowd didn't laugh. When he was finished writing whatever he was writing in his notes, he said, "What is it you think people see when they look at you?"

"This. This not male, not female body—this long, thin, just slightly feminine, but clearly not really, person."

"What would you like them to see?" Dowd asked.

"This morning in the dining hall I'm clearing my tray and this kid just reaches in front of me with his dirty dishes, stacks them on the conveyor belt, and then, like just fucking stares at me, like looking's this one-way thing, like the way you look at a screen."

Dowd's tongue clucked in dismay.

"It was like I was a cartoon character."

"What'd you do?"

"I could practically hear him writing the caption."

"What'd you say to him?"

"It wasn't like that." Noah leaned over and tugged at the hem of his jeans. He considered defending himself by telling Dowd about his "fuck you" moment with Tory Liggett and her sailor boyfriend after last week's appointment, but that would have involved more than a little truth-shaving. "The whole thing was like two seconds."

"Long enough to say something."

"You're telling me I'm wrong to be the way I am?"

"On the contrary. I don't think letting that kid 'write the caption' is at all who you are. You strike me as someone with a great deal of integrity."

Noah studied the Hopper just to one side of Dowd's head. The poster, his favorite thing in this room, showed the white sails of a heeling boat billowing out against a deep blue sea. The picture was both moody and hopeful. He wanted to look at Dowd now, but he couldn't, his visible relief at being understood having erased any and all suggestion of integrity.

"It's called *The Long Leg*," Dowd said, turning to look at the framed print.

Noah nodded.

"Pretend I'm the kid." Dowd smiled. "I'd like to hear what you'd say."

Was he fucking kidding? Role-playing? Noah could do that on his own. He slipped his phone from out of his front pocket and pretended to look at the time.

"Something wrong?"

"I'm already in a play, okay?" Noah slid the phone back into his pocket. "I don't want to spend my time in here. . . ." His mother was always telling him to practice breathing when he got angry, to bring his awareness into his body and some other stuff he couldn't really remember. It seemed to him she'd be happy if all that ever came out of his mouth was a bunch of mindful exhales.

"'You don't want to spend your time in here' . . . ? Can you finish the thought?"

"Hey, I showed up dressed as a girl five days ago, and now we're like doing psychodrama about two meaningless seconds in the cafeteria."

Dowd nodded and leaned forward, elbows on knees. "What is it you want me to know?"

Noah pulled down the sleeves of his sweater and retracted his arms. He stayed like that for a while, the empty sweater arms hanging in his lap. Dumping out the shifting contents of his mind as a way of being known was like using that Etch A Sketch on the shelf to produce a photo ID. No matter the quality or quantity, words were not going to help him explain himself, the self he'd neither arranged nor grown into, the self he was whether he was jacking off in a miniskirt or clearing his tray in the cafeteria. He pulled the sweater over his head and rolled it into a ball in front of his stomach. "Kids like me kill themselves."

As a child he had sometimes wanted to die, which he thought was probably different from wanting to kill yourself. He remembered lying awake on Sunday nights when he was eight and nine and ten, hoping he might go to sleep and never wake up so that he wouldn't have to go to school the next day, so that he wouldn't have to do the hard work of staying in his body and getting along with everyone. He had thought then that dying was something like being invisible, and that if he were dead he'd still exist, only he'd get to exist in the preferable landscape of his imagination.

"Is that something you think about? Killing yourself?" Dowd had removed his glasses and Noah saw his eyes widen, the brown becoming more amber.

"No."

"I'm glad." Dowd paused, still leaning in, the end of his tie lapping at the knees of his khakis. "What don't I understand?" he said gently.

"When you're my age, people think your confusion is predictable, harmless. A cold, not pneumonia, you know? Identity crisis. But look at me. Who'm I going to be? Half the kids here have it all planned out—career, marriage, family. I mean, what's going to happen to me? Fringe freak? *Be yourself, be yourself, be yourself*—well, fuck, that's easier for some people than others. What if myself, my *real* self, what if there's no place for that?"

Dowd looked straight at him, no arched eyebrows or upturned lips. He was quiet for a long time, his eyes maybe filling, which was hard to tell because he'd put his glasses back on. After a while he said, "Carl Jung said there's nothing more difficult than becoming our true selves." Dowd's chair was tipping as he inclined even farther toward Noah. "You're asking crucial questions, questions many people go a lifetime skirting."

Noah felt a pang of shame for Dowd, who was totally clueless about having spewed the very same page from Bartlett's once before. A phone rang unanswered out in the reception area, muffled only slightly by the distortion of the white-noise machine. Noah weighed Dowd's error against all the other stuff, which seemed hard to label. Kindness? Patience? Compassion? No, those things were disembodied. What Dowd brought, what Noah relived over and over once he left this room, was something else. It was physical, like being held, even when Dowd was sitting across the room in silence. Noah was seen. Beheld.

"When you were younger, what did you imagine your life would be like now?" Dowd prompted.

When Noah was a kid, he'd hated adults asking him what he wanted to be when he grew up. In third grade they'd had to make posters predicting their lives in the year 2030. Lots of kids just went all futuristic with jetpacks and robots and houses with monitors instead of windows. Noah's poster had shown him outside a multi-story adobe building, what he liked to think of as a Native American apartment house. He'd mixed all kinds of tribal cultures together, pasting in downloaded photos of totem poles and peace pipes, dream catchers and cowhide drums. Using Magic Markers, he'd drawn himself dressed in feathers and skins, fringed moccasins, ropes of turquoise beads. His hair was long and black, his face decorated with red and yellow war paint. Around the border of the poster, he'd designed symbols for the gods he'd invented. He could only remember a few of the gods now—Snow and Corn, Bravery and Truth. And the God of Comfort, which he'd placed, barely detectable, in the middle of the native mash-up. The teacher suggested he redo his poster. She pointed to the work of the rest of the class and said "You were supposed to draw the future, not the past."

"Want to tell me what you're thinking about?" Dowd reached down and pulled up one sock, then the other.

"What about Leah? I mean . . ." Noah shifted his eyes toward the bookshelves, the chorus line of cheesy Hopi dolls. "You never told me what you thought of her."

"For the same reason I haven't told you what I think of you. I'm not sitting in the reviewing stand in here. That's not how I think of this process. I consider myself a change agent. I'm here to help people change if they want to, if they need to."

Noah unballed his sweater, tossed it over his back, and tied the sleeves loosely around his neck. "It's the world that needs to change, not me."

Dowd jotted something down and then looked up at Noah, staring at him, deciding. His mother did that sometimes. She would look at him intently, as if savoring what was sweet but tenuous between them. It belied a panic, the desire to hoard something rare.

"Do you really believe that?" Dowd said. He leaned back in his chair, his chest broadening as he inhaled. Noah wondered if Dowd had been handsome when he was younger. You could sort of see how he might have been, in that white guy, out-doorsy way his aunt was so fond of—hands-cracked-from-oars, hair-smelling-of-wood-smoke kind of thing that seemed to turn her on.

Dowd's eyebrows were in a twist.

"What?"

"I asked if you really thought the world, rather than you, was what had to change."

"You think this is some late adolescent rebellion thing, right? Question everything, including gender. Anything for a shock?" He pressed his hands down into the sofa. "It isn't a stance. This is me. The real thing."

"Which is the real you?" Dowd said, staring acquisitively again.

Noah shook his head and reached for his backpack. He pulled out his still-damp French composition, his Sociology text, an empty iced-tea bottle, and then reached in with both hands and brought up two dark red chamois shoe bags. Keeping his eyes on the carpet, he unlaced his filthy boots, cupped his hands around the heel, and yanked out one foot, then the other. He tugged off his wool socks and slid his chapped bare feet into the black mules. He pushed the mess of papers and books and muddy footwear to the side, leaned back into the couch, and crossed his legs, his left foot swinging slightly, toe pointed at Dowd. Noah forced himself to slowly lift his chin. Even as he did, feeling a horrible mixture of fear and fury, as if his chest might just cave in on all the sadness, the very thought of that sadness infuriated him so that he looked around to see what he could harm.

Dowd placed his fingers together in a kind of steeple, breathing down over the pointed tops of them. "What do the shoes mean to you?"

Noah's ribs hurt now. Disappointment could feel like that, like you'd been beaten up the day before or long ago. He couldn't look at Dowd and he couldn't look at the shoes—either would make him cry, and he wasn't going to do that. The shoes were everything, and it was essential that Dowd understand that and impossible that he ever would. In that distance between the shoes and the man was all the isolation in the world. The shoes broke his heart every time he so much as smelled them, and Dowd. . . .

Their time was up. Doors closed gently. There was talking out in the reception area. A muffled crash. The metal coatrack must have tipped over onto a chair. A girl laughed.

Noah bent at the waist, letting his cheek graze his knee. He slid off the mules, his palms sliding over the tops as he replaced each shoe into its own bag, and then each bag into the larger bag.

"What are you feeling right now?" Dowd asked.

"I thought maybe you were someone who, like, got it, you know. I needed to believe that. But this . . ." Noah pulled one ragg sock over chipping toenail polish. "This was just bullshit today."

Dowd relaxed his body, dropped his notebook and pen carelessly by his chair, and leaned back and sighed. "I'm sorry you feel that way, but I'm glad you can be honest with me."

Noah rotated the sock so his heel slid into the proper spot. "I'm sure."

When Noah was finished tying his boots and gathering his books and papers, Dowd stood and extended his hand. "See you next week."

5

Malcolm circled the supermarket parking lot twice, looking for a spot. Great mountains of plowed snow, thawed and refrozen twenty times over, obscured the end of each row, causing drivers to inch their way around as if engaged in some sort of vehicular espionage. Leah was coming home for the weekend, and he needed to buy food for dinner. He grabbed two tote bags from the trunk of his car and yanked on a shopping cart upended in one of the frozen foothills. He pulled on the cart again, harder than he'd intended; and when it released, one of the icy wheels smacked him in the groin.

"You okay?"

The voice came from behind. Malcolm turned to see the Tsarina guitarist from that night two weeks ago at Monroe's. He righted the cart, then reached down with his glove and wiped the slush from the front of his parka. "Yeah," he said. "Need a cart?"

She shook her head, and her hair bounced up around the edges of her black Russian hat. "Strictly a basket shopper. I only ever get three things."

He smiled, and waited, gloves gripping the red handle of the cart.

She smiled back, then headed for the entrance, flanked by twenty-pound bags of salt and a pyramid display of Duraflame logs.

In the fourteen years since Laura had died, his few relationships had been pitifully easy to navigate. There was the physical and there was the emotional, with a well-defined fault line separating the two. What he knew about love was what he remembered of it and what he'd learned from working with his patients. The supermarket wasn't so big. He could find the guitarist again if he wanted to. What he really wanted was simply to run into her, in the dog-food aisle or maybe by the dairy case. He had outlived his lifetime supply of romantic optimism.

He wheeled his cart toward produce and inspected the tiers of dark bitter greens. Grabbing a bunch of ruby-stalked Swiss chard, he warned himself not to buy too much food—food he'd find himself tossing out a week from now, long after Leah had gone back to school. During her four years at Baxter, Susannah had turned up at home several times a week. When Susannah had been hired last year to teach ninth and tenth grade English at Lewis Prep in New Hampshire, Leah had predicted that her sister would be the most homesick "girl" in the dormitory. But Malcolm knew it was something more particular than homesickness that caused his older daughter to stick close to home and to call frequently when she was away. He recognized her need to be reminded, or perhaps convinced, that the living parent was, in fact, still alive, that the easily disordered universe of one's family had retained its shape for yet another day.

In the year and a half since she'd gone away to college, Leah had never before "just decided" to come home for the weekend. Her dependence on him, unlike Susannah's, had always been more practical than emotional. He was good for teaching her how to make a dock landing, how to set a pick, how to relate the conclusion of the essay to the introduction. She was not the kind of kid who flung herself on her bed and cried "Oh, Daddy, it's all so awful, I don't know what to do." Immersing his hand in a pile of shallots, he forced himself to consider, again, his insufficient capacity to father his younger daughter. Perhaps he sent her some unconscious signal that he could not withstand, never mind repair, what life inflicted. Leah had a way of looking at Malcolm or, more accurately, just to the right or left of him, as if he were beside the point and what she really wanted was in his shadow.

"Hey." A boy in an oversized Patriots sweatshirt approached him as he stopped his cart in front of the poultry case.

"Kevin." Malcolm stuck out his hand and the kid blushed and shook it. "How are you?"

The boy nodded. Malcolm had stopped treating him last spring, at the end of sixth grade. The school had referred him for "seriously rude and disruptive classroom behavior."

"Pretty good, I guess."

Malcolm glanced down toward the pork products and saw Kevin's mother. "Helping shop today?"

He shrugged.

"Couldn't help but, huh?"

Kevin smiled. "I'm on this team, now, at school."

"That's great. What're you playing?"

"Paintball. I know some kids think it's stupid, but I think it's pretty sweet."

"Woodsball?"

"Yeah, or Speedball—that's in a field. Our team goes all over— Saco, Fryeburg. So, like, I just wanted to tell you that 'cause . . . I don't know."

"Well, I'm glad you did tell me." Malcolm smiled at the boy.

"I should go." Kevin glanced toward his mother and turned to leave.

Malcolm reached out and touched his shoulder and extended his hand.

The kid laughed. "Yeah, yeah." And he shook Malcolm's hand before walking away. Malcolm consulted the shopping list he'd written out on the back of one of his business cards, then headed up the pasta aisle. Paintball? He'd told the mother to try to get the boy involved in sports or some structured after-school activity, some group. It wouldn't have been Malcolm's choice, but then again Kevin's mother was not exactly coming to her role with the zest he thought the position demanded. He couldn't do too much there. She wasn't the patient, though she probably should have been.

Malcolm was used to dealing with parents who resented his appearance in their lives. Just because a kid couldn't control himself on the school bus or an ex-spouse was determined to win custody, they were suddenly subjected to repeated inquiry by a total stranger who was trained to home in on the very worst inside of them.

When he'd told his own mother he was seeing Dr. Barnegat, one of his grandfather's colleagues, she'd allowed for a moment of what passed as respectful silence before saying, "I went to a shrink once, a Freudian. Mental masturbation, as far as I could tell." It was the summer before his senior year of prep school, and Lucy (she allowed no other form of address) was "checking in." In the five years since he'd gone to live with his grandparents in Smithport, he'd seen his mother only sporadically. She'd found him down on the dock, replacing the forestay on his grandfather's catboat. She'd handed him an invitation, a large square postcard of one of her canvases, a color field painting in shades of blue, shifting incrementally from midnight in the center to cornflower at the edges. He carefully tucked the announcement of the opening, which had already taken place, into the bottom of his toolbox where it wouldn't get wet.

"They call psychotherapy a 'helping profession,'" she had said. She'd rolled up her jeans and was sitting with her legs dangling into the water. "Perhaps someone might have shared that well-kept secret with your father."

He turned his cart into the soup aisle and scanned the shelves for chicken broth. Moving past the cans of Campbell's and Progresso, it occurred to him that he probably owed Lucy a debt of gratitude for his having learned how to cook. He'd begun fixing his own meals in seventh grade, when he'd moved with Lucy to Provincetown. Her studio had been on the water in the West End, and she'd rented another space nearer to Route 6 in which they were meant to live. But really, the A-frame in the woods was his house and the water-front studio was hers. She'd stocked the open, roughhewn shelves of his kitchen with a lavish assortment of canned foods—soup, tuna, baked beans, mandarin oranges, miniature sausages, shrunken spears of asparagus. With a can opener and a heat source, she said, he had all he needed to be self-sufficient. During those first few months in Provincetown, he would bike down West Vine after school and slip into her studio. He'd sit in the corner with his homework as she moved around the room, a palette rigged about her neck, like a cigarette girl. Her gaze traveled only between her canvas and whatever still life she'd arranged—a hundred razor blades fanned into the shape of a dove, or a bouquet of knives tied at the center with a coil of rope. Eventually she would announce that his presence was disturbing. "I see everything. Seeing is what I do. It's who I am." The one time he dared complain to her about being left alone overnight, always without warning or explanation, she had looked at him with derision. "Your father . . . he was dependent like that."

⌀

"I always pay," the guitarist from Monroe's called out as he wheeled past the tables in the deli department. "I just hand them the empty bag at the check-out." She was sitting with her hat and coat on, a book propped against her basket of food. Malcolm watched as she snaked the long slender fingers of her right hand into an open bag of chips.

"The book theirs, too?" He had turned around and attempted to lean casually against his cart, causing it to roll into a stand of baguettes.

60

"No, this is mine." She held up a copy of *Lucky Jim*. "I needed a laugh."

"Oldie but a goodie." He reeled in his cart.

She nodded. "Had to have a sure thing. When you need a laugh, you can't—"

"I'm Malcolm, by the way." He reached out his hand to her, and she looked at it for a minute, as some of his young patients did.

"Carmen Shipley—Cara. Trust me, you don't want to shake."

He smiled. What he wanted was to lick the little bit of visible salt, resting in the lovely "u" between the two peaks of her upper lip. "Kingsley Amis—scheming professor?"

She nodded. "He's merciless on the academy. Perfect for this point in the semester or maybe this semester of life, I don't know. You teach too, don't you? I'm guessing in the Psych Department. I know I've seen you around campus."

Malcolm looked behind him and grabbed one of the molded plastic chairs, nudging his cart in the direction of the other tables. "No. I work a couple of days a week in—Behavioral Health, they call it now."

"Lucky you."

He laughed. "I like kids, even big ones."

"You have kids?"

Malcolm nodded. "Two daughters, nineteen and twenty-three. You?"

"A son. Eighteen. In college, I'm pleased to say. Your cart," she said, motioning with her chin.

Malcolm turned and saw that his shopping cart was blocking a young family attempting to wedge into the nest of tables and chairs with a pizza.

"Arborio rice," she said, as he returned, the cart now an extension of his arm. "Someone in your household's a serious cook." She looked right at him when she spoke, right into his eyes. She didn't finger the pages of her book or fiddle with her shirt.

He angled a foot behind one wheel of the cart. "My younger daughter just called and told me she's coming home for the weekend, which she never does. So I thought I'd cook something worthy of the long ride."

"Nice dad."

"Just a ploy." Malcolm nodded as if in response to his own inner prodding to keep this going. "You playing anywhere in the near future?"

Cara smiled deeply and took off her hat, the glossy black braided coils nothing short of a crown. With the non-salty fingers of her left hand, she reached up to her wavy black hair and combed through one side and then the other. Malcolm watched with what he told himself was clinical amazement. She was without self-consciousness, or so it seemed. "In the summer," she started, "I tend to play a bit more after school lets out. I go through periods where I do it, the gigs come and I get into the mode. I'm lazy about setting them up, so if someone approaches me, or one leads to another. . . . I'm not really disciplined—in anything, really. Unfortunately."

"Why's that unfortunate?" he said, realizing too late that he was lapsing into professional mode.

"It's very . . . un-American to be . . ."

"Relaxed?"

"No, I was actually going to say lazy."

He shook his head. What he wanted to say was that she seemed tranquil, languid. Laura had been calm in just this way. He'd always found it comforting to be beside her physically. Her body was pleased and pleasing, and he'd made the mistake of equating that with contentment.

"Your ice cream's dripping." She nodded toward the seat part of the carriage where he now saw that a carton of chocolate chip was leaking from a side seam.

"Do you have a website or something, where you post your upcoming—"

"Too lazy for anything but a phone number." She ripped a corner from the supermarket flyer on the table and began to root around in her purse.

"Here." He slid his hand into his pants pocket and handed her a pen.

She wrote out her number and waved the scrap of paper in the air to let the ink dry. She stood and handed it to him, looking at him closely. As he was folding her number, sliding it into his shirt pocket, she reached over with a finger smelling slightly of cheddar and stroked his cheek.

"Sorry, that was . . . presumptuous. Is that even the right word, *presumptuous*? Eyelash—you had an eyelash. I'm sorry. I know I shouldn't go around touching people—it's weird—people often think it's weird. I just—"

He grazed her arm, or the puffy worn cotton of her down coat encasing her arm. "Lazy, weird—a very nice combo, really." He patted his shirt pocket, feeling the wadded-up scrap of newsprint with her number instead of muscle and rib and beating heart.

⌒∞⌒

"We kind of ate a lot on the ride. But I'll sit with you." Leah stirred the risotto with one hand and brought the open bottle of Corona to her lips with the other. Malcolm decided to keep it to himself that her chokehold on the beer, the way the mouth of the longneck remained even with her grip, was how she used to drink her bottle as a baby. By the time she'd arrived with the boys who'd driven her, the chicken was out of the oven and the salad on the table. Malcolm had not invited the boys to stay, and they'd stood awkwardly in the foyer while Leah introduced them to Merlin, explaining that no, he wasn't pregnant. He was just a really unusual mix of Basset hound and beagle.

Malcolm filled his plate in the kitchen, and Leah followed him into the dining room with a small bowl of risotto. She hadn't been home since Christmas, and he'd learned from experience not to confuse the girl who entered the house with the one who'd left weeks before.

He walked over to the stereo. "Abbey Lincoln okay with you?" he asked.

"Whatever."

Malcolm heard the clank of her spoon against the glass bowl. It was that quiet.

"This is such a relief," she said finally.

"What is?" He sliced into the chicken. The truth was that he had thought the same thing when she'd first entered the house carting the Goodwill bowling bag she insisted on using as a suitcase. Her face wasn't too drawn or tense. In fact, her cheeks looked a bit fuller than usual. She wasn't stoned. She hadn't pierced anything else that was visible, and she was moving around the house with her usual upbeat agility, as if she was trying to re-experience the rooms all at once.

"The space, the order. At school there's just always people, you know." Her elbow went up, like a wing. "And, God, the shit girls talk about sometimes, not all of them, but the shit kids my age, I mean. . . ."

Malcolm speared some lettuce and watched her eyes move down toward the yellow and violet rubber bands at her wrist. "Did something happen?"

"Madeline's grandmother died, and . . . I don't know."

Malcolm's initial impression of Leah's suite-mate Madeline was that there was nothing wrong with the sylph from Chevy Chase a summer of menial labor couldn't cure.

"She's just been so. . . ."

"Last I heard, you didn't think much of her, anyway."

"That's harsh. It's just—the grandmother dies—I mean, she's like seventy or something, and Madeline goes into hysterics. I tried to be sympathetic, but she's been using it as an excuse for everything. So like after ten days of this shit when I ask if she can please not leave food out 'cause it smells and we're going to get bugs, or worse, she tells me I can't possibly understand what she's going through. She's such a bitch. Can you believe she said that to me? She's nineteen—no, twenty—and she's never been to a funeral before."

"Maybe she's right," he said.

"What?" Leah put down her spoon.

"Madeline doesn't know it won't always feel this bad. And when she said you didn't understand—"

"*Couldn't* understand. Big difference. I told her to 'fucking grow up.'" Leah twisted her mouth. "It felt great when it came out, you know. I was just so. . . ."

"And now?"

"You think I'm an asshole?" She waited before looking at him.

"Technically speaking, yes. In that moment you were being an asshole."

"I got mad."

"Think of all the other things you might have said. Things that might have been less hurtful."

"You get mad. You're not perfect."

Malcolm looked away from her into the semi-dark of the great room. Entryway, dining room, living room, stairs leading up to the catwalk on the second floor—it was all one yawning space, and in the agitated silence between him and his daughter in this too-empty house, he had the not-unfamiliar feeling that someone was hiding, waiting to leap down from the landing and weigh in. He often wondered what it would have been like raising children with another person. There was more than a little glory in being the only one. He liked the control—as much as was possible with kids—but of course there were those times, not just the ones involving illness and unpopular decisions, but those times when you just wanted to drift, let the other adult voice at the table pipe up, wrest control, steer the craft.

He put down his knife and fork and slid around the corner of the table. Leah moved her bare feet to the bottom rung of Malcolm's chair. He studied the length of denim from her knee to her ankle. Her legs were longer than his, her arms too. She had none of his or her sister's compactness, the broad shoulders and thick muscles that made them appear just a little bulky.

"What's bothering you, really, right now?"

She pulled her feet off his chair and slid her knees under the burgundy crewneck sweater Malcolm vaguely recalled as having been his.

"This whole year, since school started in the fall, since . . . well, I've been thinking about Mom, a lot. Not that I didn't before, but. . . ." She stopped and looked around the room. "There's stuff I wish I knew." Malcolm nodded, resisting the impulse to tell her that she could always ask him anything, anything at all, about her mother.

"Did you ever feel that about your father?"

"Still do," he said.

"I have this friend at school. She's my Art History section leader, but we're becoming friends. She was adopted, and she's doing this search for her biological parents. I mean, it's kind of like that, like there's stuff about me I could figure out better if I knew about Mom."

Malcolm pulled off his glasses and rubbed his eyes. His daughter had just compared him to an adoptive parent, implying there was some more authentic connection out there.

"Your face is getting weird." She pushed back from the table. "This isn't about you, okay? I mean, this is kind of the problem, you know. The way you talk about Mom—Susannah and I always feel like, I don't know. Damage control. And Casey, this girl I've been getting to know, she told me she'd give anything to be able to read letters or notebooks—"

"I've shown you girls the baby journals your mother kept for each of you—her yearbooks from high school and college, her photo albums from before we were married."

Leah nodded. "That stuff wasn't hers. That's like going to Epcot and thinking you've seen the world. Don't laugh, Dad. I'm serious."

"Leah, even if I did have a box of your mother's journals and letters, would it be right for me to share those with you and your sister? Would it even be right for *me* to read that stuff?"

"What do you mean?"

"It's just what you said before. Some records are public and some are private. People keep journals for themselves, and when they write personal letters it's usually only to one other person."

"*Did* Mom keep a journal?"

"Let's say that your mother had been sick, that she'd known she was dying. What would she have done with all that private stuff?"

"So there is stuff? Casey said there had to be." Leah leaned forward excitedly.

"I don't really know." Malcolm had looked through Laura's metal filing cabinet only once, while packing for the move here. It was jammed with musical scores, composition notebooks, college papers typed out on onionskin, and the small leather journal he'd discovered in her underwear drawer right after she died. He'd read none of it.

"What do you mean, you don't know?" Leah's voice cracked a bit as if she were choking. She got up with her empty water glass and headed to the kitchen.

Abbey Lincoln's voice stretched from the stereo to his rapidly beating heart. This was maybe the third or fourth time in two weeks, since that cross-dressing session with the Baxter student, that Malcolm had experienced a moment of unwarranted panic. It was as if Leah, his Leah, was about to reveal something he didn't know and couldn't anticipate. Malcolm turned off the stereo, walked over to the couch and sank down into it. "Come sit over here," he said as she returned with her water. "Those chairs are killing my back."

Leah moved past him and slipped into the rocker opposite the couch.

Malcolm looked down at his hand still patting the cushion where he'd wanted her to sit. "What is it you're looking for, LeeLee?"

"I want more than an idea of Mom—*your* idea of her. Casey's helped me to realize I need my own relationship with Mom." She traced the outline of her top lip with her index finger, going around and around a few times, like a car on a track. "I want to know if she would like me."

"Mom?"

She nodded. "I need to know if she would have thought I was an okay person." Leah pulled at the cuff of her sweater and wiped the one eye that was tearing more.

"You know what?" He stopped. He stopped himself from saying what he'd always told both the girls in one way or another. *I think you're a remarkable person, and it's what I think that matters because I'm the one who's here, and I have loved you more fiercely, more powerfully, with more attention and intention than any mother and father together ever could have.* Had a patient told him this, he would have thought it megalomania. And were he the patient, he would have explained that in exchange for his marriage, he'd been granted omnipotent fatherhood.

He had the sudden urge to lie down and close his eyes. "Have you talked to your sister about this?"

Leah nodded. "But it's not the same for her."

"She was older. She had more time with Mom." Malcolm looked at Leah through a kind of haze, as if he had lit a fire and neglected to open the flue.

"Not just that. Zannah's just so much more . . . regular than I am."

The phone rang and Malcolm started, but neither he nor Leah moved to answer it. He held his breath between anticipated rings, each period of silence like the round of a fixed boxing match—no matter the assault, all that was available was the block and parry. Always he was in the position of reacting. Laura's death had rigged the rest of his life, the mopping-up was never over. Of course he'd have to tell the girls everything, had planned all along to do so once he'd prepared them, given them all he could. Just as they were about to surpass him, when they were running at full speed, he'd hand off the rest of the information. He didn't want to be forced to tell the thing before then.

When the machine came on, they both listened. It was Gordon's wife, Jane, saying that Lu Rogers had spotted Leah with a bunch of boys in the Shell station on Market Street. Please, please would Malcolm bring her along when he came to dinner on Saturday. They missed her. Jane would make sure she had a good time. It was going to be a really eclectic group.

"You said you didn't have any plans this weekend."

He shrugged. He'd been dreading this dinner party at Gordon's and Jane's and had hoped to use Leah's unexpected arrival as his excuse to stay home.

"Not that I really care, but are you mad?" Leah asked.

"That you came home?"

"No." She shook her head, and then in a rare, self-deprecating gesture grabbed on to her hair in fistfuls. "I didn't mean that, that I don't care if you're mad. It's more like I'm telling myself I shouldn't care."

"You're right. You shouldn't, but what would I be angry about?"

"Susannah says I'm always pushing." Her face flushed and she looked away from him. "And Casey's been telling me I don't push enough."

"And what do you think?"

"That Mom dying is both the worst thing in the world and as familiar to me . . . as you are."

Malcolm stood up from the couch and walked over to his daughter. He bent slightly, closed his eyes, and pressed his lips to the crown of her head, just as he had done the very first time he saw her.

6

I *had a dream my life would be so different from this hell I'm living.*
Noah stood in the wings, mouthing along with Fantine, who
was sitting on the stage, folded up like some kind of sultry
yogi. Redmond, the director, was pitching a fit because he couldn't
decide what Fantine should be doing while she sang a song of dire
hopelessness.

As they turn your dream to sh..a..a..a..a..a..a..a..me. Noah pinched the
velvet flesh of the curtains. He'd fallen in love with this Fantine weeks
ago. Off stage she was unremarkable, an extra. On stage she was the
manifestation of injustice, the embodiment of a broken spirit. When

the director finally quit interrupting her with hideous suggestions and simply let her have at it with her voice, everyone in the theater stilled. At the end of "I Dreamed a Dream," even the kids working crew applauded.

Hidden between tracks of the tabs, Noah took the opportunity to bow deeply, a Royal Shakespeare Company bow, letting his hair sweep the floor. He straightened up before the girl playing Fantine walked past, her pale lips sealed around an inhaler.

"Right, then, now, 'Lovely Ladies,' let's get on with it." From his post in the front row, Redmond called for the next number.

Noah had been in Cal Redmond's Acting One last semester and had pretty much nailed his accent, a studied RP, spoiled now and then by minor eruptions of his Birmingham childhood. On the first night of tryouts, Redmond had caught Noah "doing him" for the benefit of a few students waiting to audition.

"Ah, Burrell, you fancy yourself an impersonator?"

Noah had been unclear exactly how cutting a remark Redmond had intended. It seemed completely possible that this professor who'd been unable to remember his name until halfway through the term knew something about Noah even Noah was unsure of. He'd relived the scene numerous times, trying to get at the precise pointiness of the point. Standing stage left now, Noah could still reconstitute the hot dissolve he'd felt in that moment, as if it were happening again.

"Allison!" Redmond yelled. "Where's our Fantine?"

Noah was just coming around the stage and down into the auditorium, as Redmond shouted once more for the girl.

"Behind you," Noah said, nodding his head to where Allison was curled up with her inhaler a few rows behind the director. Noah retrieved his backpack from beneath one of the seats, took a long slug from his warm Vitamin Water, and tried not to stare as the director leaned over the girl, his feet planted in the aisle, his hands braced on either side of her.

"All right, then," Redmond began addressing the cast even before he'd turned to face the stage. "Let me have someone just so we can

71

block this number. Burrell, you're not in this one, right? Excellent, then." Redmond motioned with the back of his hand as he continued to walk in Noah's direction. "Just let Sasha chase you for your hair. No need to sing. Okay, then, let's get on with it." The director nodded toward one of his many obedient female assistants to start the music.

Noah was aware that he'd stopped moving, stopped breathing.

"Fantine, *andiamo*! Over there!" The director made emphatic use of his large shaved scalp.

Noah slowly climbed onto the stage, his whole body rebooting itself with a head-to-toe flush. He tucked his hair behind one ear.

"We're going to start with the prostitutes. Then sailors enter, then Fantine and Madame Pinking Shears, okay?"

Redmond might have picked any one of forty cast members, but he'd picked him, the one who'd need to choose whether to act like Fantine or like the awkward male everyone, or most everyone, expected him to be. As the music began, Noah caught a glimpse of Tory Liggett and her blonder bustier sidekick. They were shimmying along with the rest of the prostitutes in their sweats and T-shirts, circling their hips and giving the deserted theater an eyeful of their theoretical cleavage. He hadn't been within cringing distance of them since the chapel-bell incident two weeks before. Of course they were in this number; the scales of cosmic injustice had seen to that. Really, this seemed to happen to him more than to other people, like he was the butt of some epic joke being performed two shows daily.

"Fantine!" the director shouted and Noah leapt into the crowd of hoofing, sweating guys and girls chugging with the exertion of singing and dancing. He knew there weren't a lot of people on stage, maybe fourteen, but he felt as if he were deep inside a crowd. The girl playing the hag chased him as he snaked through the high-kicking prostitutes and the shuffling sailors. She croaked out her lines, opening and closing a pair of purple kid's scissors as she sang. Though Redmond had instructed him to speak the lyrics, he couldn't bear it. Spoken, they were even cheesier than sung. And besides, he'd had the entire score memorized for weeks. He hated that he loved *Les Mis*, everyone singing over one another in that musical hysteria that people who didn't get Sondheim called brilliant.

Noah ducked in and around the singers and dancers. Pursued, persecuted, destitute, and desperate. The exertion of so many other bodies surrounded him, and he felt distilled. He felt like himself—no, so much more, so much better than himself. During the few measures of instrumental before the sailors started in again, the girl playing the hag smiled at him and whispered, "Sick."

Easy money, lying on a bed. Just as well they never see the hate that's in your head. Don't they know they're making love to one already dead? He belted out the closing line of the number with his back to the house and his arms crisscrossing his chest in a firm embrace.

"All right." The director aimed his pen at Noah. "Thank you Ladies and sailors to the dance studio with Petra. Valjean, you're up."

Noah hopped off the stage, his whole body vibrating with adrenaline.

"You have a great voice." The real Fantine was kneeling backward on a seat in the row in front of where he'd stashed his backpack.

He shrugged, drained the last of his Vitamin Water, and wiped his damp face with the hem of his shirt.

"No. Really. If you weren't a guy, I'd be, like, worried, you know. The way you sang that. I feel like you helped me get something about Fantine that I didn't really see before."

"Ever see the movie version with Liam Neeson and Uma Thurman?"

She nodded. "I'm Allison."

He smiled. "I know. Redmond yells your name a lot."

"I don't know your name." She turned away for a moment to check who was on stage.

"Noah," he said.

"Allison!" The director looked over at the two of them.

"You okay?" he asked. "I mean, I saw you had—"

She'd already begun to walk away, even as she was patting him on the forearm. He watched her hurry down the aisle and climb onto the stage, as if she were raising herself out of a swimming pool.

⌥

It was dark by the time Noah pushed open the back doors of the theater to the courtyard behind Nelson. Even if he'd wakened from a month-long sleep, he would have known it was the beginning of a Saturday night at Baxter—the smell of steak from the dining hall, the sound of high heels on sanded walkways, and the steady stream of students on the return pilgrimage from town, damp brown bags of thirty-packs under their arms.

He felt an initial hard tap through the shoulder of his parka, turned, and pulled out his earbuds.

"More than a little scary." Each word was punctuated by an increasingly insistent finger rapping the same spot on his shoulder. Tory Liggett's real-life sailor boyfriend smelled of wintertime sweat, as if he'd been wearing a wool cap over unwashed hair for several days.

"You popped right into that femme role, didn't you? Like it was second nature." He was dressed in the same dark green sailing-team sweatshirt he'd had on the other day.

Noah took a breath in, but not out, turned from the boy, and headed back across the courtyard in the direction of the theater entrance.

"Hey, I'm talking to you."

The kid, slightly taller than Noah, probably outweighed him by thirty or forty pounds. As Noah began to run, he could hear the *whoosh* of the kid's wind pants behind him and feel the pounding of his booted feet on the granite. The Nelson Theater marked the edge of the campus. The only other college building beyond it was the president's house. The courtyard, lit mostly with solar footlights, connected the theater with a large parking area. Except for the twenty minutes just before and after a performance, it was usually

74

empty. When Noah was maybe thirty feet or so from the doors of the theater, the boy grabbed him by the back of his parka and pulled him to a stop.

Even if he'd wanted to look at the kid, he couldn't, not the way the collar of his jacket was being twisted, pinning his neck to one side. All he could see from this angle was the president's yard, where one of his kids was spinning down a snow mound at the edge of the driveway in a large pink plastic saucer.

"What the fuck are you, anyway?"

He didn't want Dowd in his head right then, hadn't appealed to him nor summoned him, but there he was, part critic, part coach. "I'm a tenor," Noah said softly.

"What'd you say?" The kid tugged on him again, and Noah could feel the heat and weight of his disgust.

"Noah." A girl called from somewhere behind him, and almost simultaneously the boy let go.

"A tenor, a freshman, a Democrat." The trail of comebacks dribbled from his mouth, but the boy was gone.

"God, that was so great in there," the girl shouted toward him. "I wish I could sing like that."

⁓∞⁓

Noah opened the unlocked kitchen door and froze. It took a moment before he recognized the deep rumble as belonging to Garrison Keillor. The radio at high volume was his mother's sole security system. He threw his coat and backpack on a kitchen chair, turned down the radio, and opened the refrigerator.

"'What are you, anyway?'" he repeated to himself, reliving the same sixty seconds over again for the twentieth time. He slammed the refrigerator closed. He hated that he was so permeable, as if his psyche was a common room where strangers roamed, freely stubbing out cigarettes on the furniture. That's what was wrong with him. Not a gender confusion, but the fact that all his borders were undefended.

He reached into the cupboard above the stove and grabbed the jug of Jim Beam by its handle. His uncle had given his mother a 1.75-liter bottle for Christmas, because that's what he liked to drink when he came over. He poured enough of the stuff into a wine goblet and sniffed it. Bourbon smelled better than it tasted.

He pulled out a kitchen chair and looked up at the mural he and his mother had painted when he was in fifth grade. There was an entire wall of very primitive-looking tropical fish and coral reefs and even a shark. They'd done it freehand and it had taken two days, two whole days during Thanksgiving break. His mother had played recordings of Polynesian and Hawaiian music she'd borrowed from the Ethnomusicology department. She'd even let Noah crank up the heat so that they could paint in their bathing suits. Noah had thought they should sketch it first on a big sheet of paper, but his mother had told him that the point was to be spontaneous. If, in the end, there was something they really hated, they could always change it. Some of the DayGlo colors had begun to crack, but the shark still looked pretty good. Noah had begged her to paint over the whole thing when he was in eighth grade, but now he was grateful that she had ignored him. As with many situations between them, whether she was authentically patient or defensively passive about the mural was unclear. She had never said anything to him about the garment bags hanging in his closet. It was possible she'd never looked. She was like that. She respected his privacy. He'd been amazed throughout high school to hear stories of parents putting electronic tails on their kids' instant messaging.

Noah got up and switched off the radio. Fucking bluegrass, what a bad idea that was. His mother had painted one more fish into the mural after he'd thought they were done and had gone to bed. He'd been adamant that every fish they included be a specific species, identifiable according to the books he'd taken from the library. But the one she'd painted while he slept was straight from her imagination—purple and orange and black—swimming, unsuspectingly or brazenly, right beneath the shark. He bent his head down to his glass, the way little kids do, and stuck his tongue in the bowl of bourbon.

He carried his drink into his mother's bedroom and gently sat down on the bed. She'd made the bedspread herself by covering a piece of turquoise silk with glue, vats of the stuff, and then covering the glue with thousands of infinitesimal colored beads. He imagined if you were naked it might feel weird. Pretty much every time you moved, you could hear beads hit the wood floor, and it didn't feel so great when they plastered themselves to the soles of your bare feet. He knew his mother was quirky, mostly in a good way. But with non-conformity there was always the possibility of the dial spinning all the way to strange. It made him a little sad that his mother's eccentricity occasionally crossed over into outright weirdness. If he ever had kids, he'd never want them to feel that way about him. Maybe that's how he could explain it to Dowd. Maybe that was really the goal, getting to be someone who wouldn't freak out his own kids.

He grabbed the remote control from the nightstand and began to scroll through the TV with the sound off. It was already after seven. He stuck his index finger in the bourbon and licked it. It was wrong to be nearly nineteen and sitting alone on your mother's bed on a Saturday night. It wasn't like he was in a wheelchair or had tubes coming in and out of him. But if he had, this is probably what he'd be doing. They were showing *The Birds* in the basement of Anderson at eight o'clock. If he got up and went, he'd be less pathetic. But if he got up and went, there was a small chance he'd run into sailor Sam. If he stayed here, he could try on a few things. He felt guilty that his mother was paying for room and board and he spent so much time back here. This was one of the things he should try to explain to Dowd. Every action came fully loaded with a possible alternate action. And each of those resulted in a spectrum of divergent consequences. It was impossible to know what to do. Everything was wrong, every move, every choice.

He turned off the TV, tossed the remote onto the bed, and walked into his room. He slid open the closet door and unzipped the canvas garment bag. He lifted the lid on the CD compartment of his old boom box to make sure his mother hadn't switched Rufus Wainwright for some south Indian chanting or something, and hit PLAY. With the sound of the first piano chord, he thought he heard a car horn. The family across the street had twin high school girls who were always signing off with cutesy little beeps of their horns. They bugged the shit out of him. He unzipped his pants and heard it again, three short toots. He walked down the hall, holding the tops of his pants together with one hand. Through the back door he could see a crummy-looking Hyundai with its lights on in the driveway. He zipped up just as Alex, the girl from Sociology, appeared fully framed, head pressed against the glass.

"Noah?"

He unlocked the door and she entered the kitchen, untying the hood of her sweatshirt and releasing a big glossy pile of red hair. "I'm pretty good at remembering addresses. I took a chance you weren't working. Nice house."

Noah laughed. "I never told you my address."

"I shovel this block. Your mother lives here, so. . . ."

"You know her?"

"Not really. She usually shovels herself."

Noah nodded. "You want to come in?"

"Nah, car's running. I'm here to see if you want to come out."

Noah could feel the light burning in his bedroom, as if he were up against the bare bulb. The closet doors had been left open, the garment bag unzipped. "I . . . don't really. . . ."

"I was supposed to work the reserve room at Baldwin, but all the computers went down, so they decided to close, and I feel like going out, doing something. You like pool?"

"It's okay."

"There's this VFW in Becket. The old guys are mostly gone by nine. We can have a table to ourselves."

"You can't just go to a VFW."

She nodded and smirked, causing her cheeks to round out under her eyes.

"I'd be oh-so-popular down at the VFW." Noah began trying to tuck his too-short T-shirt into the waistband of his pants.

"It's like this place my dad and grandpa and my uncles all hang."

"And that's supposed to reassure me?"

She stared at him, her face firming up, becoming more solemn, sad almost. "Why wouldn't people like you, want to meet you?"

"Experience tells me otherwise."

"You're totally hot. I thought looks were power in this culture."

He stared at his coat on the chair, his own coat which only an hour before had been used to choke him. "You twenty-one?"

"If you're with me, we're cool in there."

"I suck at pool."

"Get your shit. I'll wait for you in the car."

7

J ane and Gordon Stadler lived in the Captain Ryder House. It was
one of a handful of homes in town venerable enough to warrant
a navy blue plate with white lettering listing the year it was built
and the name of its original owner. Gordon had told Malcolm that was
a load of bullshit, an attempt to justify inflated prices for homes with
root cellars and 60-amp service. Gordon didn't like antiques, not antique
houses or antique furniture, or, as Jane often joked, antique women.

Malcolm and Leah let themselves into the narrow foyer, where
Leah rapidly stripped herself of her hat and coat as well as her shoes,
while Malcolm stood motionless, all zipped up, staring at the black

Persian lamb hat occupying the center hook of the combination coatrack and bench.

"What?" she said. "I don't want to track crap all through the house."

He watched his daughter stride down the center hall to the kitchen in the back. Then he slid off his gloves and reached for the fur hat. It was stupid. In a minute he would know whether *her* voice was one of the ones barely audible above the laughter and the music and the chiseling of ice from the block Gordon deemed essential for parties. He'd been wanting to stroke this hat ever since he'd first seen her wearing it in the back lot of Monroe's. The gray silk lining was frayed, which somehow seemed promising to him. The thick black label inside advertised a shop on Houston Street in New York. He looked down the hall, then swept the tightly curled fur across his lips.

"God, they'll invite anyone here." The front door opened with a blast of air and bombast from Lu Rogers.

Malcolm turned his back on her and tossed the hat back onto its hook. He slipped off his coat, then embraced her, or as much of her as he could encircle. "I thought artists were quiet, introspective types. How do you think that lie got started?"

Lu pressed him down the hall toward the kitchen, waving away his idle chatter for her own. "Why the hell would anyone tear down that house on South Cove Road? Massholes." As they passed the photos of the boys and Gordon, black-and-whites hanging in chrome frames, he knew that if he reached the next room and Cara wasn't there, the hat belonging to someone else entirely, this moment of happy anticipation would be the high point of his evening. He stepped into the kitchen, where Lu discharged another volley of disgruntled greeting, and before he even looked around, he reprimanded himself for allowing anything as retrograde as happy anticipation.

Gordon and Jane's next-door neighbors and two realtors from Jane's office swarmed toward Lu. Malcolm was freed. He slipped around the center island, moving slowly and scanning the various stations—sink, hearth, French doors, where people were grouped. Things were in his way—a blue vase filled with pussy willows, the profusion of garlic and butter, Gordon's pick-axing of the ice, Miles Davis on the stereo, his daughter's own distinctive lilt. All this made it difficult for him to see. He pulled off his glasses and unfolded the handkerchief in his front pants pocket. The open refrigerator door blocked the rest of the room. When Jane slammed it shut, Cara appeared on the other side. She was holding a highball against her hipbone and she smiled at him, causing Jane to turn and stare.

"Malcolm!" Jane was cradling a bunch of leeks, but she set them down to embrace and kiss him. "Thank you for bringing Leah. I'm thrilled she agreed to it. So, I hear you guys know each other." Jane snapped the thick blue rubber band binding the leeks. "One less introduction for me to make."

Cara smiled again.

"It's really nice to see you," Malcolm said.

Jane filled a large stainless-steel bowl with water. "Malcolm, I hate to ask, but after you've gotten yourself a drink, can you do the leeks for me? I'm kind of behind. We had this complete screw-up around driving Brendan today. Gordon neglected to inform me that you guys had group this afternoon."

Malcolm's pulse doubled. Gordon was standing by the bar, rolling a lemon between his hands. When their eyes met, Gordon winked, of all goddamn things.

Malcolm reached over and cradled Jane's elbow. "Let me get a glass of wine, and then you can put me to work."

"I could tell from your shopping cart you could cook," Cara said.

Malcolm pointed to her drink and she shook her head. "Some people actually go to the supermarket to buy food."

"I've heard." She followed him as he moved past the fire in the open hearth.

"Just one bit of shop, upstairs, just for a minute," Gordon said, putting down what looked like a dental tool rather than a bar accoutrement.

As Malcolm poured from an open bottle of Malbec, he could feel Gordon pleading whole paragraphs at him with his eyes. "Later. Right now your wife is waiting for me—"

"This will only take a second." Gordon placed his thick hand at the small of Malcolm's back as if they were on the dance floor and he, of course, was leading.

Malcolm stepped free of Gordon's reach, allowing one hand to graze Cara's shoulder. His fingertips registered the loose weave of her silk sweater and beneath that, spine and muscle, tauter than he expected. And if he hadn't been building his own fire in a place deep enough to burn everything Gordon, he would have thought about what it might feel like to run his hand up under that flimsy little sweater. "How do you know Jane and Gordon?"

"I just met Jane. Gordon was the one who invited me," Cara said.

"Really? How do you know him again?"

"Mutual friend."

"Okay, so here's the recipe." Jane pressed the heel of her hand down the center of a magazine and splayed it flat onto the counter. Malcolm was slow to move his eyes from Cara and the way her smallish breasts but broad shoulders tugged at her sweater.

"You can soak the leeks in here." She pointed to a bowl of water. "You know where the knives are. Cut on this, it works better." Jane patted him on the back by way of a thank-you.

Malcolm trimmed the root ends of the leeks and watched Cara get taken up into a group presided over by Pete Currier, the editor of the *Smithport Sentinel*. He glanced over at Jane with the same sense of guilt that accompanied decelerating on the highway when a speed trap was spotted up ahead. The wrong was unconscious, but the cover-up deliberate.

Malcolm sliced the gritty leeks lengthwise and dropped them into the bowl of water. "I never buy leeks, just for this reason," he said to Jane, who was behind him at the range.

She turned, spatula in hand, and leaned into his ear. "I've been back in Smithport for eighteen years, and I've never laid eyes on her—what are the odds of that?"

Malcolm cracked his neck and lifted the leeks from the water into the colander. "Who?"

"Cara, the woman Gordo invited."

"She's a musician," Malcolm said.

"I like music." Jane squinted up at him. She was standing directly beneath one of the halogen spots, and he noticed a flatness to her eyes. They lacked their usual glinting conviction that life was, if not mostly joyous, then certainly a real gas, a word no one but she dared use any more.

Malcolm must have stared just a moment too long. She blushed, and ran her fingers through her spiky blond hair.

He shook the water from his hands and placed them on her shoulders.

"Don't ask," she said, "just . . . you know . . . it's a party . . . let's just get through the effin' dinner party." She moved the large mass of mushrooms around the sauté pan as if the spatula was a push broom. Without looking at him, she held out her empty wine glass. "Why didn't I marry you, explain that one to me."

"You didn't know me," he said, taking the glass and reaching into the fridge where he knew there'd be a bottle of white on the door.

"You're such a nitpicker." She turned and accepted the wine with a smile.

Jane was the reason he'd moved back to Smithport from Massachusetts after Laura died. At least that's what he said when he was feeling flush with gratitude for the way many things in his life had worked out. He'd met Jane one winter weekend when he was clearing out his grandparents' house.

Malcolm had been slow to list the house after his grandfather's death and even slower to clean it out. He was the only heir. The property was his, and so was the task of tossing out the belongings of people who had lived a combined 166 years. The chore alternately loomed and receded from 200 miles away, waking him in the middle of the night, making him short-tempered with Laura and the girls.

As Jane and her clients, a middle-aged couple from New York, stomped through the cold house in ice-covered hiking boots, Malcolm continued to sift through crocheted doilies and iced-tea spoons, tie tacks and kid gloves, all of it interspersed with forty-year-old receipts from the butcher and the optometrist. When the house hunters walked down to the dock, Jane pulled up one of the ladderback chairs in the dining room. "You should keep it, you know."

He had turned awkwardly, his movements thick with layers of clothing.

"I grew up on Hatches Road, and I spent my childhood biking around here. I remember back when your grandmother still had chickens, and a beautiful white mare with strange stripes, almost like a zebra."

Malcolm fiddled with the raised monogram on a handkerchief or a napkin. He couldn't begin to guess at the uses for some of these linens. He had instructed himself, repeatedly, to sort through the contents of the house, top down, the order in which his grandmother had taught him to clean, but after months of intermittent trips to Maine, he had yet to enter his grandparents' bedroom, where he feared he'd find letters his grandmother had saved from his father as a young man, or worse, a diary she might have kept. He'd not done much more than poke his nose into the spare bedroom his grandfather had used for an office, certain he'd come upon a cache of old treatment notes. At night, he slept on the living-room sofa, something his grandmother would have despised. He'd been unable to cross the threshold into the room upstairs with the bed that had been his. As a boy, Malcolm would sometimes lie on his stomach on that bed and grip the carved maple posts of the headboard, like the positive and negative charge of everything that had happened and everything he wished had happened instead.

"It's your family's land. You should keep it, for your kids, you know."

He didn't recognize the realtor, and figured she had to be younger by at least half a decade.

"Rent it out, maybe—but keep it. Property like this on the waterfront—you'll never be able to get it back."

"My wife and I live right outside Boston," he said, as if he owed her an explanation. "Our jobs are there. Besides, we could never afford the taxes, the upkeep."

For him, the property was bound up in the accumulated grief of the people who had lived there. He needed to unload it. With the deaths of his mother, his grandmother, and then his grandfather all in fairly rapid succession, he sometimes had the strange sense that his thirties had acted upon him like a mill saw. Each loss another razing. Later, Laura's death would cap off the decade and take him down to bone.

He suggested then that Jane buy the house, and she laughed. Seeing her clients begin their return from the waterfront, Jane walked to the front hall. Malcolm followed, stooping to collect the splintered bits of kindling littering his grandmother's braided wool rug.

"Apart from the fact we could never afford it, my husband is just this side of urban," Jane said. "He likes sidewalks." She blushed, and Malcolm remembered thinking that she loved the guy—just a passing thought. After Laura died and he decided to move back to Smithport, it was Jane he called for help finding a house for himself and the girls.

❦

Jane brought the food to the table and Gordon assigned the seating, sandwiching Malcolm between Cara and Leah. Gordon never sat at the head of his own table, an empty gesture at democratization because no matter where he sat, he was the impresario of these dinner parties.

"What do the kids you go to school with say about it?" Gordon served himself some pasta from the bowl that was passed to him. His program for the night had begun, a discussion of a much-publicized instance of cyber-bullying that had ended in the suicide of a Portland high school student.

"It's like if you're genderqueer in high school, you should be put on the endangered-species list." Leah reached a little too far for the butter and then began slathering a piece of ciabatta.

Nobody spoke and she looked over at Malcolm. "What?"

Pete Currier asked her to repeat what she'd just said.

Leah looked around the table, her face reddening slightly.

"I've never heard that before, that term," Pete's wife said. She ran Smithport's recreation department and was overly fond of predicting the next generation of headliners in the police blotter of her husband's paper.

"What term?" Leah placed her buttered bread on the side of her plate.

"'Genderqueer,'" Gordon said with exaggerated annunciation, before beginning to laugh.

"That real, or did you coin it?" one of Jane's realtor friends asked.

"You know, like trans people." Leah looked across the table at Gordon.

"You mean like undecided?" Jinx Currier asked.

Her husband laughed. "Bisexual, hon. The term is 'bisexual.'"

Leah laid down her knife softly. "Lots of people feel those terms—gay, straight—are limiting. No, well, actually more than limiting: that the words themselves have caused a limited consciousness. And that we should look at gender along a continuum. And really, if you think about it, that's probably much closer to what's true for most people."

"Did you know about this?" Gordon asked Malcolm from across the table, as if he'd been hoarding some hot new trend all to himself.

"It's just come up in a kid I'm working with. Something, maybe like this. I just downloaded a bunch of literature in the library yesterday—haven't gone through that much of it—but 'genderqueer' did come up in the subject headings."

"How about you, Patrick, you run into this?"

A physician's assistant in Baxter College's health services, Patrick was the next youngest person at the table after Leah. Patrick finished swallowing and wiped his mouth. "Pushing the envelope on everything is what I run into."

Malcolm leaned close to Cara, who had become unnaturally still. He saw that she was gripping her fork tightly but not moving it. "He calls on people," he whispered. "It can be very unnerving."

"This is really good, this pasta," she whispered back.

"Jane's a great cook." Malcolm wondered what it was about the scene, whether it was the dynamic or the topic that was making her uncomfortable. Gordon had a tendency to run his dinner parties the way he did therapy with groups. He strapped on the head lamp and went in, focusing, redirecting, searching. Malcolm usually loved nothing better than listening in the wake of Gordon's surgical strikes, culling the data, verbal and nonverbal, that Gordon elicited from people slightly undefended by alcohol and camaraderie. But tonight there was Leah to tend to and Cara and this rotten crap with Gordon and Jane; working on the puzzle of the characters around the table would have been self-indulgent.

"So are they like not having sex?" Gordon asked.

"Just sounds like fear, to me." Lu Rogers reached for the immense wooden salad bowl. "Get your shorts in a twist over *gender identity*, and then you don't have to make it with anyone."

Malcolm heard Leah snort, but the conversation had already begun splintering. "I conveniently forgot about this." Leah reached for the wine.

"It's the second time we've listened to *Kind of Blue*," Cara said, holding a platter of vegetables toward Malcolm.

Jane pushed back her chair abruptly and strode off toward the stereo, her annoyance unnoticed by Cara, who had just placed a hand on Malcolm's thigh underneath the farmhouse table. Malcolm became acutely aware of his daughter's presence on the other side of him.

When Jane sat back down, Cara asked her what kind of music she liked to listen to. He saw the squint in Jane's response and, again, that flatness. Leah put a hand on his shoulder, trying to get his attention.

"Dad," Leah finally said, a bit too loudly, "I think I might go after dinner." She looked down at the cell phone in her lap. "Those guys I got a ride with want me to hang out with them at Baxter."

"Hmm?" he said, turning as if he had a stiff neck, not wanting to discourage Cara's hand, his thigh having taken on a life of its own.

"You can get a ride, I bet," Leah said with a little smirk.

"I'm sorry, Lee," he put his arm around her. "What're you asking?"

"For the car keys."

"Wait 'til everyone's done."

"I didn't mean right now. Jesus."

"I'm sorry, I'm having trouble hearing." Malcolm looked down at the table. Jane had made the plates, hand-thrown. Each one had to weigh a pound and a half. The oversized silverware clanked against the crackle-glazed crockery. The full goblets thudded when they hit the wooden table. Voices dipped and rose through anecdote and response. And then there was the deafening sound of that hand on his thigh.

The hand patted him. "I can take you home."

"Do you even know where he lives?" Jane said, the tone obviously getting a jump on the words. "Way the hell on the Twin Harbors side of Smithport."

"The dark side of town," Malcolm said.

"Leah, honey, you take my car, and Gordon will drive me over tomorrow to get it." Jane stood up and headed toward the kitchen.

"What should I do, Dad?"

Malcolm placed his right palm over her wine glass, and then stood up, but not before pressing the fingers of his left hand into that warm hand on his thigh.

He found Jane in the back hall, digging through her purse.

"I can get into fifty houses in town, but I can't find my own car keys."

She was standing amidst a sea of boots and skates, running shoes and sandals. "You seem a little stressed," Malcolm said, laughter cresting in the next room.

"Perceptive." Her back was to him. She unzipped the pocket of a ski parka. "Is he having an affair with her? Is this . . . her driving you home . . . is that . . ."

Malcolm placed both his hands on Jane's shoulders and pivoted her toward him. "Jane. I'm the one who wants to have the affair with her."

Jane brought her arms up on the outside of his and covered her eyes and began to cry. "Oh, God, I'm such an idiot. Such a fucking idiot."

Jane wouldn't look at him, and Malcolm was unsure how to proceed. He was strangely eager to tell her how he felt about Cara, to tell her he was infatuated, preoccupied, nearly lobotomized with the idea of her. But his joy could only add to Jane's suffering in some strange funhouse-mirror way. Clearly she knew enough about Gordon to be suspicious. Just as people had different thresholds for pain, he suspected they had different thresholds for the truth.

"Just hold me. Can you just hold me, like really hug me?"

Malcolm pulled her to him. Her back was warm and slightly damp beneath her silk blouse. He could feel her silent sobbing, her head bobbing against his ribcage.

"Who's going to love me?" she whispered.

"Dad?" Leah stopped a few feet before she reached them.

Jane lifted her head and pressed her hands against her eyes. "Your dad's just making a house call, that's all," she said, then laughed. "You know, it's probably better if you take your father's car." Jane shut off the light in the hall and began walking toward the kitchen. "Then Cara will have to give him a ride, and who knows where that will lead." Jane turned, addressing Malcolm now. "The girls and I have been thwarted in our every attempt. . . ."

Malcolm watched, as if she had completely disrobed back in that hallway, and was now retrieving the discarded layers of her costume—irreverence, spunk, wit, competence. Everything she needed to continue on. He was ashamed at his relief, deeply ashamed for holding up his end of the rug while she swept all the crap back beneath it.

⚭

"Well, I think that we change the world energetically. I think that what we do, how we interact with others, the loop inside our heads, what we're thinking and feeling—yeah, I think that has an effect." Cara had pushed her plate toward the center of the table and was talking softly.

"And that's it?" Gordon challenged. "That's all that's asked of us? Be nice, think nice thoughts, and the world will change . . . energetically?" Gordon smirked in Malcolm's direction, a smarmy train conductor commanding him to get on board. Malcolm refused to meet his gaze, and instead surveyed the table. Certainly he'd missed something. Whatever it was had caused most everyone at the table to become subdued, as if a noxious gas had been let loose.

"Those things aren't limited. Everything affects everything else. It's all connected." Cara was very still as she spoke, moving only her eyes and her jaw. Her lack of urgency, her disinterest in convincing Gordon of anything, of winning him over to her side, fascinated Malcolm.

Gordon nodded and pressed his lips together. Jane poured herself some more wine, and everyone waited.

"If you don't mind my saying, it sounds like a lot of New Age bullshit." Gordon looked right at her.

"Actually," Cara paused. She smiled. "Actually, Gordon, I do mind your saying that, but apparently you feel you have to say it, and say it in that way."

Malcolm relaxed, leaned back into his chair. He'd been worried that Cara was one of those people for whom being passive and being patronizing were just a hair's breadth apart.

"Dad," Leah whispered into his ear. "This could go on like forever."

Malcolm pushed away from the table and reached into his pants pocket for the car keys. "You've only had the one glass, right?"

"So far."

"It's the kind of night where there could be black ice."

"I'm probably just going to end up staying with Erin at Baxter, okay?"

He grabbed Leah's hand under the table and squeezed it. A few moments passed, as if her attention were elsewhere or she were considering the small thing he'd just said, but then, he felt it, the squeeze back, all the rings on her fingers digging an affirmation into his flesh.

"It's not that late," Cara said, her words barely audible over the growling of her ancient Saab.

Malcolm looked at his watch and put on his seatbelt. It was 12:20.

"That thing about musicians being night owls? Totally true." She pulled away from the curb.

"You have a plan?"

"I try never to have a plan."

"Really?"

She nodded in the dark, then sped through a stop sign. "Just trying to stay ahead of that godawful engine noise. I like to get out of neighborhoods as fast as possible, before someone calls the police."

"I'd be happy to look at it sometime for you."

She turned and searched his face in the dark car.

"I used to work on boats a lot. Eventually, even when you work on sailboats, you end up learning about motors. It's always the most screwed-up part of any boat."

"I don't picture you knowing about cars, engines, that kind of thing."

"Well, how do you picture me?"

"Naked."

"No. Really," he said.

"Really," she said, her eyes straight ahead, her gloved hand on the gearshift.

"I wish I could be sure that was a good thing."

Now she turned to him, the crease at the top of her hat dipping down a bit. "Well, of course you can't be sure."

"No," he said and looked out at the snow illuminated by the waxing moon. "Do you tend to see people naked? I mean, is that just part of how you perceive the world?"

She stopped at a traffic light. They waited. There were no cars.

"You mean, am I one of those people who goes around undressing everyone with their eyes? No. It's not like that."

The light changed, and Cara eased the car into first gear. "What's it like then?" He didn't think anyone had ever said that to him, that they pictured him naked. Even when he and Laura were first together, and they'd be apart for a while, talking on the phone, no, she never would have said that. She might have said that she missed him, maybe even that she missed him being inside her, and. . . .

"I don't really know where you live. I mean I know it's *way the hell on the Twin Harbors side of Smithport*," she said in a passable imitation of a peeved Jane.

"Where do *you* live?"

"Near campus, on Freeman."

They were coming to the edge of the college now; the fieldhouse and the rink were up ahead. A group of darkly clothed students walked by, one walking backward so he could keep talking to the rest. "If we went to your house, could I get you to play some music?"

Cara abruptly turned the car into the service driveway behind the alumni house and palmed the shift into neutral. She unfastened her seatbelt. Pivoting her whole body toward him, she leaned over slightly and swept her lips across his cheek. He reached out to her with his arms extended, but when he tried to narrow the space between them, his shoulder belt locked, pinning him against the seat. She fumbled for a moment, feeling around for the release button. As soon as he was free, he clasped his gloved hands behind her neck and pulled her toward him. He moved his lips over hers, feeling his way to that arch, all at once plump and firm, warm and cool, the entry to everything. He was unprepared for her tongue, which as he took a breath slipped into his mouth. Her hat slid down over her face and he grabbed it, holding it now behind her neck. He thought about the mesh sweater she had on, but there was no way to get to it beneath the innumerable layers of down and fleece, Gore-Tex and fiberfill, not to mention the elaborate system of padlocks and pulleys, moat and drawbridge, that were the two-way zippers and snaps, Velcro, and drawstring. Her tongue was moving around parts of his mouth he hadn't been aware of. She was pressing him from inside his own mouth. And he wished he could press the length of his body against hers, with nothing in between, nothing at all.

"I've wanted to do that since I first saw you in the parking lot that night at Monroe's."

He nodded. She had moved back against her seat, replacing her hands on the wheel. A security light at the rear of the alumni house suddenly shone onto the hood of the car. He placed the hat on her head, then pulled off his gloves and tucked her hair behind her ears. She put the car into gear and turned up the defroster. He reached over again as if to make one more adjustment to the hat, but stopped. Letting his hands come to rest on either side of her face, he ran his thumbs down the sharp slope of her cheekbones.

"I've wanted to do *that*, since I first saw you that night in the parking lot."

⁂

Her house was cold. She moved around with her coat on, punching at the digital thermostat with her gloves. There was a candle burning in the bathroom, and as he closed the door he could smell patchouli. He unzipped his coat and his pants and when he went to flush, the metal handle was freezing. It almost felt as if a window were open. He looked back at the candle. How could she have left the house for the night with it burning?

"Want something to drink?" she called to him from the kitchen.

He walked down the hallway that bisected the house, passing several closed doors, each of them painted a different shade of purple.

"I know I have bourbon." She was filling a teakettle with water, the bell-shaped sleeve of her coat dangling dangerously close to the faucet.

Malcolm looked around the narrow kitchen, the only solid wall completely covered with a kitschy marine mural. Small as the house was, it was bigger than the car. Big enough to have to make decisions, to choose where to move, where to place your feet, your hands, your lips. Her back was still to him, the dim red of her coat, the luster of that black hat, the same color as her hair. His fascination with her was almost immobilizing. He wanted to watch her, listen to her, study her. Maybe if he had a drink he wouldn't need to keep telling himself to interact. He took off his parka and draped it over one of the kitchen chairs.

She struck a match and lit the burner. He came up behind her and lifted her hair away from the back of her neck and kissed her. Malcolm was barely taller, the perfect height to move his mouth behind her ears. She unzipped her coat and he brought his arms around her front, just as she reached up to open the cabinet above the stove. She set a bottle of cognac on the counter beside the range, and turned.

"I'm sorry it's so cold in here."

He grabbed both her hands in his and blew on them, re-gripped them, tried to feel the weight of them. He wondered if her masterful fingering on the guitar was linked to an extraordinary sense of touch. He slowly raked his fingers through hers. The kettle let out a rasp and she switched off the gas, took hold of his wrist, and led him out of the kitchen and down the hallway.

Her bedroom was small and spare, except for the bed and its beaded coverlet. It was like an enormous glittering gemstone in the center of a plain white box that was only barely big enough to hold it. She lit the votive candles lined up on the pine bureau. He watched her hold the match until it seemed to be burning her fingertips. The candlelight made the beads jump and sparkle, as if they were blinking like the lights on a Christmas tree.

He hated to take off his glasses, to compromise his ability to see Cara, but it was so dim in the room anyway. He watched her unzip her short boots, and he folded his glasses and placed them on the bureau with the candles and a few pictures. He fingered the frame nearest him, its edges decorated with shells or beads, he couldn't quite tell.

He hadn't had sex since August, that one time with Nina Hunt, and he was primed to meet resistance. But Cara seemed unimpeded by all the things that slowed or stopped most everyone else. She was seated on the edge of the bed now, and as he moved toward her he thought he heard her whisper something. He was close enough to touch her before he realized she was chanting, speaking, not in English and without any particular intonation. Her hands were pressed flat against her heart. He withstood the urge to place his hands on hers, to unzip her pants, to tug at her sweater, to run his finger along the inside of her thigh.

"A little prayer. I try to say it every night, you know, without exception."

Speaking now would have been graceless. Besides, he didn't really want to know who she was praying to or what she was praying for.

"I knew you wouldn't think that was weird. I mean, I'm not usually comfortable doing that in front of anyone else. But you . . . you're very open, you know?"

He was far from what most people would consider open; he only knew what it looked like well enough to fake it. He knelt down on the floor, pushing the wide leg of her pants slowly up past her knee as the room filled with the sound of rushing water, the source of the river a white-noise machine on the nightstand. Her calf was soft and smooth, and he slid his palm around it several times before running his hand past a scar on her kneecap, then up the inside of her thigh just to where he felt hair and moisture. He snaked his index finger under the lace edge of her silky panties and she made a noise that almost sounded sad to him. He stopped and tried to make out her expression, but the room was too dark and his sight too blurry. She pulled on his arm and he let her trouser leg fall. She lay back on the bed and waved for him to follow. He had the fleeting feeling that he was setting off for someplace nearby but completely new.

⌒∞⌒

It was still dark when Malcolm woke the first time. The candles must have just gone out. He smelled the acrid smoke, imagined it rising like a fog above the bureau. Or a mist in the rain forest, the white-noise machine having cycled to a different sound in nature. He looked over to make sure Cara was still beside him, then closed his eyes and waited for the sliding feeling that almost always accompanied this kind of waking. He remembered that his car wasn't here.

He took a deep breath. He had to titrate the present with the past.

⌇∞⌇

A Saturday afternoon in spring, the kids off with Laura's parents. He was on the front steps, having just returned from the hardware store with a washer for the downstairs shower head. Laura was tugging at her gardening gloves, the knees of her jeans muddy and moist, her head framed by a rhododendron that had finally burst into full, dark pink blossom. She moved past him into the house, and he watched her through the screen door he'd just that morning swapped for the storm. His eyes followed her down the darkened hall until he could no longer see her but could only hear her, landing hard on her bare heels, kicking off her pants, turning the loose knob on the bathroom door. And none of the millions of things that had been chipping away at the back of his brain two minutes before amounted to anything then. He felt a flood of embarrassment or gratitude or, possibly, greed for everything that was, and even for everything that had been back in that old orbit of his childhood. Because without all of that, it would be impossible to know this, the intensity of this appreciation.

He placed the brown paper bag containing the washer on the kitchen table, which was covered with unread newspapers and the remains of a turkey sandwich, and he followed her down the hall. She had gone to clean up and found the shower head dismantled. She turned toward him in the doorway in her sweatshirt and underpants, and he could tell she was going to say something about the unfinished project, but instead she just looked at him, and they walked toward their bedroom holding hands, the way they only did now with the girls.

The bed was still unmade from the morning and all the windows were open, the shades snapping against the sills, then sailing straight out toward them in the middle of the room. It was an amazing thing to love someone all the way to her very back wall and in so doing catch a glimpse of the infinite. The wind picked up, and out in the yard he could hear things being blown about, knocked over, taken down. Inside, the cool air raced across their bodies, the smell of honeysuckle all about them, almost as if life were too sweet to be endured.

That was May, and then it was September.

"Malcolm," she'd said his name, tentatively, as if she'd never spoken those particular syllables before. It was Leah's first day of first grade, Susannah's first day of fourth. They were walking back to the house after the school bus had pulled away. He was looking at the crab apple, wondering whether they should spray it, when she said, "I'm falling in love. . . . She's in the a capella group." The gerund especially frightening, as if it were happening in that very moment, right before him. Almost as alarming as the pronoun that followed.

Down in the basement with the dryer on so that the kids wouldn't hear, he'd tried to tell Laura it was only about sex, her and this woman, this Elizabeth Lang, and maybe that could be a good thing, for the three of them. He'd actually told her that it turned him on.

And then there was the session with the marriage counselor he'd found for them, who asked why he needed to pathologize his wife's desires. "If you love her, you need to respect her." And Malcolm had looked straight at him and said, "What the fuck do you know about her, you just met her."

Less than an hour before the state trooper came to the door, the cruiser's lights bathing the kitchen cabinets in red, Malcolm had been angry enough with Laura to have killed her. He'd been making dinner for the girls, when she told him she needed to take his car to rehearsal. Her car was on empty, and she didn't have time to get gas. He was stirring the macaroni and cheese with a wooden spoon, one Leah had teethed on as a baby, and he thought about how good it would feel to bite down into that wood.

Laura had slipped her right arm through the sleeve of her raincoat, his keys already in her hand.

"Why the fuck should I let you drive my car to . . . meet your lover while I'm here . . . babysitting?"

"You can't babysit your own children. That's called parenting."

"I get to have a say over some things, Laura. You can't take my car."

"Malcolm, this is my job. And I need to get to my job. Just cut the shit, just for tonight, all right?"

In one fluidly dissociative step, he turned from the stove and grabbed her hand. He repeatedly shook the fist clutching his car keys, as if he were trying to drive the mercury in a thermometer back down to normal. When she didn't drop the keys, he reached over with his other hand and squeezed her wrist.

She looked up at him, her eyes filling with tears. "You're hurting me."

"Good," he said. Her wrist was tiny, and he knew he could break it without much more effort.

"Malcolm, listen to me—"

"Listen to you?" No, he wanted to silence her, erase her, make her feel what he now felt, as if he'd never scratched the surface of this life, as if everything had been a trick to make him think he mattered.

"Daddy." Susannah stopped on the threshold separating the hallway from the kitchen, and the car keys dropped to the tile floor. "We're starving."

"Get your sister," he said. "Dinner's ready."

⌘

By the time Malcolm woke again in Cara's bed, it was light. He rolled on his back and looked up at the ceiling. He didn't need his glasses to see that it was peeling. He reached over and touched his fingers to the tips of Cara's hair splayed on the pillow beside him. He was here in this bed in this moment with this woman. Apart from wanting to have sex with her again and again and again, there was nothing else he could think of that he wanted, except to paint her ceiling.

When he could ignore the urge to urinate no longer, Malcolm pulled on his boxers, inched his way blindly to the bureau, and felt around for his glasses. He instinctively looked up and down the hallway before crossing into the bathroom. He turned on the light above the sink and looked at himself in the mirror of the medicine cabinet. After squeezing some toothpaste onto his index finger, he swished it around in his mouth and rinsed. He finger-combed his hair with a little water and passed his hand over his chin. He might have opened the medicine cabinet, looked around, tried to piece together the puzzle. But to what end? There was a great freedom in knowing little more than the fact of her body and the way it moved through space toward his. He switched off the light and wondered if this lack of curiosity was a symptom of incipient senility.

There was just enough light in the hall to see the framed drawing hanging to one side of the bathroom door. It was a pen-and-ink illustration of a mythological creature, half horse, half man. Even the head was divided, with something like a drama mask, tragedy and comedy on either side of the face. It was a small piece with a lot of intricate detail, a little obsessive maybe. There was a bleakness to the lack of color in so fantastical an image. Malcolm wondered whose idea it had been to place the picture in a red frame. Certainly not the artist's. Outside he heard a car slow, then the slap of the Sunday paper as it hit the sidewalk. Before he turned out of the hallway, he leaned in and inspected the drawing more closely. The duality of the creature's face was not happy/sad, as he'd first thought, but rather masculine/feminine.

8

Noah had swapped his two dinner shifts at Homefires for lunch shifts until *Les Mis* was over. Since coming on at eleven, he'd only had three deuces and a single. He'd replenished the bar fruit, topped off the salt shakers, and folded all the napkins on the linen supply shelf. He looked down at the toothpick log cabin he'd constructed at the bar and reached into his backpack for *Interaction Ritual*.

He couldn't concentrate on his schoolwork. He hadn't been able to since Saturday night when Alex had driven him home some time close to three and come in for a toasted cheese sandwich. In her case, two toasted cheese sandwiches. He'd spotted the strange coat on the kitchen chair as soon as he'd closed the door behind them.

"You do have cheese, right?" Alex opened the refrigerator. "God, I hope it's American, orange American."

"My mother has . . . company, I think." Noah looked down the hall in the direction of his mother's bedroom.

"Oh." Alex walked away from the open refrigerator and dropped into a kitchen chair.

They were both pretty buzzed. They'd only bought one pitcher, but her uncles had repeatedly refilled them from their own pitchers. It hadn't been a bad night. He wasn't wild for pool, but they'd played a video trivia game that was decent, and, much as she'd promised, everyone had treated him well. Her uncles, all partners in a land-scaping business, were young and only got younger as the night went on.

"What're you doing?" He'd turned from the counter where he was fixing the sandwiches to find Alex seated at the kitchen table, zipped into the strange parka.

"It has fleece inside. I was cold. You know what this coat smells like?" She pressed her nose into the collar of the coat. "It smells like perfume."

Noah walked over to Alex, bent down, and inhaled. He raised his nose into the air like some kind of hound, then lowered it to sniff again, covering her mouth with his palm to stifle her laughter. As he pulled his hand away from her mouth and wiped it on the front of the parka, he noticed a little sailboat pin. He thought for a moment about Tory Liggett's boyfriend; maybe he'd broken in, done something to his mother, and was now waiting to—

"Patchouli?"

"It's not patchouli." Noah pulled the toaster oven's plug from the outlet before the timer binged its self-important, overly bright chime. The coat smelled like his mother, like the essential oil she dabbed on her pulse points. "Sandalwood."

He tore off two pieces of paper towel and served Alex, then himself.

"Ketchup?"

Noah brought a bottle of ketchup to the table and poured each of them a glass of orange juice.

"My dad's slept in the basement since like I was five or something." Alex ripped at the hot bread. "Everyone says she's nice, your mom. She deserves to be happy, don't you think?"

"And sex makes you happy?" Clearly, he was still drunk.

"It's what I hear." She stood and started opening cupboards. "If I'm going to put ketchup on this, I'm going to need a real plate."

"Above the dishwasher." As he watched Alex stretch to reach the top shelf, still zipped into the coat, he wondered if she'd ever let him dress her.

"Want one?" she asked.

He nodded. "You've never had sex?"

"You have?" she asked.

He shook his head. "I didn't go to Smithport High." As if that explained his virginity. Yeah, definitely still drunk.

"Why not?" She sat back down in her chair and upended the ketchup bottle.

"Why didn't I go to Smithport?"

She squirted out a design of ketchup, a blood red Jackson Pollock thing all over her food and part of the plate.

"Attractive."

"No, why haven't you had sex?" She dipped her index finger into a pool of ketchup.

"Why haven't you?"

"No one's ever asked me?"

"Oh," he said, dumbly. So fucking dumbly. "Yeah."

"I work for my uncles in the summer, and there was this girl, you know like from somewhere near Boston, we did her family's yard every week. They have one of those big houses out by South Cove. We fooled around a couple of times the summer before my freshman year. But then this past summer when I saw her again, it was like none of that ever happened. You have any carrots?"

"What?"

"Carrots in ketchup, excellent."

He got up again and opened the crisper drawer in the refrigerator and pulled out a half-filled bag of baby carrots.

"If you were going to do it with someone, who would it be?" She reached into the bag he'd tossed onto the table in front of her.

He couldn't tell her that he wasn't really sure of the difference between being attracted to someone and being sexually attracted to someone. There were people he was drawn to the way you were drawn to a scenic overlook or pulled in close by a phrase in a piece of music. Some people were like well-designed objects, pleasing to the eye and maybe the spirit. You might want to be near them, maybe touch them the way he'd always wanted to touch the white marble Rodins at the MFA. But that was all or enough. He looked at her now, a carrot in each hand. From the first moment he'd met her, he'd had the weird desire to touch her. But he didn't think it was sexual. He wasn't sure what that was, really.

"How honest can I be with you?" Definitely too much beer. Shit, why couldn't he keep his mouth shut?

"Not very," she said, using the carrots as paintbrushes in the ketchup.

He stared at the side of her face as she chewed. Some part of him wanted her to know what had happened to him outside the theater tonight without having to use words to tell it.

"Kidding. Jesus. What're you so serious about?"

He looked down at his plate and peeled some of the cheese, now cold, from the bread.

"'Dog food, laundry detergent, chicken broth—'" Alex was reading from a small beige card she'd pulled from the pocket of the parka. She turned over the card. "Huh."

"Guy's got a dog. That's promising."

She nodded. "So, when are you going to show me your shoes and shit? You got that stuff here?"

⌘

His dead lunch shift was nearly over. He'd been reading the same two pages of the Goffman for twenty minutes and hadn't absorbed any of it. Humiliation was very noisy. He closed the book and slid it down the bar next to his toothpick log house. Before he and Alex exited the love shack early Sunday morning to go back to the dorms, he'd taken her into his bedroom and showed her Leah's clothes. Now, three days later, he was still mortified. In Sociology yesterday, he'd arrived early and sat against the far wall, just to avoid seeing her. At least he hadn't dressed. And she hadn't asked him to, either. And he hadn't shown her everything. He hadn't allowed her to poke through his closet. Instead, she sat in his wooden desk chair, swiveling around, while he pulled out one dress, a sundress, very demure, and one special-occasion dress, the black one with the cowl drape in the back.

He reached into his backpack for the highlighter pen and pulled the cap off between his teeth. He'd finally made a friend at Baxter and he didn't want to screw it up, which he was pretty certain he'd done. If only he could just contain himself, things would be more normal, more dependable and predictable and not so crazy. *He* wouldn't be so crazy. That's what he wanted to tell Dowd. His problem wasn't gender confusion—it was him, something more basic than whether he was Noah or Leah. It was, Uncle Billy had told him more than once, his complete inability to sac up. He said it like he'd made a diagnosis, discovered a genetic marker. Uncle Billy, what a douchebag.

Noah looked up from the book he still wasn't reading and saw his mother and one of her friends walking toward the entrance of the restaurant. Gretchen or Monica, something like that. Shit. It was nearly two, and he wanted to leave. He shoved his work into his backpack and waited until he heard them come through the front door before he exited the bar and greeted them with menus.

"Noah, goodness. What're you doing here?" She seemed genuinely flustered by his presence. "You remember Charlotte."

Noah looked at the woman. She was small and blond, and like most of his mother's friends she wore little makeup and was dressed in an odd mixture of revealing and concealing attire, a spandex tank

top beneath a voluminous caftan-type jacket, big enough for four of
her. What did these women call this style? She extended her hand
and when he shook it, the double helix of silver bangles on her arm
jingled with pointless festivity. He led them to a table by the window,
and as Charlotte pulled out her chair, he noticed her boots: Miu Miu,
pretty sick, especially in cobalt.

Noah went to get a water pitcher from a stand in the back. Charlotte's chair was empty when he returned to fill their glasses.

"Since when are you working lunches?" his mother asked.

"The show."

"Oh."

"You might want to order soon. It's after two."

"Gonna kick us out?"

"The soup is a seafood chowder."

"Have you tasted it?"

He rested the pitcher on the butcher paper covering the table. "You
dating someone, Mom?"

She looked up from the menu, her expression a Cubist concoction.
While some parts were clearly recognizable, the whole wasn't anything
he'd seen before. Charlotte's armful of silver bangles announced her
return to the table.

"Noah says we should order soon. I didn't realize how late it was."
His mother picked up her menu, placing it like a screen in front of
her. When he didn't move from the table, she said, "Can you give us
another minute?"

"What would you like to drink?"

His mother lowered her menu just a bit and looked across at
Charlotte.

Charlotte looked at her watch. "Is Edie still making that
sangria?"

"I can check for you."

"I'm fine for now," his mother said, still not looking at him.

"I'm fine for now," he mimicked as he headed back into the
kitchen. Crap. He had to read half of *Adam Bede* by tomorrow, and

he knew it was going to be a late rehearsal. He'd thought he'd be out of here by now. His own mother was jeopardizing his studies. It must be nice being Carmen Shipley—just breezing around, eating lunch at three, having sex all night, not having to explain anything to anyone. Not having to explain yourself, translate all the time for the rest of the world.

When he returned to the table to report back to Charlotte that there was a cauldron of sangria available for her to swill, a man had joined their party.

"Noah, this is Dr. Stadler."

"Hi, Noah." The guy reached across Charlotte and extended a hamhock of a hand.

Was this the guy? Noah shot his mother a glance. "Would you like a menu?"

"Nahh. I'm just horning in on their lunch for a while."

Hornying in's more like it. He'd seen this guy somewhere before.

"Noah's a freshman at Baxter," Charlotte said, like it was some brilliant segue.

Dr. Stadler looked up at him, and Noah felt the muscles in his back tighten. Doctor of what, he wondered. Half the people in this town, at least the ones his mother knew, anyway, called themselves doctors. Doctor of Philosophy—let me operate on you. The guy's too-blue eyes were all arrogant sympathy. Noah rested the edges of his teeth together and tried not to grip his jaw. Oh, yeah, you got it all figured out, Mr. Doctor of computer science or linguistics. Mr. I-know-your-mother-in-a-way—"I'm worried that the kitchen might close, so why don't I try to get your orders in now."

"You can bring me a coffee," Dr. Stadler said.

Quel dick. Jesus.

As he walked away from the table after taking their orders, Noah listened for the distinctive patter his mother adopted when she was talking about him. She didn't know how to be defensive. But all the same, when her speech got slower, and the space between her words expanded, he knew that someone had said something, or maybe a lot, and she was attempting to transpose his tune into a more accessible key.

But he only heard laughter, uproarious laughter from Popeye and Charlotte. Today, he was just the waiter, invisible. A good thing sometimes.

"So what?" he said aloud, as he swung open the door to the empty kitchen. Luis must have been out having a smoke. So what if she was fucking some guy. She deserved to be happy. He poured sangria into a brandy snifter, something Edie'd cribbed from Ina Garten, and slid open the reach-in for extra fruit. His mother wanted *him* to be happy. She tolerated his choices, his behavior. Just because she was tolerant, though, just because it all flowed over her, the rock in the stream mindful not to disturb the very water, didn't mean she couldn't be disappointed. The Buddha himself would have formed an opinion, if not a judgment. He grabbed a basket and plucked some rolls from the warming drawer. Certainly he was not the kid she'd dreamed of having. She was doing her best. Who could blame her for not wanting to know him, for not trying to get to know him the way he knew himself.

"I'm giving them a few minutes." His mother was standing in the rear of the restaurant as he swung back through the kitchen doors. "They don't see each other that much."

"Oh," Noah said. He paused with the drink and the bread basket in his hands, like some figure in a religious painting.

"I'm counting on you being at the house during spring break when I'm in the Azores." She swept her thumb and forefinger around the corners of her mouth as if clearing it of something.

"I was at the house Saturday night," Noah said, the bread and wine still held aloft in his hands.

"You were? When?"

"Late. Whatever. Just take these to the table, please." He thrust the sangria and the rolls in her direction.

She peered back toward the dining room. "In a moment."

He looked over her shoulder. The room was flooded with sunlight, and Popeye and Charlotte were making out.

"I don't have time for this today." He left his mother in the narrow corridor outside the kitchen and noisily approached the table. Stadler had lost his beefy forearm to Charlotte's boxy top. He looked like a vet, sleeves rolled up, trying to birth a calf.

"Food'll be right up, with that coffee you asked for."

"Noah, right?" Stadler's hand was still hidden under Charlotte's tent of a jacket. "What's your major?"

"I don't have to declare 'til next year."

"What have you taken so far that you really enjoy?"

"Intro to Acting. I should probably check on your food."

"Noah's in the spring show, right?" Charlotte said brightly.

He nodded.

"Do you dance?" Noah felt the man's eye's scan him up and down.

"Are you a medical doctor?" Noah asked, just as his mother sat back down at the table.

"He's a psychologist," Charlotte said, with misappropriated pride, as if she'd been the one to put him through school.

"Are you over at Behavioral Health, too?" His mother uncovered the loosely swaddled rolls.

Stadler pulled the little porcelain butter dish toward himself. "Malcolm's at Baxter two days a week." The man stuck his enormous dinner knife into the butter ramekin, nearly upending it.

Monroe's. The crier. This was the guy he'd seen sitting with Dowd. The guy he thought. . . .

"Malcolm told me you've been in private practice together for a while," his mother said.

Noah heard the kitchen door open behind him. There was no reason for him to be standing here, tethered to the side of the table. His order was up.

"He pointed out your offices in Watson's Mill when we drove past on Saturday night," she continued.

Noah unstuck himself, sprang back from the table, walked to the far end of the dining room, and pushed open the doors to the kitchen. Luis was talking on his cell phone, hosing down the sink with the spray nozzle, listening to Rush Limbaugh. Noah looked down at the stainless-steel counter, completely empty except for the two white plates heaped with spinach and topped with grilled salmon. He slid the plates onto his left arm and backed through the door. He couldn't feel the hot plates on his skin or the breath in his body. He had disappeared, just ceased to exist, and no one, no thing had taken his place.

9

As Susannah's car crossed over the bridge into Twin Harbors early Sunday afternoon, Malcolm had the uneasy feeling he was being taken for a ride. The girls had surprised him, arriving unannounced while he'd been away with Cara for the weekend. It was Leah's second time coming home in a month, and when Malcolm began to inquire about that, Susannah fixed him in the rearview mirror and said, "We'll talk when we get to the diner. But not about your . . . trip, Dad. We don't really want to know."

"The hell we don't." Leah punched her sister in the arm.

"Christ, Lee." Susannah's eyes moved in a triangle from her sister to the road ahead to Malcolm in the rearview mirror. "All I'm saying is, don't feel like you have to get all open about it. I mean, go with your gut. And trust me, your gut will tell you to keep it to yourself."

⌒∞⌒

Cara had called Malcolm on Friday morning and asked him if he wanted to run up to Montreal with her overnight to hear some jazz. Driving home yesterday, they'd pulled over twice, and eventually succumbed, checking into a hotel in Dixville Notch, *the* hotel in Dixville Notch. They'd glimpsed the place in the distance, a preposterously grand structure alternately obscured and revealed as they traveled beneath granite cliffs toward the entrance.

"I've always wanted to stay here," Cara said as Malcolm exchanged his credit card for a room key. Looking around the lobby, he understood that the resort wasn't so much resting on its laurels as impressing its impressive past on the run-down present. Most everything inside their room on the third floor felt deeply familiar to him. The bed, the dresser, the little writing desk might have all come from his grandparents' house. Even the soap in the bathroom was an old-fashioned brand, utilitarian and unperfumed, but redolent just the same.

Cara finally stepped out of the clothes she had begun to remove bit by bit hours earlier in the car, and Malcolm pulled back the bed covers, pulled her down toward him, the last of the day's light barely visible through the lace-curtained windows. As she began kissing him, he could hear kids just in from skiing and skating, running the length of the hall, shouting and laughing, a father singing, "She'll be coming around the mountain. . . ." Cara had her hands in his hair, then on his back, her thumbs tracing his torso as they moved down and around until everything gathered together, magnetizing into an impossible tension. He urgently wanted to take his time and wanted to have it all right then.

The shower was running when he woke up and, maybe because it was evening and not the start of an entirely new day, he let himself sink back into the satisfied looseness in his limbs. Now doors were opening in the hallway with families going down to dinner. His grandparents had brought him to places like this as a kid, New England resorts with dining rooms the size of cruise ships, the three of them at the same table three times a day, the missing son, the missing father, the missing generation so palpable in that sea of rollicking clans on vacation.

Cara emerged with her hair in a towel, the rest of her damp and naked, and it was as if she'd caught him dwelling in some ancient pain. When he knew her better he would explain the necessity of crossing back, crossing over, like returning to visit the old neighborhood or the old country. Now and then you had to hear your native tongue, you had to remember that in this present, this new land of asylum, no matter how fluent you became, you were always speaking a second language.

It wasn't until they'd pulled up in front of her house today that Cara told him she would be leaving for the Azores the next day.

"Six hundred miles in a car together and the subject never came up?" he said.

"We're researching and recording some indigenous music." Cara was already out of the car. "I've been kind of dreading it so, well, I . . . compartmentalize." She leaned back in, across the front seat, and kissed him hard on the mouth, then grabbed her overnight bag from the trunk. Malcolm remained seated, stunned by the split-second sensation of everything being out of scale. Cara, her house, her car in the driveway, and even her suitcase, loomed over him, a tiny passenger on a stalled Lionel.

⁕

The girls had insisted on the Abenaki, an old stainless-steel diner where smoke and grease mixed together in equally viscous parts. They busied themselves with the menu, affecting nostalgia, reading item after item aloud, discussing the pros and cons of the Belgian waffles.

"It'll be like that frozen runny stuff if you get the strawberries," Leah said.

Susannah raised her eyebrows. "I don't care."

When the waitress had taken their order and with it the big fun of the laminated menus, Malcolm wrapped his hands around his coffee mug and asked, "What's going on?"

Susannah looked at Leah, and Leah looked down at the table. Susannah took a deep breath, more of a gulp, Malcolm thought. "This is probably going to sound awful, Dad, but if something ever happened to you—"

"Which it will," he said.

"There's things we won't ever know," Susannah said. "Things we should know."

"Okay," Malcolm said, watching Leah stack marmalade packages in front of herself on the table.

"So, like, we've been wondering—"

"Do you still love Mom?" Leah said without looking up from her teetering tower of jam.

"I'll always love your mother."

Leah shook her head.

"I don't think that's what she means," Susannah said.

"I'm not talking about *fondness*." Leah pronounced the word derisively.

Were they really asking him if he was romantically in love with someone who'd been dead for years? "I've lived without her longer now than with her. I'm a much different person. I've had so many experiences without her—"

"Would you choose her now?" Leah asked, still not looking at him.

"More coffee?" The waitress slid their plates onto the table.

Malcolm stared down at his eggs and listened to the hiss of fatty meat frying on the grill behind the counter, the clacking of plastic glasses in dish tubs, the slamming of the cash register drawer, the clearing of every phlegmy throat in the place. "I'm not sure I really understand what you're asking," he said after a long while.

"Who you are now, right now," Leah continued. "Let's say you got seated next to her at a dinner party . . . you know what I mean . . . not that exactly . . . but, you know . . . would you want to ask her out? Would you be attracted to her?"

"Are we talking about Mom now, or are we talking about my going away—"

"Don't want to talk about that," Susannah said, syrup poised in midair.

"Cara and I—"

"That's okay, Dad. We're happy. I mean, frankly, I, for one, was getting worried about you." Leah swirled a piece of pancake in a deep pool of syrup. "Is this the first time?"

"God, Leah, really," Susannah said.

"Are you asking me if I've had sex in fourteen years?" Malcolm looked across the table at his younger daughter.

She shrugged. "I don't know. I just never saw you like the way you were with that woman—Cara, right?—that night at Jane and Gordon's. Your face had that, you know. . . ."

"No, I don't know."

"You were, like, juiced." She shifted her attention momentarily to paw at her phone with a sticky-looking finger. "And when you walked into the house today, Jesus. It was like we'd caught you—"

"She's a musician, a guitarist. She plays at Monroe's sometimes. She's. . . ." He pulled a thin napkin from the dispenser at the edge of the table.

"This isn't really. . . . What we want to talk about. . . . It's not really about what's happening now," Susannah said.

"Well, can you tell me what it is about?" Malcolm asked.

Susannah looked over at her sister. There was a long pause, during which Malcolm imagined the girls holding hands beneath the table, crossing their fingers, rubbing a lucky rabbit's foot. "Leah's been going through her own stuff about Mom this year. And I've been talking to her. We've been talking a lot, and recently I realized. . . ." She stopped and retrieved her wadded-up napkin from under her plate. She squeezed it in her fist a few times. "Sorry," she said, looking over at Leah, "I just can't. Not now. Not here."

⁓

Without speaking, Malcolm got into the driver's seat. Susannah slid in beside him and Leah got into the back. He drove down one salt-bleached road after another, headed for the water. He watched as they passed the stacked traps in side yards, the shrink-wrapped boats, the yellow and brown Christmas wreaths, the red bows shredded by the wind. He cracked a window. A storm was on its way. He could smell it now, the fish coming to the top to feed before all hell broke loose.

He stopped the car at the chained entrance to the state park. It was closed for the season. He pulled onto the sandy shoulder, and word-lessly they each got out of the car and followed him to the fire tower. As he began spiraling up the white wooden structure, he could hear them lagging behind. Occasionally he caught a syllable or two, before the wind swallowed up the whole word. When he was on the third tier of the tower, they were still only on the first. He peered down at them. With each revolution of his and theirs, they looked different. Once they were touching each other, then they had switched sides. Leah had given Susannah her scarf to wind around her head. Each time he came around and caught a fresh glimpse of them as they progressed, he was surprised, as if he expected them to disappear permanently when they were out of sight, as if he deserved it or even desired it.

At the top, he lowered himself onto the splintering bench that faced east. Everything in view was a shade of gray, the sky, the air, the water, even the pines appeared more silver than green. He listened. There were gulls, a distant motor, osprey, some harlequin ducks, maybe. Hard to know what it was you were really hearing.

The girls panted up the final set of steps. Susannah slumped beside him, and Leah walked to the far railing, leaned over, and looked down. For Leah there seemed to be no difference between being three feet off the ground and three hundred. He'd never ridden with her on a Ferris wheel or a chairlift that she hadn't leaned over the safety bar. Inside a gondola or an observation tower, she would invariably press against the glass. Right now he could feel some version of himself reaching out and grabbing hold of her hood, just clutching it.

"Why does she do that?" Susannah asked him vaguely.

He could come up with some clinically formulated response about risk, aversion, danger, impulse control. But, really, he didn't know why this particular girl, his daughter, did this.

"I always feel like I'm going to faint when she does it. I mean it actually causes a physiological response in me," Susannah said.

He nodded and put his arm around her. When Leah was done torturing them, she came and sat on the other side of Malcolm. He grabbed her mittened hand in his gloved one. "It's natural for you guys to have questions about Mom. Leah and I have talked about how that never ends, really."

"Why should we have questions about things you could answer?" Leah said.

Susannah turned her body slightly to let the wind push the hair out of her face, and as she did, a hank of it slapped Malcolm's own dry lips. "It's like, well, we both have the same feeling, Dad, like you've been . . . protecting us from something."

Malcolm realized that the template for this interaction was neither conspiracy nor intervention—but a parental circling of the wagons. He had mom and dad on either side of him and they were closing in.

"The thing is, Dad," Susannah continued with therapeutic calm. "We know you'd do anything for us, if you thought it was best for us. We know that. We've lived with that our whole lives. But we just don't feel like you've told us . . . everything."

Malcolm felt the girls beside him, but heard their voices sounding from the rocky outcroppings still visible at mid-tide. Susannah seemed to be talking in concert with the crashing of the waves. Silence as the water receded, crescendoing accusation as the water slammed into the rock ledge. *Everything.* No one wanted to know *everything*; they only thought they did, as if the whole truth were a select club from which they couldn't bear to be excluded. But once invited into certain clubs, people often made for the exits.

Little had been kept from him as a child. His mother talked about all topics in the same way, whether it was how you calculated the distance of a thunderstorm or how your father had killed himself. All information was imparted as if it were just that, information. He'd used his own upbringing to create the negative of it for his girls. Even with their mother dying, or perhaps especially because she had died, his girls had offered him a childhood he could craft. He'd lost a parent so he knew just where to blow in the insulation, round the sharp edges, create a solid, sturdy vessel, a safer passage.

He nodded now, as if finally agreeing after a decades-long argument with himself. "There is information I have that I haven't shared with you. You've both always been . . . perceptive." He paused. One last reprieve. There was no way to warn them that certain secrets changed everything once they were unleashed; that sometimes the shadows lingering at the edges of dreams were preferable to unwieldy facts. Having been protected the way he had protected them, they wouldn't have understood. He'd acted based on his own history. Everyone was always fighting the last war.

"We're not blaming you, Dad," Susannah said. "We know you loved Mom—"

"But we don't know that, Susannah," Leah said now, her posture suddenly erect in the bracing cold. "That's the whole point."

"Hey, let's hold up here." He'd been staring down through the gaps in the floorboards, looking for the little bits of light between the wood, but he jumped up now so that he could stand and look at both of them, their eyes tearing, he couldn't tell whether from cold or sadness or anger. "I have a feeling—"

"We know," Susannah said, attempting to regain control of the situation. "I mean, we know about the affair, okay, about . . . whatever, that woman. Matt found a letter from her in the box of tapes you sent, you know, so he could put Mom's recordings on CD. It was wedged into the flaps at the bottom of the box. Elizabeth Lang. Her business card was stuck into a couple of the cassette cases, too."

"I don't know what letter you think you found—"

"Dad!" Leah stamped her boot on the decking of the fire tower and for a moment Malcolm imagined the whole thing collapsing, the principles of integrity uniting the structure reversing, releasing the three of them into a whirlwind of cascading wood. "We just told you we know you were having an affair, and you're still trying to manage—"

"I wasn't the one involved with Elizabeth Lang," he very nearly shouted, as if they were, in fact, already tumbling into that chaos, the destruction so much louder than his voice. He stopped and stepped closer to them and began again. "About two months before your mother died, she told me that she was in love with someone else, a woman, someone she sang with—"

"Mom was gay?" Leah blurted out, as if she'd just gotten to the end of a suspenseful book.

"Well, wait, wait a minute . . ." Susannah said, and already the process had begun, the uncovered secret needed to be shaped to fit the space they'd each allotted for the truth.

"I'm not sure I'm going to be able—"

"How could you not know that?" Susannah said.

"When someone wants to keep a secret—" he said.

"Were you like trying to—" Leah began.

"I mean, that seems like such a huge thing—"

"Well, what did you *say*, when she told you?"

"What happened after that? Was that the night? Did she drive off—"

"No," Leah yelled at her sister. "He just *said* it was two months before."

He'd hoped the outdoors would be large enough to accommodate this scene, but it wasn't. The air was dense, the sky was a ceiling, the landscape pressed back.

"Did you really not know?" Leah asked, squinting into a strange new light that was emerging through the clouds.

He shook his head. "I thought things were fine. I was focused on work, on you guys, on the future. The track."

"What did you . . . I mean, were you going to get divorced?" Susannah asked tentatively.

"We hadn't worked it all out." Malcolm remembered one early-morning discussion. It was the end of September and they'd both woken before dawn, still sleeping in the same bed. And Laura had said that she knew he'd been waiting his whole life to live in a family, a real family with parents and kids. That was the one gift she'd always been certain she could give him.

"Were you mad?" Leah asked, poking at a hole in the knee of her jeans.

Malcolm nodded.

"Did you know her, Elizabeth, the woman Mom . . . ?"

"I met her. After. You did too. She came to the house about six weeks after Mom died. And she brought you gifts. It was a few weeks before Christmas."

"The calligraphy set," Susannah said. "We came home from some-where, me and Lee, and she was in the living room, and you were showing her pictures of Mom. God, that was her?"

"You remember that?"

"I don't," Leah said.

"She shook my hand when you introduced us," Susannah said. "She was very tall. I don't think a woman had ever shaken my hand before. Me and Lee thought. . . . We were worried that she was a girlfriend, and that you were going to tell us you were getting mar-ried. Too many Disney movies."

"I can't believe you remember that. It was the only time she came to the house. She wanted to meet you."

"And you let her?" Leah balled her fists inside her mittens.

Malcolm looked at his younger daughter, her contempt instantly aging her.

"Why? What would you have done?" Malcolm spoke more harshly than he'd intended.

"If I were you in that position?" She forced her thumbs back into their rightful place in her mittens. "Told her to stay the fuck away from my house and my kids."

"She didn't want *us*, Leah. She wasn't going to take *us*."

"Were you ever going to tell us this?"

What he'd imagined was that their mother's story would surface in the wake of an event that dwarfed it—marriage, birth, illness, cataclysmic, apocalyptic disaster. Or, when one or the other of them came to him saying she loved a woman. "I never told anyone," he said.

His daughters looked up. Susannah first, a wind-chapped confusion on her fair, round face. And then Leah, her head cocked just slightly as if she were partly engaged elsewhere.

"What do you mean?" Susannah asked.

He couldn't tell them, his daughters, what it felt like to have drawn this tight circle about him and their mother, only to have the danger come from within. When she was done with him, there was no one left to tell. He was barely there to register it himself. Malcolm turned his wrist and pushed back the cuff of his parka to get a look at his watch.

"Time up, Dad?" Leah asked.

"Jesus, Lee." Susannah pulled up the collar of her coat. "Is anyone else, like, so cold they can't sit here another minute?"

"Next time you visit Dad, remember it's Maine and not Newbury Street."

"For Christ's sake, Leah, we're not going to figure this all out today." Susannah looked up at Malcolm for confirmation, then seemed to think better of it and turned her attention to the flaking paint on the wooden platform. "I mean, it's going to take, like years or whatever to. . . ."

"*Process*," Leah said.

Malcolm stood, looked one last time toward the water, and began down the stairs. He felt around in his coat pocket for the keys. He would get in the car, turn on the engine, start the heat blowing. That was as far into the future as he could safely project.

10

Noah had cancelled two appointments with Dowd, and then there was spring break. Dowd was both the guy he wanted to talk to and the guy he needed to talk about. It was all fucked up.

The bells in the tower rang. Now that he was finally keeping an appointment, he was late. He berated himself, each deafening stroke another lash, impelling him toward Dowd's office. He skidded a few times, his sandals sliding and catching on black ice. Kids with frightening orange-brown tans ambled along, some still suffering the consequences of that last blast in Cabo. This place could so piss him off. While they'd been on the beach, he'd spent spring break in rehearsal and hanging out with Alex. They'd shoveled together one morning, and he'd made a hundred and thirty dollars. His right shoulder still ached from that.

Alone in the elevator, he combed his hair and retucked his shirt. For someone who was so angry so often, he didn't like arguments. The goal, as far as he could tell, was to avoid conflict. He'd considered denying his knowledge that Dowd was the guy his mother was seeing, simply erasing her familiarity with that asshole Stadler, doubting that the *M.D.* in her contact list on her cell was somebody other than her medical doctor. The fact was that he really didn't want to know the facts, at least he didn't think he did.

The elevator doors opened. The waiting room was empty, and the receptionist was reading a textbook. Dowd's door was ajar, but Noah rapped tentatively anyway.

Dowd greeted him as usual with that open face, broad grin, and hearty handshake. "It's been a while," he said.

"Sorry I'm late." Noah sat down and pulled his legs up Indian-style. "So, how've you been?"

Noah nodded. He looked around the room, trying to gather some animosity, but the place was as he'd left it—institutional, with splashes of idiosyncrasy. It smelled like carpeting, and it felt safe. "I think I saw you," Noah blurted out the fabrication, a decoy duck to flush out the truth.

Dowd had bent down to pull up his socks, but he stopped. "Oh, really?" He was being all Fred Rogers, acting like he didn't have a clue. "When?"

"Do you know what I'm talking about?"

Dowd shook his head, that dumb grin stuck on his face.

"Maybe not, it was really late and dark and stuff." Noah looked out the window. "I've been doing what you told me, keeping a journal, charting my . . . *feelings*." The word had all the integrity of a product placement, and the larger claim was something of a lie too. The thing with Tory Liggett's boyfriend had happened over a month ago, and he'd never written about it. When he thought about the incident now, it was, depending on his mood, either completely incongruous with his sense of self or utterly definitive. And that seemed too insane to set down on paper. Plus, he'd signed on to the superstition that if he began writing about it, the confrontations would continue, some inverted Scheherazade kind of a thing. In the last four weeks he hadn't seen the guy, not even at a distance. Maybe he'd been conscripted, tied to the mast, swallowed by a whale.

"Have you noticed what might trigger certain feelings?"

Like picturing someone—anyone, especially you—getting it on with my mother? Yeah, that had "put him off his feed," as Alex liked to say. Truthfully, he had experienced one particularly weak and childish moment, when the possibility and the coincidence of Dowd and his mother seemed proof of the existence of God. The rest of the time, it was just fucking weird. "I don't know. Not really."

"How's the show coming?"

"Fine."

"Made friends with anyone in the cast?"

"Yeah, right." Noah pulled his fleece over his head and tossed it beside him on the couch.

"Ludicrous question?"

"I've never been Mr. Popularity, but at Baxter it's like. . . ."

"What?"

Noah just shook his head.

"What?"

"It's just like there's me, and then there's everyone else."

"In what way?" Dowd asked.

"You know those conveyor belts, moving-sidewalk things they have at really big airports? It's like everyone else is on one of those, and I'm on the other side of the half-wall, standing still looking at them." He tied the arms of his fleece together.

"You feel like you're standing still?"

"More like everyone's together and moving forward and I'm . . . I don't know."

Dowd said nothing. He just waited.

Noah shifted again. "I don't know. I mean, I'm not part of things. Like if you were going to use a compass and draw a circle—you know, I'd be out beyond the edge of the circumference."

"And what do you suppose would be the radius?"

God, why did Dowd have to dress Noah's every metaphor with a pair of cement shoes? Maybe geometry was inadequate to the task of explaining his relative place on the planet. Alex was clearly outside the lines, but she didn't seem to care or even notice. His mother was often on the edge of the circle. His uncle was way out, thankfully on the opposite side from Noah. If his mother flirted with the boundary, then what did that say about Dowd? And his father? Supposedly, jazz musicians, especially back when his father had first started playing, were all about being outside the mainstream. No, they were still within the realm of normal compared to him. The circle could have been redrawn at any moment to include them, even Alex. But he didn't think it could ever be redrawn to include him.

"Your face just changed expression. What're you thinking?"

Noah made another knot in the sleeves of the pullover. "That you don't get what I'm really talking about. When I say I'm over here, and everyone else is over there—maybe you can't possibly really understand, like, the intensity of my difference. It's like, I don't know, everyone else's being complies with the laws of gravity or something, and mine defies it. That's how extreme it feels."

"That must be terrifying."

The word bore straight into him, causing a lump in his throat. The incident outside the theater had been terrifying. He wished Dowd knew about it in that custodial, archival way a doctor knows of his patient's long-ago childhood illnesses. It bore no relation to the person he wanted to be to Dowd, or to himself. "This thing happened a few weeks ago and. . . . It's stupid, really. I mean, it's . . . I wasn't even going to tell you." He stopped, and shut his eyes, hoping it would help him to say everything he needed to say. "There's this thing with this girl. . . ."

"Oh," Dowd said.

"No, not that kind of thing. This girl's in the show and she's just a real bitch, like she's my personally assigned bitch for some reason, you know. Like she's just on me, and. . . ."

"And what?"

"And nothing. I mean, I don't even know why I'm telling you this. It happened like a month ago and. . . ." Noah opened his eyes and fixed them on the window, another gray sky.

"What happened?"

"She's a cunt," Noah said.

"And what did this cunt say or do?"

Noah looked over at him and smiled. "She just likes to fuck with me, that's all. So, like one day, after rehearsal, she catches up with me out in that courtyard behind Nelson, you know—"

"Where the parking lot is?"

"Right. So, I'm like a few steps ahead of her and she yells out, loud. People are walking by and shit, and she yells, 'So what the fuck *are* you, anyway?'"

"What'd you say?"

Noah picked at the cuticle on his thumbnail, working on it until it began to bleed. "You can't lie to me, okay?" he said, wishing Dowd knew enough to call him out on his own lie.

"Why would I lie to you?"

"Why wouldn't you?"

Dowd slid the notebook under his chair and looked at Noah. "Trust gets earned."

"Yeah, that's why I even dressed for you, you know. I've never done that. No other person has ever seen me like that. Shit, I wouldn't have done that if I didn't trust you."

Dowd nodded.

Noah looked over at the clock.

"Go ahead, there's time."

Noah wondered if seven minutes was enough, or too much. "I met the other guy, the guy you work with." Noah fixed his gaze on the carpet. It was wheat-colored and bumpy, that kind of bubbly texture that would leave an imprint if you fell asleep on it. "Dr. Stadler."

He heard Dowd clear his throat, but he couldn't look at him.

"You met the other partner in my private practice," Dowd said flatly, neither statement nor question.

"Yeah, I waited on him and his girlfriend or whatever, where I work." Noah planed his hands along the tops of his thighs, pressing into his muscles. He inhaled deeply.

"How did you know he was my partner?"

"He's talkative. The girlfriend, too." The exhale was too noisy. He felt his face flush.

"Noah?" Dowd called to him softly from the other chair, but it might as well have been from another dimension. He looked up at Dowd finally. He couldn't bear it if Dowd was being dishonest with him, sleeping with his mother and not addressing it now. Every time Noah left his room, he was engaged in the backbreaking work of bringing the hard truth to light. To think that Dowd didn't have the strength to do the heavy lifting . . . he didn't want to know that.

"My mother . . ." he started but didn't really know how to continue. His eyes welled up and the lump that had formed in his throat several minutes earlier broke loose. His mother's life had been pitiful. Dead husband, weird kid, and now when she had the chance to be with someone, all he could think about was what it meant for him. His mother had never shamed or teased him, never tried to herd him in any particular direction. Apart from that one yoga class when he was nine, his mother had not forced him to do or be anything other than himself. He could feel his whole face expanding, three, four times its size, hot and heavy. He attempted to cover its enormous surface with his hands. She deserved more. His mother deserved someone like Dowd, maybe even Dowd himself, no, especially Dowd himself.

"Noah, what's happening right now?" Dowd's voice was soft and close, almost as if Noah were murmuring to himself. Noah felt a hand on his sweaty back and realized that Dowd had gotten out of his chair and was crouching beside him. He spread his fingers just enough so that he could see one of Dowd's shoes, right there beside his own foot. The fact that he would do that, cross over that expanse of carpet, get out of his assigned seat, made Noah cry all the harder. Love existed. He sobbed for its flagrant presence in this room, as well as for its skulking absence almost everywhere else. "It's not fair," Noah burbled.

"What's not fair?" Dowd clapped his back with splayed fingers and patted him gently.

Most everything was obscured by the fact that Dowd was comforting him. He'd endured an entire childhood without an adult male doing that. If his father were alive, he wondered if they would still hug. For the millionth time, he acknowledged how lucky he was that his mother was the one he'd been left with. And for the million and first time, he considered how his every problem would have been solved if his father had raised him instead. Even in his fantasies, it didn't occur to him to be deserving of both.

"I'm fine," Noah said. He shifted slightly, and Dowd slowly raised himself to a standing position, took a few steps back, and sat down on the couch.

"I'm fine," Noah repeated.

"If you can, I'd like you to finish that thought. You said, 'it's not fair. . . .'"

Noah wiped his face on his sleeve and looked over at Dowd— the checkered shirt and the solid tie, the wire-rim glasses, and the choirboy haircut.

"What's not fair?"

"My mother . . . she's dating someone."

"Ah," Dowd said, a bit too enthusiastically.

"It's not fair for me to ruin it, you know?"

"How could you do that?"

Noah turned his long fingers toward himself.

Dowd raised his eyebrows in mock naïveté.

"Showing up."

"Oh. I see. You're so offensive that your very existence will send this guy running? You're a pretty powerful character then, aren't you?"

"It's not like that. That's not what I mean."

"You feel responsible for your mother's romantic happiness and unhappiness?"

"Stop making me sound like a psycho." God, why wouldn't this session end? "All I'm saying is that she waited until I wasn't around to even have a love life. So, like, I get it. I get that I'm an obstacle. And I don't want to screw it up for her."

"Did it ever occur to you that she was just focusing on one thing at a time—that she was devoted to raising you, and when you were out of the house, her thoughts naturally turned to other, undeveloped aspects of her life?"

Dowd began working on his knuckles from left to right—a ploy to get patients to talk—anything to cover over that sound. Noah looked out the window.

"What's unfair? I'm still not clear about that."

"For me to wreck things for her, I told you."

Dowd paused and Noah saw that he was about to start on the other hand. "I'm wondering if that's all that's unjust."

"You really don't know what I'm talking about, do you?" He had no followup. He was at the edge of the precipice.

"I have some thoughts—but I'd rather you expressed them."

No kidding. Story of my life. He stared at Dowd. The guy was so earnest. He couldn't dissemble if he read the manual. "I've been the biggest disappointment of her life. And she deserves to be happy."

"We all deserve to be happy—you included. Do you know for a fact you've been a disappointment to her?"

"Do you know that I haven't?"

"What I know is that if you were my son, I'd be immensely proud of you."

Noah looked down at his flip-flops, a remnant of Bogota Blackberry on one toenail.

"Children have the tendency to believe they're omnipotent. So, if Mom's unhappy, let's say—it must be my fault. Magical thinking."

Noah narrowed his eyes.

"It would be pretty natural to feel some jealousy in regards to this guy."

Noah bit the inside of his cheek. "Because I want to sleep with my mother?"

"Because the two of you have been a closed system for so long—some fear of being displaced?"

Noah felt a small cave-in beneath his rib cage. Why didn't Dowd understand that he was always displaced, a permanent exile?

"Hey, have you considered that you might actually like this guy, that he could be a positive addition to your life?"

Noah nodded, truthfully.

Dowd stood. Their time was up. "So, do you have plans to meet him?"

11

When they emerged from the theater, Malcolm was unsure in which direction they should walk. They'd driven the forty-five minutes to Eastland to catch a late-afternoon showing of *The Thin Man*. And now, of course, the movie had put them in mind of a drink. This was the third time they'd gotten together in the ten days since Cara had been back from the Azores. But it was the first time they'd ventured beyond his house. They were like the hibernating bulbs Laura's mother buried in black garbage bags in her basement, waiting out an inhospitable season in an unnatural habitat.

"Thin," she said, looking back at the old-style movie marquee. "Too thin?" She slid her arm through his.

He smiled in the semi-dark, pushed up the sleeve of her coat, and looked at her watch.

"It's six," she said.

"Why don't we go to Monroe's or the Squire? Someplace closer to home, then we won't have such a long drive."

She nodded but didn't say anything.

He slid his arm from hers, placed it around her shoulder, and guided her to the car. As he started the engine, she pulled a CD from her purse and pressed it into the slot in the dashboard. Her music (she had yet to arrive at his house without her iPod) invariably surprised him. This time it was opera. In what language, he couldn't tell.

"*Lakme*." She clipped the plastic CD case closed. "Leo Delibes. Forget you recognize the *Flower Duet* from a commercial."

He patted her knee and she took his hand. The movie theater had been underheated and Cara's fingers were icy. He'd gotten up once at the start of the film to complain to the fifteen-year-old who seemed to be in charge. That was when it had started, the compression in his chest. Right now, with one hand on the wheel and one in hers and his eyes on a tree strung with buoys, he felt his chest might just collapse into his back. He'd been unable to get that girl to do what he wanted, simply make the theater warmer. Had she acquiesced, he would not have been forced to endure these waves of generalized angst, cresting every few minutes in the standoff with his own recalcitrant girls.

It was Sunday afternoon, and he'd dreaded Sundays his entire life. It was gray and cold, early April in Maine which was to say still winter, in the middle—no, past the middle—of his life, and he'd sat freezing in an ancient movie palace gone to seed, watching a film that had been made during the Depression with the express purpose of distracting people from the rotten reality of their lives. It was an anesthetic, and nothing caused despair like an anesthetic that failed to numb. Nick and Nora and the idea that something abiding existed between them, something that alcohol and witticism and boatloads of money only served to deepen, infuriated him. He was treating a couple now, Joe and Eileen, a blue-collar version of Nick and Nora who spent the first ten minutes of every session trying to elbow him out of the dynamic with their well-honed shtick. He didn't want to think about them and the fact that he wasn't getting very far with their problems.

He and Cara were nothing like Joe and Eileen or Nick and Nora. They didn't quip. In fact they could go, as they were doing right now, long periods without talking. Their tendency toward silence, which only a few days before he'd considered companionable, struck him now as symptomatic.

Every dirty pile of spring snow they drove past made him more and more anxious. It had been three weeks since he'd told the girls about Laura, and neither of them had called or texted. Leah was conveniently unavailable when he phoned and hadn't returned any of his messages. Predictably, Susannah wasn't as good at surgically removing him. She picked up sometimes, always after he'd started leaving a message. Mostly he just heard her sighing in response to his questions, sighing the way the newly grieved do, as if there wasn't enough air to make the whole sad truth go down. Then after a minute or two she would tell him she had to go. That was it. That was the extent of his communication with the only two people he loved and who he thought loved him.

Malcolm inhaled and exhaled and tried to listen to the music. He jacked up the heat and set the fan to furious. There was so much cool wafting off Cara. Cool as in hip, as in insulated from trouble, as in remote. Her calm was making him sad.

She lowered the fan speed and increased the volume on the stereo. It was taking too long to get dark out. Everything beyond the car windows on this road was grim. He didn't think he could stand another rusted swing set, another pile of busted lobster traps, another random package store with a chained ice chest out front. Who stole ice—frozen water—in a place where there was nothing but water and cold temperatures?

"You're sighing," she said, turning down the music.

He nodded. God, she sounded like him at the office. She had simply said it like a fact, but not a fact that she had to do anything about.

Up until now, his relationship with Cara was eighty percent physical, and Malcolm wasn't entirely sure who she was out of the bedroom. Maybe until this afternoon he hadn't been interested in finding out. What did they talk about, really? Books and movies, music to some small extent that he could follow, local politics—all the stuff that allowed you to chalk out the vaguest outline of the other, like the silhouettes the girls used to bring home in grade school, with the features, the specifics, rendered opaque by black construction paper—all the better to project every fantasy and every grudge. Malcolm tried to remember who it was who said that your most honest assessment of someone was in the instant of the initial meeting, before you began the inevitable process of fashioning him into the person you needed him to be.

What had he thought about her that night in the parking lot of Monroe's, where he was about to turn in now? Whatever clarity he might have brought to that moment had, even then, been clouded by having watched her perform for much of the evening. He'd already begun to spin a story about her. When he'd met her outside, he remembered thinking she'd been laid-back, even though she was cursing into the phone.

He'd been certain she was talking to a lover—who else at that hour? Maybe in another time zone. But she'd told him in one of their post-coital discussions that it had been a long while since she'd been in a relationship. She'd married young and had been widowed at twenty-eight, left with a baby to raise on her own. When he asked where she'd grown up, how she'd met her husband, she'd teased him, saying "it's always about the past with shrinks, isn't it." And if he asked anything at all about her son, she changed the subject.

"Scene of the crime." Cara shut the door of the car tentatively, and Malcolm walked around to make sure it was closed all the way.

"The bar okay?" he asked as they walked down the long back corridor into the restaurant.

"How about over there?" She pointed to a small table by the far windows.

"Okay," he said, unconvincingly. The hostess hugged Cara and one of the waiters waved. No sooner were they seated than an elderly woman with a long white braid wrapped around her head greeted Cara. Malcolm excused himself. He pushed open the door of the men's room and walked over to the sink. He should have just told her that he had work to finish for tomorrow. He should simply have driven her home when they got out of the movie. Because he could feel it, he was going to start an argument—merely as a way of figuring out something that was confounding him. He waved his hands in front of the towel dispenser and nothing happened. He waved again, then banged on the machine. He was bugged and so he was going to bug her. It was that simple. Everything had been fine until this afternoon. The sex was good. She had a fondness for sucking him which he could call up every time he glimpsed her tongue while she spoke or ate or drank. She was concealing something. His antennae were tuned to deception, if nothing else. He banged the machine again, this time noticing the little wheel beneath the dispenser.

"I'm surprised you don't know Becky," Cara said when he returned to the table. "She was in the registrar's office for years and years. She lives down the block from me."

Malcolm opened his menu.

"Pete came by while you were in the restroom. There's no soup tonight. The special is meatloaf with garlic mashed potatoes. And there's a prawn appetizer."

"Would your husband have ordered the meatloaf?"

Cara looked up at him, her reading glasses sliding to the tip of her nose.

"Well, you never talk about him. I don't even know his name."

"Russ. Russell was his name." She continued to look right at him, almost as if she were staring him down.

"My wife's name was Laura."

"Yes, I know. You've told me that."

"So would Russ have gone for the meatloaf and the garlic mashed potatoes?" He ducked beneath her gaze and looked down at the menu.

She placed her glasses in their case and reached across the table for his hand. He could feel the toughened pads of her fingers, so different from the creamy tops of her hands. "He tended not to eat meat."

"How did he die?"

She removed her hand and curled her hair behind her ear. "A stroke. I know I told you that."

"I didn't mean what did he die of, but how, the circumstances? What was it like? For you? Were you with him?"

The waiter came with Cara's red wine and Malcolm's scotch. "I'll give you guys a few more minutes."

"I could tell you all this," Cara said, stroking the stem of the glass. "But . . ."

"To what end? It's not happening now, in this moment, is it? And we're here in this moment, you and me."

"Really?" He shut his menu and looked out across Spring Street at the summer people's hardware store, its window an embarrassment of copper weather vanes. "That's what you think? That the past happened once and has nothing to do with us now?"

"I'm sure that's not true for you. I'm just saying it is for me."

"You aren't curious about what happened to my wife?"

"You told me, when we were driving to Montreal."

"Well, there's more. Just like there's more about Russell." What had begun as a rational plan, tell her something intimate, meaningful about his life so as to get her to do the same, was turning now into a much less controlled imperative. He felt his own story building in him, the pent-up pressure of it potentially violent, and he wanted to unleash it on her, a water cannon blowing her equanimity and serenity to hell. "If we're going to know each other in any kind of substantive way, then you need to know things about my life. No, more than that, you need to *want* to know."

The waiter appeared at the table, but Malcolm couldn't look up at him. "I'm not sure we're all that hungry right now, Pete," Cara said.

Malcolm lifted his drink, and a ring of water broke apart and ran down the gray card stock of the menu as he handed it to the waiter.

"I am interested in knowing you in a substantive way, an essential way," Cara continued once the waiter had left. "But your essence, Malcolm—that has nothing to do with your story, or what you think your story is. I'm not convinced that this, this thing couples feel the need to do, talking, telling, serves any purpose but to perpetuate illusions."

He could feel his mind bifurcating. He wanted to grab hold of her argument and not let go until he'd ripped it into the bite-sized, mindless nuggets on which he knew it was founded. And at the same time he wished he could make her the subject of a case study, the examination of her Byzantine system of defenses as gratifying as its destruction. He rattled the ice in his glass. "There's something I'd like to tell you. Something I only just told my kids. It's the reason they're not talking to me now."

"You're going to tell me something confidential as a way of hooking me, can you see that?"

"No. I can't. I can't see how my confiding—" He stopped, aware that his anger was about to edge out his reason, even while she sat there placid to the point of affliction.

"You need to trust that things will unfold as they should, without forcing issues, hurrying us along in some predetermined direction." The words came out evenly spaced, without emphasis or inflection.

He looked around the mostly empty dining room, the dark walnut of the tables and chairs solidifying a slow-to-form and slippery thought. Wariness born of woundedness, open mind, open legs, less than open heart—that was a scenario he could work with. "What are you afraid of, Cara?"

"Everyone has a different comfort level, Malcolm."

"Why don't you ever ask me about my kids?"

"You do . . . *this* for a living." Her fingers were sliding up and down the stem of her wine glass. "You talk to people about very personal things."

"Well, mostly people talk to *me* about very personal things and I listen." He smiled now, but she wasn't looking at him any longer. "You never talk about your son."

"Our lives with our children are private."

"What does that mean?"

"I don't choose to involve him in this, just as I don't choose to involve you in his life. It's how I've always had to conduct myself."

He turned his body so that he was no longer facing her but looking in the direction of the mostly empty bar. Two couples sat huddled at the center, sipping one another's cocktails and picking off one another's plates. He envied their easy familiarity. He'd thought that life would feel much more like that than it ever did for him.

"You compartmentalize," he said.

"Yes, I suppose so."

"Are you married?"

"Malcolm, please."

"Compartmentalization. The hallmark of the adulterer."

She reached for her wine, then put it down without drinking. "I think I'd like to go home."

"I'd like to stay," he said.

"I wasn't asking for a ride. I can walk."

"I'd like you to stay—just 'til we finish our conversation."

"I'm not sure I read you correctly. I thought, my impression was that you were . . ."

"What?"

"Non-judgmental. But now I see that it's really the opposite. You have expectations—"

"Expecting simple biographical information is an unreasonable expectation?"

"Rigid expectations, and when they're not met, when people fall short—you're right there to remind them. Maybe it's a holdover from your work." She slipped a five-dollar bill from her wallet.

"I'll take care of that," he said, and she began to replace the money.

"Thank you."

"Do you tend to do this?" he said, trying for a level tone.

She stared at him blankly, and he struggled to recapture what he'd found so exotic, so thrilling about her face the first hundred times he'd looked at her. "What?" she asked flatly.

"Duck out at the first sign of conflict?" He was vaguely aware that in some irrational chamber of his heart he was holding her personally responsible for everything that was wrong with the way people went about not loving one another.

"There's never a need for conflict. And I choose not to engage in it when someone else introduces it."

"Really? And this works for you—this degree of non-engagement?"

"How well does your intrusiveness work for you?"

He'd been gripping the sides of the table with his forearms, trying to hold her there, to keep her from leaving. In his practice, he'd long ago abandoned the desire to convince patients of anything. But Cara's belief system, as it was being acted out with him now, actually seemed dangerous—a public mental health menace. "What if," he began, almost wildly, as though his life depended on it, "what if everyone operated this way? Would you really want to live in a world where no one extended themselves for anyone else—a world where there were no demands on you and no expectations from others?"

She stood and began to button her coat. "Would I want to live in a world where people were free and not attached to outcomes?"

He rose beside her and placed his hands, perhaps too heavily, on the shoulders of her down coat.

"Malcolm, please," she whispered.

He reached back for his jacket and threw some money onto the table. "I'll drive you home." As they walked past the bar, he looked once more at the chummy group sharing dinner and noticed what he'd failed to discern before. All four of them, two men and two women, were deaf, gesticulating in the air, tapping one another on chests and wrists to gain attention. They were wordlessly talking up a storm.

12

Malcolm pulled up to the semicircular drive in front of Lewis Prep and parked in one of the four visitor spots. Susannah's dorm, Hoyt, was down beyond the chapel, he was pretty sure, though he'd only been here one other time. He was taking a risk, coming without telling her. He'd driven three hours on a Friday afternoon, not knowing if she would be there, or if she would even see him. It had been nearly a month since they'd trudged up the fire lookout. Cara's exit from his life on Sunday had only served to underscore the girls' silence. No one was calling.

He walked toward the squat stone building housing the school's main office. The whole trip might have been a fool's errand, but now that he was here, he wasn't going to waste energy or effort in wandering around the campus. He entered into a lobby of marble floors and leaded windows. The heat was up too high, and the whole place felt a little fevered. Boys and girls loitered in the reception area, their self-conscious hilarity verging on violence. Malcolm was both anxious and angry, and he didn't think anything could be as funny as these teenagers insisted.

A shuttle bus was leaving for the mall, and a few girls came sliding into the lobby, racing and skidding across the smooth floor. Two were joined by one iPod, the "Y" of the headset's cord stretched between them. He tried to remember Friday afternoons when he'd been a student at Chapman. The Christmas Eve just after his thirteenth birthday, his mother had driven him from Provincetown to his grandparents' farm in Smithport. After pacing the living room for an hour, she announced that she'd promised an aunt—some aunt, any aunt, was how it had sounded to him—that she would spend Christmas with her in New York. And she wished them all a happy holiday.

On Christmas morning, Malcolm gave his grandparents the bird-house he'd made in shop, and he opened his gifts—all from them, his mother's only gift having been universal relief at her departure. Then he'd sat at the kitchen table, waiting until his grandmother was bent over a skillet of French toast before announcing that he couldn't live with Lucy anymore, and that if they made him go back with her, he'd run away. The stove, with its cache of compartments for keeping food warm, was the same one his grandmother had cooked on when his father was a boy. Looking around the old boxy kitchen that morning, Malcolm felt a rush of nostalgia for a time he couldn't have known, a time when that stove had been state-of-the-art. He listened as his grandmother slid the large cast-iron skillet off the burner, then pulled out the chair next to his. She was as old and outdated as that range, but also as resourceful, replete with hidden gadgets and gizmos that actually worked. Even so, he felt sorry to have to tell her this.

"You don't have to do anything that you don't want to do, Malcolm."

"She's crazy, Nan." He saw her wince.

"She loves you in her way."

"You always say that."

"And how will you feel about going to junior high here in town?" He shrugged.

"And what about next year? Your father went to Chapman. Grand could make some inquiries. I'm sure there's an entrance exam, but I don't expect that would be a problem for you. No, not at all." She paused, pulled a handkerchief from the pocket of her woolen robe and blew her nose. "You're always welcome here, Malcolm, always. But I should have to think a boy your age would be happier with a bunch of other boys than with two old codgers like us. You think about it. You talk to Grand about it, see what he advises. And when your mother returns, after the New Year, Grand will sit down with her." She took both her warm bony hands and cupped them around his on top of the table. "And we'll have to figure about getting your things up here, too."

He was embarrassed to tell her that he'd brought all his things. Some he'd put in an old pillowcase, and the rest, what little there was, he'd placed in boxes and wrapped as if they were gifts. His mother hadn't even noticed.

∞

A boy with a lacrosse stick offered to show Malcolm the way to Hoyt, but he said he could get there himself. Back out the double doors, the air was rawer than it had been two minutes before. He followed a paved path as it rounded the library and a Victorian gingerbread cottage that he guessed was either the infirmary or the headmaster's house. The layout of the school was no different from that of a small college. But as he walked, he sensed the disparity in the ruling regimes. Leah had dubbed the place "Lose Your Rights Prep" after spending a day last August reading all the posted regulations while helping her sister move into the dorm where she would serve as resident adviser. Certainly, the citizens here required a semi-visible yet omnipresent totalitarianism, as opposed to the constitutional monarchy at an institution like Baxter. He'd been surprised by the rigidity of boarding school. The absoluteness of the schedule, the routine, was a comfort. While some of his teachers and classmates might have been unpredictable or unfair, they were the anomalies; the prevailing culture of the place was of orderliness. Chapman showed him that the world could make sense. In the years he lived with his mother, he'd often felt as if he were on a raft made of cloth, trying to stay afloat and as dry as possible atop nothing more than a pile of threads laced across water. When he was at his grandparents', he was never free from the threat of his mother "swinging by and scooping him up," as she liked to describe her spasmodic maternal impulses. And no matter what they said, his grandparents seemed as powerless as he to stop that great bird of prey from sweeping in and carrying him off. Boarding school provided a more formidable protection from his mother. Even Lucy was disinclined to scale that institution's ivy-covered walls.

He made his way toward a small pond and across a footbridge. Competing raps pounded from speakers in open windows. He hadn't forgotten the conflict that had caused him to drive all the way here, but as he opened the front door of Hoyt and paused in the entrance, Susannah's remove seemed completely separate from the fact that she was his daughter and he merely wished to see her. He'd fantasized with obsessive repetition while driving here today about knocking on her door and having her throw her arms around him while crying, "oh, Daddy," as in "oh, Daddy, this has all been so stupid."

The hall was longer than he'd remembered. The wooden floors were dusty and scratched, the lighting dim. The faint smell of sweat and rotting orange peels hadn't figured in his daydream. He unbuttoned his overcoat and pulled off his gloves. The bulletin board announced a semi-formal that had come and gone, an extension of the Reduce, Reuse, Recycle challenge, and a mandatory meeting Sunday at 4 P.M. to "discuss the recent rash of insensitive pranks." That one was signed *S. Dowd*.

Her room was at the end, by the emergency exit. As he moved down the corridor he listened to the roar of blow dryers, the clacking of keyboards. So many children during the most hazardous years of their lives. Other people's daughters in his daughter's care. He wondered how that had happened.

He stopped in front of her door and listened. It could be difficult to determine where sound originated. He heard singing from deep inside one of the rooms on either side of the hall. Susannah had been a member of the concert choir in both high school and college, but Malcolm could never quite shake the feeling that she sang out of a sense of duty. Watching Susannah during a performance of *Messiah*, Leah had whispered, "This is for credit, right?"

He knocked loudly and waited for her footsteps. Leah came down hard on her heels, but Susannah tended to bounce slightly off the balls of her feet. Spring and shuffle. His need to see her was so fierce, he could feel her now on the other side of the scarred oak door.

"Daddy."

Her hair was wet, and a trail of watery footprints spread behind her. He didn't recognize the kimono robe she was wearing. All the years of washing and folding the girls' clothes had afforded him detailed knowledge of their wardrobes. But now there were all sorts of things he didn't know. "I just came up to say hi."

She opened the door more widely, they hugged, and he entered.

"It's gross in here. Sorry, Dad."

The room was overheated and dim, lit only by a string of blinking snowflake lights outlining the two windows on the far wall. "I got you out of the shower. I'm sorry," he said. He looked around for a place to put his coat. He could feel the sweat breaking out across his back and chest. They were in the sitting room; the door to the left led into a bedroom and a bathroom. Malcolm looked at his daughter again, the fancy bathrobe. He turned his shoulders slightly toward the open bedroom door and caught a deep whiff of coconut. Perhaps he was interrupting something. Her boyfriend, Matt, taught at a large prep school about an hour away. He'd landed his job first, teaching earth science and coaching the ski team. When Malcolm had expressed some concern that Susannah was limiting her job search because of her desire to be near Matt, she'd looked at him blankly. "If I told Matt I wanted to teach in Whoville, he'd come with me, Dad. Don't you know that?" What Malcolm knew was that Matt was not given to fits of speculation. He and Susannah had met during their sophomore year at Baxter, and so all six and a half feet of him had been in and out of the house a fair amount. Once when Malcolm had referred to Matt as "a good boy," Susannah had accused him of being patronizing. "He's just as smart as you are, Dad," she'd said.

"Yes," he had said. "But will he be as smart as you're going to be?"

"I just want to brush my hair," she said now, tightening the robe around her waist. "Give me a second. You want something to drink? Water, tea?"

"No. Thank you. But I was wondering if I could take you to dinner."

She'd already left the room, and he heard her rummaging through things in the bathroom. "Just a minute," she yelled over music coming from a laptop in the corner of the sitting room.

Every inch of wall space in the small room was covered with photos of friends and family. The combination of blinking light, loud music, and hundreds of disembodied smiling faces triggered an attack of vertigo. He pulled one arm from his overcoat and sat down on the only couch he and Laura had ever purchased together, maybe twenty years ago, now covered with a remnant from a fabric store. He left the coat on the couch and moved toward the window, pushing the sash up. It wasn't until he'd fixed his gaze on the pond outside, the little footbridge and the three kids crossing it, that he registered the voice coming from the computer speakers. It was Laura.

Malcolm leaned his head into the fresh air and felt the window slowly slide down on his back. Had he imagined that walking into this room would be like entering her room at home, when, after a fight, the muffled sounds of crying allowed him ready access? He used his shoulders to push the window up again and tucked his head back inside. He loosened his tie. These rooms were hers. The stuff inside might be familiar to him, but he was in her home now. There was nothing inevitable about this reunion. He sat down on the old sofa and tried to take a deep breath.

Susannah returned wearing sweatpants and a sweatshirt. She pulled a painted metal chair from its place at a covered card table and dragged it opposite the couch. He spent a few moments just looking at her. Partly that's why he'd come. He'd forgotten how she looked, exactly how she looked. He had to see that she was okay. In fact, he had to see that she was alive. This falling-out with the girls had set off a familiar anxiety reaction. He'd become convinced that one or both of them would die.

"This," he swung his thumb back and forth between them: "it's been tough."

"Yeah." She picked up a bottle of nail polish from the coffee table that separated them and tightened the cap.

"It's a little early still for dinner, but I was hoping I could take you out."

"Matt's already on his way."

Malcolm nodded. "Well, then, do you have a few minutes now?"

"Sure." She pulled back her wet hair and he saw the two damp spots on the front of her sweatshirt just above her breasts. Last week a patient, two months post-partum, had leaked breast milk out onto her shirt. Stupidly, he'd moved toward her with a Kleenex box.

"You sure you don't want some tea?" She put her bare feet on the table.

He shook his head. "Listening to Mom, huh?"

She nodded, then folded her lips as if to seal them shut. Sitting across from her, he sensed that nothing but tea was to be made available to him. His ache for her was now indistinguishable from his ache for himself. They were silent for a moment, and then Susannah spoke. "I can't help feeling. . . . It's like you lied to us about the very thing that is us, you know?"

"Do you want to know why I did what I did?" He realized he'd been hunched over, as if protecting himself. He straightened up, pressed his back into the sprung springs, and continued. "You're old enough to see this from a larger perspective. You're old enough to understand that I come to all this with needs, too."

She stood up and walked over to her laptop, turning down the volume. Now all they heard was the low murmur of Laura's voice in the background. "Dad, we know you're—"

"Let me finish, Susannah. You think I lied to you and your sister, and I want the chance to explain, and I want you to listen."

"Jesus, you came here to 'talk,' and now you're yelling at me."

He was fairly certain he wasn't yelling, and he wasn't going to let her sidetrack him into debating his tone. "There is nothing more important to me than being your father and Leah's father. Not just since your mother died, but from before, from when you were born. I was determined to create for you what I never had." He was scared to pause for fear that she would interrupt him. "You know, meeting your mother, it was like, everything that had been wrong got righted. It was miraculous to me, and then the boat didn't just capsize, it turtled. And I just couldn't let that happen to you." He watched her as he spoke. Her expression was flat, closed. "I didn't do what I did out of malice," he began again, somewhat more desperately now. "Had you been older. . . . The sexual component of it . . . it was simply inappropriate to share with a six-year-old and a nine-year-old."

"You had fourteen years to tell us the truth." She folded her toes into the ragged edges of her sweatpants and looked up at him. "Who've you really been taking care of all this time, huh?"

Finally, air blew in from the open window, causing the string of lights to rattle and the vintage cloths serving as drapes to flutter and flap. A girl laughed outside. A door creaked open. Reggae spilled into the hallway. For a moment Malcolm had the feeling that he was in some kind of playhouse. Susannah's chair scraped the floor, and he listened to her walk into her bedroom. When she came back, she was holding a pair of ski socks. She stood by the couch for a moment.

"I've been going to a therapist in town. I feel like you pulled the rug out from under us. Everything keeps moving. Like there's no solid ground."

Had he looked up at her then, looked at her round, young face and seen the pain that she felt, the pain he'd caused, he would not have known how to proceed, what to do or say next, or who to be. Survival could be a shameful instinct.

She sat back in her chair and crossed one foot over her knee and began putting on her socks. "I wake up at two and four and five and wonder what's next. Maybe you're really not our father, maybe we're not related—me and Lee, maybe . . . I mean, what other facts—"

"Zannah—" He stopped now, hearing his own voice in his ears. "There's nothing else. I know you think I made a mistake. And now, I guess, I hope you can come around, at some point, to believing that I did the best that I could."

"No," she said loudly. She put both feet down on the floor, one sock still in her hand. "No. You were capable of a lot better. That . . . that secret—not the best that you could do." She was crushing the sock in her hand. "Why are you even saying that? That's *not* who you are." She stopped herself, took a breath, struggled to shift into neutral. Looking straight at him, she said "I'm so disappointed."

Malcolm watched her rub her finger over the sock now draped on her knee, back and forth, back and forth, trying to spark some warmth, some comfort. Was she really asking him to once again understand her without her having to do the same for him? He looked at his daughter and felt as unforgiving as the couch he leaned back into. A history of abuse had led to so many sprung springs. Metal, meant to cushion, now cut. For a month he'd registered a mounting sense of unfairness each time Leah didn't pick up the phone, each time Susannah ended a call while he was still talking. But now, on the receiving end of this punishing appraisal by his older daughter, he allowed his fury to cascade. She had no idea how impossible this all was, no idea how he'd cobbled himself together, scavenged from teachers and books and movies to make himself into a decent adult and an effective parent.

How dare she tell him he could have done better, that he'd fallen short of *her* ideal? He had spoiled them. That was the problem. He had extended himself again and again, stretching himself to the point of distortion to reach them and make them feel known. They'd never had to worry he'd forget when to feed them or where he'd last left them, or the way to their rooms when they called out in fear. They had lived with the certainty that he loved them and put them first. Wasn't that more than enough?

Malcolm stood up and lifted his overcoat from the arm of the couch. "I'm sorry I disappointed you," he said. He began walking toward the door, aware that Susannah wasn't moving, or even turning in his direction. "And you should know"—he stopped with his hand on the doorknob and turned back toward her—"that you've disappointed me, too."

13

E ven through his clumpy mascara, Noah could see there were too many people in the living room. He hated that about the bungalow; the living room was like a fucking stage, anybody on the street was front row center. Alex turned off the car and went around to the trunk for the two bags of chips she'd insisted on bringing. Noah had argued with his mother about this party. He'd tried to explain how completely tacky it was to make a big deal of his being in the ensemble. She'd said it was a Friday night, and she didn't need his permission to entertain her friends, many of whom would be going to *Les Mis* anyway, some of whom would be playing in the pit. He didn't have to come if he didn't want to, but she hoped he would.

"Your mother's going to think I'm a total Neanderthal because I've never stepped foot in the music department," Alex said as they walked up the driveway. "You got any salt? Someone's going to slip here."

"If my mother thinks you're a Neanderthal, it won't have anything to do with your not taking music."

She punched him in the arm and it actually hurt.

"You're nervous," he said.

"No. I just. . . . It would be good if I could, you know, kind of position myself. I try to do that. Throw out a couple of things people can get their hooks into so they aren't left to their own deductive devices about me."

Noah stopped and looked at her. The family next door had a floodlight that stayed on night and sunny day until it burned out. Alex looked a little vacant in the center of its glow. "You're my friend," he said, placing his palm on the top of Alex's head, which was a good four inches below his own. "That's your handle."

He kept walking, and she leaned against a dirty white pickup that Noah didn't recognize. "I'm sorry," she said.

"About what? What's the matter?" Noah felt a flutter of apprehension, as if someone were calling him into a cave when what he really wanted was to stay out where it was light and bat-free.

"I *am* nervous. This is like your family and your mother's friends and shit." She reached into her jeans pocket and pulled out a rubber band and began putting her hair in a ponytail.

"Actually, Al, it looks really nice down. Leave it alone. You look good."

She nodded obediently.

"You already get along with me, and I'm the asshole. My mother's nice, like totally blissed out, you know. She meditates. Zen energy oozes off her. That's what I'm told, anyway."

"I've seen her. She's really beautiful and—"

"Me, too," he said, "and you're not intimidated by me." He shook his bottom and widened his eyes, acutely aware that his stage makeup had hardened and tightened. "Come on, I've got to get this shit off. Look, we'll go in, say hi, get a beer, and then you come into the bathroom with me while I wash all this off. We'll ease you in, all right?"

Starting up the four steps that led into the kitchen, he reached and took her hand. He'd been touching her a lot lately, his hesitancy and self-consciousness giving way to a call to place his hands on her. He thought he might tell Dowd about it sometime in the uncomplicated future, but how to describe the feelings he had around Alex? He wanted to say that it was love. But it was a kind of love that was tough to understand. It was like that spotlight on the side of the Cavanaughs' house. Bright and warm, probably unnecessary—what was it illuminating?—but insistent nonetheless.

"Our very own thespian," Uncle Billy yelled out when Noah and Alex entered the living room already crammed with people. His mother kissed Alex on the cheek when he introduced her. Then she hugged Noah and whispered, "What a performance, what a gift, Noah." They pulled apart, and he attempted to wipe some of his foundation from her scarf while making a few quick scans of the room, relieved to find it Dowdless.

"Just the ensemble, Mom, cast of thousands."

She shook her head. "You stood out."

"You're supposed to blend when you're in the ensemble."

She shook her head again. "Just wait, it's only your first year. Honestly, honey, your presence. . . ." She swallowed hard and then let the rest of the guests and their congratulations flood in.

"I've got to get this crap off my face." Noah grabbed Alex's hand and began to tug her toward the hall and the back of the house.

"She in the crew?" he heard one of his mother's friends say a bit too loudly. "She go to Baxter?"

"Throw your coat on my bed, Al," Noah said. "Then get us a couple of beers and come in here." He pushed open the bathroom door and pulled his sweatshirt over his head. Reaching into the medicine cabinet, he grabbed the cold cream his mother had bought for him the last time he did a show. He looked at the little bit of drugstore makeup she kept on the narrow glass shelves. His own stash, good stuff, expensive stuff, was in a Tupperware container at the top of his closet. He wondered what it would be like to need next to nothing to accurately reveal yourself. His uncle only needed his hunting jacket and a few days' growth of beard to reflect to the outside world how he felt inside—predatory and gruff. Noah plucked a cotton ball from a Ziploc bag at the top of the cabinet and began to make sweeping trails through the cold cream on his face. What about Dr. Dowd, Mr. Neutrality? The Eagle Scout attitude beneath the button-downs and the corduroys. A handy combo of morality, compassion, and knot-tying skills sufficient to solve any problem. Nothing like the image his own father projected from those old photos—a man who wanted nothing more than to convince you that indoor plumbing and electricity were conspiracies spawned by the military-industrial complex.

"In the name of the father and the son. . . ." Alex paused on the threshold of the bathroom. She sipped from one bottle of beer, then brought the other bottle up to the center of her forehead, down to her chest and across to each shoulder. She laughed and he was relieved. He had recognized her panic out in the driveway as the gigantic, frenetic kind that blots out everything but the panic itself.

"Here." She placed his Stella on the edge of the sink and sat down on the closed toilet seat. "Like watching my dad shave when I was little," she said.

He looked over at her, his face still half covered in the thick white cream. "Hardly." He cupped his hands under the faucet, splashed off the rest of the cold cream, then dried his face on the front of his T-shirt.

"You okay?" He pushed back the plastic shower curtain, designed to look like a sheet of music, and sat on the tub, the edge of which he realized too late was wet. He knew she would probably say that she was fine, no matter what. He wondered if there was an evolutionary advantage to keeping the lid on your real feelings. There had to be some benefit, some purpose, some sense to living side by side with parents and friends and still, no matter how well you knew them, only parsing out little bits of emotional truths, at federally accepted limits of one part per billion, a safe non-toxic level.

"I don't know," she said, looking not at him but at the back of the bathroom door, where his mother's chenille robe was hanging, the beige belt grazing the floor. "I think maybe I should go home."

"We don't have to stay—"

Someone in the hall knocked loudly on the bathroom door.

"Jesus," Alex barked. "Where's the fucking fire?"

Noah had never heard her yell before, not in anger. And he pretended to read the score on the shower curtain for a second or two before making eye contact with her.

"This the only bathroom?" she asked now, softly.

He nodded.

They navigated the crowded hallway to his room and, once inside, they sat down on his bed, her head on his shoulder, his hand on the big boulevard of her thigh. "We got talking about hypothermia in my Russian Lit class the other day." The bed moved as she crossed one heavy leg over the other. "You get to this point where you're so cold that you stop feeling cold—and then, like, you're delirious and you just fall asleep and. . . ."

He could hear people leaning against the other side of the closed bedroom door. As a kid he used to fear that his door wasn't an adequate barrier, that if during one of his mother's parties people needed more room to dance or another place to talk or even another person to talk to, they might just barge in. So few of his mother's friends had kids, and they tended to view Noah as some kind of novelty, one more example of the kitsch Cara collected.

"It's kind of perfect, really, when you think about it."

"Dying from hypothermia? No, it's not," he said. "Maybe you should talk to someone."

"Yeah, like anyone over at Behavioral Health ever helped anybody. They send depressed kids to the top of the tallest building on campus."

"You're sick." He stood and reached across to his dresser top where he'd placed his beer. It was warm. "That's not true, about Behavioral Health. There're some good guys over there." He wasn't sure why he hadn't told Alex about Dowd, other than that he hadn't told anyone. "I know kids who . . . I've been going . . . seeing this one guy there. I've told him everything, you know—the wardrobe, all that stuff. He's . . . been helpful." Noah sensed Alex stiffen a bit as he sat back down next to her.

"Really?"

"Why would I lie about something like that?" he asked.

"To make me feel better, like I'm not such a psycho. Your timing's suspicious."

"I've never heard of somebody lying about being in therapy when they really aren't."

"People lie about everything."

"I'm not people, Alex." He tried to nudge her forward so that he could get his arm around her.

"I'm not in the mood," she said, and he laughed, glad to see some spark of her old self. He let his hand dangle down over her shoulder onto where he expected her breast to be. She must have been wearing a sports bra or a torso wide bandage, because he couldn't really feel anything other than a kind of plateau. He listened to her breathe and felt his own chest rising and falling with hers. He wondered what it was like to be so solid. What it felt like to stand on legs that thick, put on a coat over such broad shoulders? He moved his hand from the front of her chest to her hair and let his fingers run in and out of its kinks. What was it like to shake your head and sense all that hair behind you? He'd seen her one day when she'd just come out of the shower. Her head was about one-tenth the size when her hair was wet. As he watched it air-dry over the next hour or so, he told her she reminded him of a Chia pet.

"Stop it," she said. He could smell her beer breath as she exhaled.

"What?"

"Stop touching me." She swiveled her shoulders and shook him off.

Noah got off the bed. "Sorry," he mumbled. He could feel his face heating up and the familiar rush of shame coursing through his body. He heard a cork being pulled from a bottle, smelled the burned stuff on the bottom of the oven, and he wished he were out there in the kitchen or the living room instead of in this gloomy space with her. He wondered if she'd make fun of him in a day or two about therapy. She might, as a joke of course, slip it in while she was scraping the ice off her car or ripping open a bag of pretzels with her teeth.

Noah moved his fingers slowly across the top of the bookshelf, and when he felt his incense holder he decided to light a stick. With the door closed, the small room filled quickly with sweet smoke. Somewhere in his scent-addled consciousness, he registered the sound of crying. Alex was sobbing. He looked around for Kleenex, but knew that he'd have to leave the room to get some. He moved toward the foot of the bed, then away, walked to the door thinking he would just run across the hall to the bathroom, but she wouldn't know that he wasn't leaving for good. In desperation he reached into his top dresser drawer and pulled out a lone athletic sock. He walked back toward the bed and reached toward her with the sock, but she didn't see it. He took a risk and placed it in her hands, but she didn't break her stride. Maybe this was hysterical crying. He started murmuring "shhhh" and "it's okay."

"No," she mumbled. "Nothing's okay. It's so fucked up. You have no idea how bad it is."

"Yeah!" Someone out in the living room turned up the volume on k. d. lang. Christ, his mother's friends could be so annoying. He looked around the room through the fog of the burning incense. Only the contents of the dresser top were clearly visible; everything else was vague, like a topographical map. The heavier and more grim she grew beside him, the lighter and more ashamed he felt. Who was he to be happier than Alex?

"I'm sorry. I'm ruining your . . . I'm such a bitch, such a bitch. You probably hate me."

"Well, I do kind of hate you." He waited for her to laugh. "Did something happen?"

She shook her head. "And it never will. I'll always be alone. I don't know what I did that was so bad to end up so alone." She mumbled all this through barely separated wet fingers, and then she began to weep again. He didn't know what to say, but he had the sense that the universe was somehow depending on him to save her by saying the right stuff. It was like coming up to a car wreck and trying to get the driver out with nothing more than a big pile of slippery words. Maybe he was overreacting, thinking that she was in some desperate fix, that gasoline was leaking and any minute there'd be an explosion.

"Alex, you aren't alone, though. I mean, we—"

"My little sister, she's sixteen and she has this boyfriend, and he calls her and drives her to school and brings her gifts and can't keep his hands off her. And I came downstairs the other day, and they were in the kitchen making a pizza and making out. I mean, I'd never seen two people kiss like that up close, like they were inhaling each other."

He offered the sock again. Loneliness, that was something he understood. Inclusion, exclusion. "Is it about love, or sex?" He was sure that his need to ask this question was further unnecessary evidence of his complete freakishness.

She reached for the sock in the darkness and blew her nose loudly. "What the fuck? What is this?"

"I didn't have any Kleenex."

She looked up at him. Her cheeks were wet and her lips were just heading toward rawness. It occurred to him to kiss them, salty and a little beat up. He wasn't sure what desire was, but he knew that it was something with more integrity than curiosity. His urge to kiss her was not unlike wanting to stand on high ground during an electrical storm. "Alex," he said a bit too loudly, as if to refocus himself, "you can't kill yourself because of sex." He moved into a kneeling position on the edge of the bed. "It would be like—I don't know—killing yourself because the toy inside the cereal box sucked. But when you really think about it, you'd buy that cereal anyway, for the cereal. The toy's just a gimmick. And you're above that." He was having one of those moments of complete conviction, his ambi ways lending him panoramic vision.

"No one's above sex." She twisted her hair into a knot behind her head, and Noah watched as it slowly unfurled, big thick hanks moving as if alive.

"It's sex and love. That's the point. That's what Katie has, someone who loves her . . . body and soul."

"I love you body and soul," he said. God, he was speaking in song lyrics.

"Nice, but not true. You don't stay up nights fantasizing about me."

"How do you know?" he said.

She rolled the sock up into itself. "If you do think of me that way, most likely it's 'cause you want to *be* me, not because you want to *do* me."

For the second time in only a few minutes, a flood of humiliation swept through him, followed quickly by an onslaught of fear. His whole body was pulsing, and he hopped off the bed where he'd been perched weirdly like a too-big boy in prayer. Of course, she was right. If she brushed against him accidentally, he'd get an erection. But thinking about her couldn't produce the same effect. Still, he didn't like being told what he felt. "How do you know how I feel about you? Maybe you can't understand what I'm talking about."

She didn't move or say anything. Whatever thin connection had been sustaining their discussion disintegrated, and the room swelled smoky and dark. Alex stood and picked up her empty beer from the nightstand and walked out, closing the door softly behind her.

Noah spent a few minutes considering how unfair this was, given that everything he'd said was totally true, then he grabbed some shoes from the bottom of his closet. His mother's friends couldn't be concerned with anything as sensible as not parking other people in, so chances were good that three or four shitboxes were now blocking Alex's car. The folding doors to the hall closet had come off their tracks, and Noah wrestled them open wide enough to grab his mother's coat and hat.

The sidewalk was slippery and Noah was attempting to race along in clogs. He slowed to a shuffling trot, fixed the Persian lamb hat more firmly on his head and buttoned the red down coat, the sleeves barely coming to his elbows. Had he said the right things to Alex, he would not be roaming the unlit streets of his mother's neighborhood desperately looking for her now.

Halfway down Freeman he did a quick 360, just to be sure she wasn't behind him. Her car had been blocked in the driveway, and her parents' house was too far to reach on foot, so most likely she'd gone back to the dorm. Unless, of course, she'd headed somewhere else entirely—down to the water, up to a ledge. Everyone talked about suicide at some point. He wondered if Dowd could tell who to really worry about. He wondered if he'd ever been wrong.

As he rounded the corner from Freeman to Cutler, he paused and listened. His own breath was ragged and the loose change in his mother's pocket jingled loudly. He needed to reassure himself that when he stopped moving, whatever sounds he thought he'd heard behind him stopped too.

Once on Cutler, the student rentals became more frequent and the junk on the front porches less practical. In order to get to their dorm, he'd have to go down Meecham, which somehow had become the unofficial address for much of the hockey team and some of the sailing team. Kids were partying, mostly with windows and doors shut. Still, as he walked he could hear the electronic cat scratch of someone fucking around with an amplifier and then what sounded like a bunch of guys yodeling. He instructed himself not to look around, simply to pick up his pace.

A car slowed behind him, the tires making a slurping sound on the wet pavement. Now seemed like the right time to get off this street. He looked around lamely for a stick or a spare tire iron. He was in the middle of a long block. His only option would be to cut through some snow-crapped side yard.

"Cara! Stop! Please!" An old Subaru wagon pulled up to the curb. The driver killed the brights and put the car in park.

"Noah?" Dr. Dowd was framed in the open car window.

Noah was unsure about whether or not to step off the curb and move closer to the car. Dowd was staring so intently at the hat on his head that Noah had no choice but to remove it. "Cara—Carmen Shipley's my mother."

"Excuse me?" Even in the darkness, Dowd looked sick.

"You thought I was my mother."

The blinker was still clicking inside the car, flashing a little bit of orange light on the sidewalk up ahead. "I'm sorry. I didn't realize—"

"Yeah, I know."

Dowd looked immobilized.

Shit. This was going to take time, and he needed to find Alex. "The party's just getting going. I mean, you know where the house is, right? I'm sort of—"

Dowd's brow furrowed under his pick-up-sticks hair.

"The *Les Mis* thing." Noah had never seen this particular expression before. Dowd was always so programmatic, and now he looked as if someone had pulled the plug on him. "Actually, you know, it's kind of like really weird that you came by just now." Noah moved toward the car, hoping the advice he needed might be rapidly dispensed from this particular take-out window.

14

Malcolm had let Merlin out at seven and then gone back upstairs to bed. Hours later, the dog's barks landed like a verdict. It was as if while he slept, Malcolm had been found out, tried, and condemned. As the dog accused from somewhere in the yard, Malcolm repeated to himself what needed to be done and in what order. *Get up, go to the bathroom, go downstairs, let in the barking dog.* Sun poured into the room. The shades covering the four windows had, one by one, lost their spring action, and Malcolm had removed them without replacing them. Even still, he was a long time coming to the surface of the day. So many excellent reasons not to.

He'd driven back from his abysmal meeting with Susannah in a kind of oblivion and ended up snaking the streets of Cara's neighborhood with the desperate idea that she might somehow help him. When he saw her out walking, he couldn't believe his good luck. His presence could appear accidental; he wouldn't have to bear the indignity of intent. But, for the second time in two months, Noah had tripped him up by tricking himself out in drag. And then he'd begged Malcolm to drive him around looking for his missing friend.

"She doesn't know." Noah had loosened his seatbelt so that he could reach the fogged-up windshield, creating a widening porthole with the back of Cara's suede glove, the motion releasing traces of Cara's mossy perfume from the coat he was wearing.

Malcolm lowered his window all the way.

"She's got red hair, my friend, like a lot of red hair."

Malcolm nodded in the darkened car, and hit the brakes midway through a crosswalk where two undergrads on skateboards had appeared out of nowhere. He dangled one arm out the open window, using the cold air, counting on it to ground him. "When you say she doesn't know. . . ."

"I mean, my mother."

"What exactly is it she doesn't know?"

Noah sighed and attempted to stretch his long legs. "That you're my therapist or whatever, or that I even go to a therapist or that. . . . Can we, like, not talk about this right now?"

Malcolm drove on, rapping his knuckles against the iced-over car door. The Subaru took a speed bump, and Noah's knees slammed against the glove box. "So, your mother doesn't know that I've been treating you?"

"I just said that."

"But you've known that your mother and I were—"

"Yeah."

"You've told me a lot about yourself, Noah. But you didn't think you could tell me that?"

"It wasn't that *I couldn't tell you*." He lowered his voice to a pompous bass.

The sting of being mocked was impossible to delay, unlike the humiliation of having been tricked, which, Malcolm knew from experience, could be held off until he was alone. "You know—"

"Hey, I'm sorry. It's just, like, really weird, okay? I don't mean to be rude or whatever."

They'd found the girl a little before midnight. Alex? They'd spotted her down at the Baxter boat launch. Noah had seen her tucked between two racks of Baxter sailing team Lasers and 420s. The moon, almost full in a clearing sky, had helped. Malcolm remained in the car while Noah got out. She was crying, or had been crying. Every few minutes she dragged the sleeve of her coat across her face. Malcolm was nearly mesmerized by the image of Noah crouched in front of Alex, in an attitude of offering.

Noah had put Alex in the front seat to be closer to the heater fan. Malcolm drove slowly, giving himself time to assess the girl's condition. She was no longer crying. She was quiet but lucid, and she seemed to murmur some kind of thanks when Noah reached between the seats to stroke her hair.

When Malcolm returned the kids to Alex's car, he saw Cara through the living-room window, the party still going strong. She was leaning in close to a woman, her head of dark hair inclined toward the woman's head, her hand on the woman's shoulder, as if she were sharing a confidence.

"Thank you." Alex shut the door and looked back into the car at Noah.

Noah slid to the passenger's side of the back seat. "I don't want her to drive by herself."

Malcolm had the impulse to tell him that he'd make a great husband someday, a great father. He hadn't been able to parse the boy's relationship with this girl. "Alex is lucky to have such a good friend," Malcolm said.

Noah had his hand on the door. "Yeah."

"I know we can talk about this on Tuesday, but . . . when did you know that your mother and I—"

"Remember I told you I met that guy, the other guy you work with. That was like before spring break." Noah was sitting at the edge of his seat, twirling the black Persian lamb hat on one finger. "I didn't really want you to know, because then it would ruin everything. If you found out, I knew you'd pawn me off on someone else."

"I appreciate your telling me that." Malcolm looked again toward the living-room window, the house filled with people having fun, before turning back toward Noah. "It helps me understand . . . a lot of things."

Malcolm walked into the bathroom, urinated, flushed. He brushed his teeth, then went downstairs and made his way through the empty house to the kitchen door to let in Merlin. He picked up the dog's water dish and exchanged the slimy water for some cleaner stuff. He dumped yesterday's coffee, rinsed the carafe, and started a fresh pot. Thankfully, he hadn't run into Cara last night. He tried to recall Noah's mother as he'd been imagining her in their sessions. The patient's mother was a cipher compared to the flesh-and-blood Cara. What a ludicrous business, trying to read the story of someone's life from an oblique perspective. Noah's mother was considerate, but not caring enough to confront her son's true identity. Was Cara the same? He listened to the coffee maker gurgle and hiss, looked into the living room, out the windows onto the bay. It was still sunny but strangely ominous farther out over the water where the sky was the color of slate. "Our lives with our children are private," she'd said to him the last time they were together, the words rearranging themselves now to reveal rather than conceal.

Merlin ran to the door just as a snow squall began to swirl from out by Peck's Island. A blast of obscuring white flakes came jetting at the living-room windows even as the late afternoon sun poured in. Merlin didn't bark but wagged his tail rapidly enough to jingle his collar. Malcolm walked over to the kitchen door to see what had gotten the dog's attention. Jane was outside, carrying a bakery box and a bottle.

Malcolm made a fire and opened the wine and cut the string from around the box. He placed the pastries on the coffee table and tossed Jane a plaid blanket. She sat cross-legged in the rocker by the fire with her mittens still on.

"I know it looks weird," she said, trying hard to sound breezy, "but this particular cabernet with those chocolate bombe things are excellent."

He placed his hand on her shoulder and walked back to the kitchen for some glasses and plates.

"I didn't call first," she said, as if this were the beginning of an explanation. "You must have things you're doing this afternoon."

He poured her some wine. "Talking to you."

"Did you know that night I made an ass of myself at our house? When I thought it was the music teacher, Carmen? Did you know about this . . . woman then?" She placed her glass on the table. "No. Don't say anything. He's your friend. Of course you knew." She was looking past him out the windows. "You must think I'm such a pathetic fucking idiot."

"I'm sorry." Malcolm reached down and pulled a burr from Merlin's flank. "I'm sorry I wasn't able to be your friend and Gordon's at the same time."

"You mean you're sorry you lied to me."

Malcolm put down his glass. The window was behind him, but he could tell, by the way the light in the room was shooting through the wine, that the front was passing. "I'm sorry I hurt you, Jane." He knew his voice sounded flat, too controlled, as if none of this really mattered to him.

"He's had affairs before, you know? I know you know." She pulled the blanket more tightly around her shoulders and rocked back in the chair. "Nothing's real, that's what it feels like. All my perceptions, useless. I was going along thinking things were bad, but I didn't know he had a whole other life, bigger than the one I shared with him." Her anger had begun to give her a kind of glow.

"I thought the rotten thing that was happening was happening to both of us—but, really, it was only happening to me—and my kids. He does this and walks off into a romance, and me and the kids are stuck in a tragedy." She abruptly planted the heels of her black boots on the floor beneath the rocking chair, halting it mid-rock and propelling herself slightly off the edge of the seat. She used the opportunity to reach for the wine bottle. The blanket slipped off her shoulders, and Malcolm stared at her sweater, a leopard pattern. "I'm forty-six. If I live another thirty years, I'll go like half my sexual life not having sex. I'll have cats but no sex."

"Is that what's worrying you?"

"Yes," she said, slamming down the glass. "As a matter of fact, it is."

"There's more to life than sex. You know that."

"No. Maybe *you* know that." She looked over the red rims of her glasses at him. "Sorry, that just slipped out."

Malcolm released a sigh that sounded like a final exhalation. He fought the urge to turn from Jane and look at the weather on the water, to go upstairs and crawl into bed, to box her up for a later date. It scared him that he could keep talking to her almost robotically when she was in such distress. In the first year or two after Laura died, he had often found himself reading to the girls or playing with them, even driving with them in the car, only to have no clear recollection of the recently elapsed present, the sense and substance of it, an hour or two later. All he knew was that their bodies had been close to his, that they'd eaten, arrived at their destination; meanwhile, he was embroiled in some frantic discourse.

"You know in the movies when someone gets cheated on, they're the underdog, a kind of noble victim or something, and you always root for that person," Jane continued after a moment. "But it's nothing like that in real life. There's no moral high ground or whatever. Because there's no morality in love. You're simply no longer the desired one. Movies never show how embarrassing—that's not even the right word—worse even than embarrassment—"

"Shame." Malcolm leaned back into the soft cushions of the couch.

"Shame, yes, thank you." Jane slipped off her boots and tucked her feet to one side in the chair. She was small, but solid. Her animal print sweater and pink socks and red glasses screamed whimsy. Life was a party, her yellow spiky hair a perpetual party hat. None of it was serious business.

"Can you even begin to imagine the gossip? I hope they move, far, far away for ever and a day." She rocked in the chair slightly, her wine rising and falling in her glass, a burgundy tide.

Malcolm grabbed a fresh log from the stack by the hearth and opened the fireplace curtain. He *had* imagined the gossip. He had been concerned that his and Gordon's practice might become associated with Gordon's infidelity. And of course it would get out that the woman was a patient. In these interconnected small towns, his success as a therapist depended on being a non-persona, on keeping it out of the papers. He had thought about this often when the girls were still at home. Having a kid's name in bold face in the police blotter was the kind of publicity that could seriously hamper his livelihood. He had never said this to them; he didn't need to. They saw the way other parents deferred to him, how kids they didn't know ran up to him on the street, the late-night phone calls that caused him to head to the emergency room. Professional partnership was like marriage. Half the comfort was the sense that it wasn't all on you, that you weren't in it alone. Maybe it was time. Maybe Gordon would move far, far away and leave his referrals behind.

"You wouldn't consider sleeping with me, would you?"

Malcolm was still rearranging the fire, and Jane's voice drifted toward him and up the flue. He could hear her laughing behind him, and he began to laugh too, until he turned and saw that she was crying.

He reached back to the coffee table and grabbed a napkin to wipe the soot from his hands, then tossed the napkin into the fire. It flared up a gaseous blue. "Of course I would consider sleeping with you." He sank back into the couch. "I would consider it, but I wouldn't do it."

She bit her lower lip. "No. Because that would be wrong. And you would never do the wrong thing, would you?"

He looked at the vanishing wine in the bottle and wondered if she was drunk. "If we did that, Jane, then we couldn't do this. We wouldn't have this."

"Yeah, and who'd want to give up *this*? Because *this* is really fucking great."

"You don't need me to have sex with you. You don't need Gordon. You have more friends and more energy than anyone I've ever met. You *are* the life force, for chrissakes. One day, when I was telling Gordon that I hated keeping a secret from you, because I loved you, he said, 'Yeah, everyone loves Jane—'"

"But no one wants to have sex with her. Everyone loves me, but no one is *in love* with me. No one's under my window singing to me, or sending me notes or surprising me with trips."

Looking now at her costume, he thought she couldn't have arrayed herself with more armor, couldn't have worked any harder to come across more ironic. And here she was talking about romance. Everyone wanted to be someone's beloved. Unconditional, perfect, romantic love, the missing piece of the self, placed in someone else's puzzle box.

Jane pulled off her socks, tugging from the toes like a toddler or a striptease artist. She shoved the fantastical pink socks into her boots, stretched her legs, and pointed her red-painted toes in his direction.

"Just stretching, don't worry. I'm stopping at the socks."

He smiled, but he *was* worried. She was far more potent than he right now.

"He told the boys, you know, he told them about her. He actually believes. . . ." She stopped and looked up at Malcolm. "He believes the truth can set him free. You know, maybe it can, but what about everyone else, and what about all the time he was lying?"

"How're the boys doing?"

She pulled one of the empty brown liners that had cupped the chocolate pastries and began folding it like a fan. "They're overly solicitous of me."

Malcolm watched her tuck the little fan between her toes. "You should talk to someone."

"Yeah, right. Who should I call? Oh, oh, I know, the social worker from the high school who—"

"I could give you a name or two in Portland."

"I'm not sure I'm so hot and heavy for therapy or therapists right now. Christ. You're all a bunch of whack-jobs." She pulled the fan from between her toes. "I know you'd rather be dead than sitting here talking about all of this—"

Malcolm moved to interrupt, and she held up her hand.

"But I don't really care," she said. "You owe me. Sheer guilt, alone."

"You're angry—"

"Spare me the shrink-speak, okay? You betrayed me. You of the high road."

The sun had disappeared again. The room cooled and darkened as if the bay water had pooled into the house. Behind him, Malcolm pictured a few random whitecaps, the first glimpse of Enoch's Rock, now that it was mid-tide.

"Remorseless, both of you. You don't even feel guilty. That's a problem, Malcolm. I accuse you of something, and you respond by telling me the obvious, that I'm angry. You know what, the two of you are a pair. You deserve each other." She uncrossed her legs in the chair and bent to retrieve her socks. "Don't you ever take responsibility?"

He noticed the little bit of ripped frill at the top of her anklets, the same kind of socks his girls had worn as toddlers. He'd long suspected that adults were just a duller, muddier version of children, adult life a steadily fading reprint of a once-ecstatic and insistent original. His adult patients were rarely as interesting as the younger ones. He wondered if he should expect an ever-leaking interest in his own children. Perhaps the reversal had already begun. He would be less and less intrigued by them, less sympathetic, less attached.

Jane was standing now. She reached for her red scarf, which she'd thrown on the armchair beside her, and began to wind it around her neck. "Apparently you thought I was posing a rhetorical question." Her voice dropped a bit with each word.

"It sounded more like an accusation. You know I take responsibility." The sadness he'd felt only seconds before transformed into irritation. "In a world populated with takers, the only damn thing I've been known to *take* is responsibility. So, actually, I'd really appreciate your not laying that on me, all right?"

She turned her back to him and put her palms up to the fire, as if braced against its warmth. "I'm sorry," she said. "I don't really know what's going on with me. I'm clearly not behaving like myself." She let her arms fall to her sides, her body unnaturally still for so long, Malcolm wondered if she was breathing. When she did move again, it was to get her coat from the rack by the door.

"You know, earlier when you were talking about no longer being the desired one. . . ." He moved toward where she was standing on the doormat, buttoning her coat. "About the shame . . . well, I know about that." He needed to give her something before she left. "A few weeks before Laura's accident, she told me she was in love with someone else."

Malcolm could hear the lack of affect in his speech, unsure of the proper inflection for telling this too-old story right now. He listened to the refrigerator motor, the wind causing the house to shift and creak, a downdraft in the fireplace, as if someone were moaning from up inside the chimney.

Jane put on her mittens, trimmed with feathers at the wrist, and walked back to the coffee table. Using the heel of her hand, she rammed the cork into the nearly empty wine bottle, picked it up, and walked to the front door. Just as she was stepping outside, she turned toward Malcolm and said flatly, "You must have been really angry."

Malcolm heard her car back down the gravel driveway. He grabbed the blanket off the rocker and unfolded it in front of the fireplace, Jane's lemony scent trapped in its weave. He took off his shoes and lay down on his side. The gray cold of the room chilled his back more than the fire warmed his front, but that was to be expected. He was asleep in a wine-soaked, sad slumber before he could chide himself for lying down in the first place.

꒰◯꒱

The home phone rang. Malcolm rolled to his back and shook his left arm to get the circulation going. The outdoor lights had come on, the sky edging toward black. Whoever had called hung up without leaving a message, and Malcolm curled his back toward the chilly fireplace and tried to return to where he'd been. On a train, moving from car to car, each time stepping across an icy threshold before sliding open the next door and entering the next warm, brightly lit car, looking at every face, looking for one of the girls, for a little girl. He knew she was alone and he had to find her. He heard his cell phone in the kitchen where he'd plugged it in that morning. He rolled carefully to his knees and leaned on the coffee table as he stood. In the darkened kitchen, he looked down at his phone. One missed call from Susannah.

He hit CALL and walked toward the windows overlooking the water.

"Oh, Daddy," she breathed. "Oh, good, you're there."

The view, the water, the first star, the trees at the edge all receded like Enoch's Rock. "What's the matter?"

"Leah . . . I'm hoping she's with you."

"No." He leaned against the windowsill and then forced himself to walk into the kitchen and look out into the driveway. As he moved through the house, he listened to Susannah chatter and breathe.

". . . stuff, you know, some stuff. And then she borrowed my car like right after she got here this afternoon. She said she was running to CVS and she'd be right back. And like now it's almost eight."

"It's a little past seven," Malcolm said. Susannah had a tendency to exaggerate.

"That's four hours, Dad, that she's been missing."

"What did she say about why she'd left school for the weekend?"

There was a pause on the other end.

"Susannah, I'd appreciate your telling me what you know."

"She made me swear not to tell you."

Malcolm stared at his own impenetrable reflection in the living-room window. He could feel his ear getting hot, and he realized he was pressing the phone to the side of his face with excessive force. "What happens when you call her cell phone?"

"It rings on the sink in my bathroom. Do you think we *should* call the police?"

"Susannah," Malcolm barked, "if there's some reason you think we should call the police, you better tell me."

"Oh, Daddy. Some graduate student . . . the section leader in her Art History course, has been, like, stalking her."

"What do you mean?" Malcolm pulled out a dining-room chair and sat down stiffly.

"Calling all the time, showing up wherever Lee happens to be, writing notes and e-mails."

"How long has this been going on?"

"I don't really know."

"Jesus, why didn't she tell me?" Malcolm put the receiver to his other ear and rubbed his chin. "She's reported this guy, right? Reported him to campus security? Talked to the dean? Something?"

"She was afraid to."

Malcolm couldn't remember Leah ever being afraid to do anything, and he wondered who the creep was who'd so frightened his daughter that he'd altered her. He felt a shift in his chest, like a pile of half-burned logs sliding and collapsing. Maybe he was the creep, his revelation having so shaken her that she'd begun to crumble from within. "You should have told me, Susannah."

"She asked me not to."

"All because—"

"It's complicated, Daddy."

"No, Zannah, it's not." But even as Malcolm spoke those words into the molded plastic that passed for a connection to his daughter, he knew he was wrong. Even before Susannah betrayed her sister and told him everything she knew, he could feel it there in the pauses and the sighing, the clipped, reined-in way Susannah was speaking. He got up from the chair and turned out the two small lamps in the room. Then he cupped one hand around his face and stared out at the bay, desperate to look at something more immutable than himself as she finished up with him.

"She was scared, Daddy. She was scared to tell you. There was a little thing between them, I guess. A little kind of . . . some kind of relationship or something, I don't really know."

"A hookup?" he said.

Susannah sputtered. "Jeez, Dad, easy. Anyway, she was worried you'd be angry."

"When was the last time I got mad at you, either of you, for having sex?" And it occurred to Malcolm in that moment that she was pregnant. Or worse.

"The grad student's a woman."

"Oh," Malcolm said, just as the thought of H.I.V. had flashed into his mind. "Oh."

"She was worried you'd. . . ." Susannah started to cry on the other end of the phone.

"Oh," he cooed. "Okay."

"And now we don't know where she is, and I was really hoping she was driving down there to see you. But she would have gotten there by now, and what if this woman really is crazy and she, like. . . ."

"Have you tried Madeline or the other suite-mates? Maybe she went back to school, or maybe she called to say where she was going."

"I called some of the numbers on her cell phone. No one's heard from her today."

"Is that grad student's number on there?"

"I don't know."

"You got Madeline's number?"

"Yeah."

"Give it to me."

15

On Tuesday afternoon, Noah sat beside his mother on the couch in Dowd's office fingering the turquoise choker at his neck. When he'd finally told her everything, she'd brought out a cigar box of jewelry for him to "paw" through. He'd accepted the box warily, wondering if it contained stuff she might share with a daughter, good stuff, or whether she was simply making a contribution to the dress-up trunk. It would be just like his mother to make no distinction. In keeping with her Buddhist philosophy of organization, all was one.

"You look very nice," Dowd said.

Both Noah and his mother said "Thank you." Noah laughed and his mother blushed.

"So that we're all clear, this is about you today." He pointed at Noah.

"And my mother. Me and my mother." Noah looked over at his mother, who'd surprised him with a text message that morning asking when his next appointment was and whether she might join him.

⠙⠕

After being up with Alex most of Friday night and doing two performances of *Les Mis* on Saturday, Noah had found himself still in his pajamas late on Sunday afternoon, hunkered beside his mother. They were in the third hour of watching an ancient video of a British TV series she dug out whenever she felt sad. The unending complications of the lives of some uber-rich Edwardian family and their servants worked on her like a designer drug.

Noah was physically exhausted, his legs numb from the job of holding up the rest of his body, but he was also strangely charged, as if a deep and persistent current was working through him. Something about what had happened with Alex and Dowd had rearranged him. It could be done. People could be honest about themselves.

They'd paused the tape right after Lady Marjorie set sail on the *Titanic* so that his mother could go to the bathroom, and, just as she was coming back into the living room, stepping over the big tangle of wires needed for the tiny TV and the wheezing VCR to reach the coffee table, he said, "Can I tell you about something?"

She knew. She didn't really know. She kind of suspected . . . something, but didn't know what it meant.

"It doesn't *mean* anything," he said. "It's just who I am."

"Okay," she said. "That explains the clothes. I mean, I do hang things in there from time to time, and I thought, I don't know, maybe you were hiding an illegal immigrant or, maybe this was the safe place for a friend's clothes, you know, a friend who couldn't keep them in

175

his own closet." They both stared for a while at the slightly blurred image of a butler proffering a silver tray with a sealed envelope on it. And then his mother hit PLAY.

Hours later, as they were finishing off a carton of Hunan chicken, Noah muted the barking hounds mid-foxhunt.

"I've been going to Behavioral Health."

His mother placed her chopsticks mindfully on her empty plate.

"I think you know the therapist." Noah began to busy his hands with the metal hanger on the Chinese food carton. "Dr. Dowd."

"Oh."

"I know he's the guy. . . ."

She lowered her plate to the coffee table. "How long have you been going to him?"

"He didn't know—not until the other night, during the party when I was out looking for Alex. He . . . I ran into him on the street."

"Oh, God. Really?"

"I'm sorry." Noah successfully freed one end of the metal handle from the carton.

"For what?"

"If my . . . knowing him, fucks it up for you. He's a pretty cool guy. A really cool guy, actually."

His mother pinched a grain of brown rice from her lap and deposited it on her plate. "We stopped seeing each other a week ago."

With a final tug, Noah released the other end of the metal from the paper container and began the work of joining the two jagged ends.

"We're very, very different people. The last time we went out," she paused and tucked her hair behind her ears, "he got mad at me for not talking about you, and I told him—"

"What do you mean not talking about me?"

"You're the most important person in the world to me. I need to really trust someone—"

"Before you drop the freak bomb?"

"Before," she began measuredly, "I let them in on what really matters."

He must have squeezed too hard. The wire gave way, breaking into uneven thirds. He didn't believe her. He was a liability to her in almost every situation—except for this one, where they sat around in loungewear and watched old videos all day. "I never talked about you, either." He screwed a piece of the broken wire into the water chestnut on his plate. "I never told him you were on the faculty. I just wanted to be me in there."

She nodded, and Noah unmuted the TV.

"How did it all come out, that he and I . . . ?"

On the screen, the hounds and the horses were still racing through the countryside.

"That guy that day at Homefires. Your friend's boyfriend."

"Why did you want your mother to come today?" Dowd asked.

"It was her idea. There's things she's scared to talk about with me that we need to maybe talk about." Noah could feel the clasp of the choker catch on a neck hair. "She doesn't believe in talking much, anyway."

Dowd did that annoying eyebrow thing in the direction of his mother.

She smiled, then looked down at the ground. Noah turned a bit so that he could see her on the couch beside him.

"It's just that I'm not—I'm not sure if I'm saying the right thing." She looked from Dowd to Noah. "I want you to be happy and fulfilled. And I'm uncertain of the part I still play in that. Does that make sense? Maybe you're all grown up, and I'm just an interfering adult, a clueless adult."

"What makes you think that?"

She reached for the box of tissues on the table beside her end of the couch. Noah couldn't remember the last time she'd cried when she wasn't watching a screen. She'd cried the other day when the *Titanic* telegram arrived on that Brit show.

"You're very mature. You always have been, which I guess wasn't easy for you in school. You're smart, Noah, in a way that I'm not. I've always trusted you to figure things out for yourself."

A wave of grief rolled through him. Nothing she'd just said was news to him. He'd always sensed it. And for a moment he allowed himself the barely perceptible flash that the other parent had died. It had happened—the thing he always feared—orphaned.

"How does that make you feel?" Dowd asked, looking at him sternly.

"What she just said?"

Dowd nodded.

"It's not true."

"Which part doesn't sound true to you?"

"She's helped with lots of things. Just not with this."

"When you say 'this,' what do you mean?" Dowd asked.

Noah lashed himself with the back of his own hand. "This. My gender twin set."

Dowd looked over at his mother sympathetically. "Bundling all your parenting into one neat pile of 'not needed' might be a way of not having to deal with Leah."

His mother jerked her head.

"I told Dr. Dowd that *Leah* is how I think of myself, you know, when. . . ."

She nodded, a bobble-head on the dashboard of a careening car.

"You didn't explain that to your mother the other day?"

"That's what we were going to name you if—"

"I know."

"It was your father's mother's name."

"She had a lot to take in, enough for one afternoon," Noah said, answering Dowd.

Dowd nodded. "Sounds like you take care of her, you're protective of her."

"She's pretty low-maintenance as mothers go," Noah said.

"That's interesting. You both think the same thing of the other—that you're self-sufficient. That's convenient. Two people who need next to nothing." Dowd removed his glasses and dug into his pants pocket for a handkerchief. "What would it take for you to feel that your mother accepted you—"

"But I do, I do!" His mother practically jumped from the couch.

Dowd held up his hand, an emotional crossing guard at a hazardous intersection.

"It's not that," Noah said. "Of course she accepts me. She's not, like, going around making jokes at my expense or even complaining about me to her friends, I don't think. She had that party for me the other night."

"Well, then, what is it you'd like from your mother that you haven't already received?"

Shit. Why did he talk like that? Like feelings could just take up residence in a 3-D world along with junk mail and big box stores. "I want her to be curious, to ask me stuff about myself, real stuff."

"Can you give her an example?"

"Well, it's like she's not interested enough to exert the effort."

"You didn't answer my question." Dowd was refolding his handkerchief in these anal little triangles.

"It can't have been easy not having siblings," Noah's mother rushed in. "I worried all the time when you were younger that your childhood was lonesome, that you were missing out by growing up with only me."

"Did I ever make you think that?" he said.

"No. But I grew up with a house full of people and—"

"Maybe *you* felt deprived?" Noah said. "Maybe you feel cheated right now. No husband, and your only kid is a freak. A total freak." He'd fantasized about saying this to her. It was right up there with two or three other statements he felt crystallized his existence. And whenever he'd rehearsed the moment in his mind, his pulse quickened and his eyes teared. He could choke himself up just thinking about saying this to her, but now it felt rote. This whole thing, having Dowd here, there was no way for it not to be self-conscious and artificial. You could almost feel the camera in the corner. He paused, stared up at the painting of that tilting boat cutting through blue water, and tried to work his way back to a place of feeling. "And now I've wrecked this." He motioned between his mother and Dowd.

"Oh, Noah. No." His mother reached over and laid her hand on his thigh. "No. You haven't ruined anything. That was Malcolm's decision. Don't ever refer to yourself as a freak." She began to cry. "You're my gift from God."

Noah slid toward his mother and reached an arm around her heaving shoulders. He sat like that for a while, one arm around her, completely disoriented. This room had always been a place that called out the truth, even if he didn't always tell it. It was like a chapel, or something, a destination for being honest. But now the space had been desecrated. The office had filled with a mess of swirly feelings, some of them his, but some his mother's and some even belonging to Dowd. He was strapped into an ancient, herky-jerky carnival ride. From the underside of his dizziness, he heard Dowd.

"How are you feeling now?" he asked.

"Like this was a mistake."

"Why?" his mother asked, sounding alarmed.

"Where's it going to get us?"

"Don't say that, Noah," his mother said. "You have to give me a chance, to catch up. I can do this. I didn't have the best model, you know. Grandma and Dieter weren't exactly warm. They were loud, gruff, and I hated that. I vowed to be different with you, calm. It was always a firestorm with my brothers and sisters. But you think that the calm was just as empty as—"

"I never said empty. Where did you get that?" Noah asked.

Why wasn't Dowd steering her in the right direction? He slid back to his end of the couch and folded his legs beneath himself.

"You think I'm dispassionate? Is that why you're so—"

"What?" Noah said. "So what?"

"I'm not enough, and you're too much. You're everything, everybody, every feeling, every gender."

In the long silence that followed, Noah felt himself fill with anger and then empty to the point of despair. Up until this moment, he couldn't imagine anything sadder than his mother having had a love affair and never getting around to mentioning him. But being despised was no easier than being denied. Too much? What did that mean, that he was too much? Too much of what for whom?

"I know that sounded like a criticism—" his mother began.

"Well, *yeah*," Noah said.

"I guess I was really talking more about myself, my own insecurities. We say we want our kids to be better than us, more evolved. But the reality is harder to take. I just need some time to catch up. You're way ahead of me, you know."

"Why didn't you ever get married again?"

"Oh, Noah." She wound her fingers into the ends of her shawl. "That's so complicated."

"Maybe it's really none of my business."

The cell phone on Dowd's desk began to buzz, and Dowd got up and silenced it. "Sorry about that." He sat back down and leaned forward in his chair. "I don't understand why your question about your mother's not having married again isn't your business."

"It's personal, I guess, private," Noah said.

"And you're the closest people in the world to each other."

Noah looked at Dowd and wondered what it would feel like to be the closest person in the world to him. "Mom," he turned his body toward her, "I worry that you're basically a loner, and I am too, and I'll never find anyone either." He flashed a look at Dowd.

"I just. . . ." She exhaled. "I thought I was doing the right thing, being a good mother. You were my main concern. And I suppose if I'd met the right person—"

"I don't think so. Who would have put up with me, you know? Who besides you could have really accepted me? Uncle Billy's my fucking uncle and he can barely stand me. What men who you know actually really like me?" Noah pushed the sleeves of his shirt up past his elbows, exposing the dark hairs on his thin pale forearms. "How long have you been waiting for me to go to college? I bet even this year was like a disappointment. Here I am, around all the time—"

"Noah, please stop," she said coolly. "You're ranting."

Dowd raised his eyebrows but didn't say anything.

"I'm telling you the truth. I'm sorry if you don't like the way I'm telling it."

"Well, I can't listen to yelling."

Noah had his mouth open when he saw Dowd making a "T" with his two hands.

"If I may?" Dowd said. "Cara, do you really think Noah was yelling?"

"He was raising his voice, and it sounded threatening to me." Noah could feel her body grow rigid at the other end of the sofa. "I don't do well when people yell." She turned her shoulders so that she was very nearly facing the wall.

"Jesus, Mom."

"Maybe," Dowd looked at him, "maybe that's an accommodation you need to make when dealing with your mother, okay? If you want her to hear you, you need to talk in a way she can better understand you."

Noah wondered if Dowd knew this from firsthand experience.

"Thank you." His mother's head began bobbing. "That's right. That's how I feel."

"Every adult male I meet—I try him on, you know? Would my dad have been like *this*? Would he have treated me like *that*? What would he have thought about me? How well would he have hidden it?"

"Your father adored—"

"When I was two. What if he had lived and saw how I turned out, you know? Maybe I would have driven him away."

"Your father wasn't like that. He would never have judged you the way you're describing."

"You don't know that."

"Yes, I do," she said softly. "And I wish that you did too."

"There's a difference between being tolerated and being. . . ."

"What?" Dowd encouraged him.

"You know. Embraced."

"What are you trying to say?" His mother was crushing a tissue between her knuckles.

"Being understanding, that's intellectual. You can learn those lines, say the right thing. I mean, someone can be accepting of you and still not . . . I don't know." Noah broke off and looked at the bookshelf.

"I'd like you to finish that thought," Dowd said.

Noah looked at him. The simplest way of finishing the thought would have been to point to Dowd in his corduroy blazer and chinos and say to his mother: *Make me feel the way he makes me feel. Go out of your way to love me.*

"Sometimes I think you're scared of me," Noah said, not at all sure that was true.

Cara cleared her throat. "You're on a path I can't really . . . identify with, and so—"

"And that gets transmitted to me, that you think I'm a freak. You should be able to identify with anybody. The fact that you can't, makes me feel like I'm so different. Like I'm some other species. That's the loneliness—not being an only child. You make me feel alone." He couldn't look at her now, so he turned toward the window. Supposedly the trees were budding. He'd heard that on the radio, but you couldn't really tell, not from up here on the sixth floor. He felt her rise from her end of the sofa. He looked over as she bent to pick up her handbag.

"I . . . I really can't be much good in this process right now. I need to—I need time to mull what's happened. I'm not quick enough to talk and think simultaneously."

"It's important that you stay now, Cara." Dowd spoke gently but firmly to her.

Noah watched his mother's face redden. She was already at the door, winding herself into her shawl. "I don't like being ganged up on. How would you feel if someone told you that you'd failed at the most vital relationship in your life? How would you like it if someone told you that you were a bad father, that your daughters didn't feel loved?"

Dowd, who had been in the process of moving toward her at the door, stopped short as if hit from behind, coming to an off-kilter halt in the middle of the room. Noah looked away, afraid that his mother would exit and Dowd would topple, and he'd be left here alone. "It's important," Dowd began slowly, dragging his rough fingers across his lips as if trying to reanimate them, "to this process, that we make the most of these strong feelings. This is how we progress. Trust me, I won't ask you to do anything in here you can't do, okay? I know it's painful. Really, I do. This is the effort we make for love."

His mother dipped her head in acknowledgment and sat back down, wrapped in her clay-colored shawl.

Noah had endured some long silences in this room when it was just him and Dowd. But the vacuum created by three people not speaking was exponentially worse.

"Just by being here," Dowd finally began, his gaze regaining focus, "you're showing Noah that you can take the kind of emotional risk he needs you to take."

"You think I send a message saying it's not okay for you to be who you are—well, isn't that what both of you are telling me? That my love is inadequate, that my temperament—being reserved, let's say—is an insufficient way to be?" She removed the shawl and placed her hands on the empty couch cushion between them. "Noah, what you're up against—that's not something I can help you with. Your . . . suffering, the suffering you've already experienced and the suffering still to come, that's an internal battle. You think if I accept or embrace you, you'll have won the battle. That's just not so."

"Why can't you prove to me that anything's possible? Why can't you live like that?" He tried not to raise his voice, tried to sound imperative, but not hostile. "Dr. Dowd makes me feel that way, like I should challenge all my assumptions, everything that makes life small. He could make you feel that way too, I know." He had not meant to say this last bit, but there it was, an accidental snip at the end of a delicate surgery.

"What you just described—about possibility, about freedom." She looked directly at him, and he could see his incision. "I find all that in music. So you don't need to worry about me."

"Fine." Noah pulled at the cuffs of the shirt he was wearing, her shirt that he'd slid from her closet unnoticed, like so many other things he'd helped himself to all these years. "Whatever," he said, standing now. "But I'd like you to worry about me."

16

Malcolm cracked open the door to Leah's bedroom, checking to make sure she was there, monitoring the pile of quilts for a rise and fall. It was his third such patrol since he'd gotten home from work, and probably his twentieth since she'd shown up at the house very early Sunday morning. She'd arrived without so much as a backpack or even a purse, dressed in her sister's pajama bottoms and a Lewis Prep sweatshirt. She told Malcolm that she was very tired and that she would talk to him after she'd slept. She looked and smelled less than clean to him. As he walked with her up the stairs, he suspected that she had spilled gas on her boots.

She sighed deeply after every few steps, her breath hot and metallic in the space between them.

She'd slept straight through Sunday, and he'd canceled all his appointments on Monday. Each time he entered her room, he found her in bed, ostensibly asleep. When he'd tried to rouse her for dinner, she'd begged him, her cracked lips barely moving, to just let her sleep. This morning, after his appointment with Noah and Cara, he'd returned home to check on her, and in the later afternoon, when he had three sessions in a row, he'd asked Gordon to swing by. Just to make sure she was breathing.

Gordon had told Malcolm that he shouldn't let it go on. That tonight he had to wake her or threaten her with hospitalization.

Malcolm had made eggplant parmesan. He'd kept the door to her room open, certain that the scent would wake her. He needed to get her to at least drink some water. The oven timer beeped as Malcolm sat down on the edge of Leah's narrow bed. He turned on the small sailboat lamp on her nightstand. "Okay, baby girl, this is it." He got up and switched on the ceiling light. Leah pulled the topmost quilt over her head. One of the few indications that she had gotten up while he was out of the house were the additional comforters, as if no amount of covers was enough to warm her. The timer beeped again from downstairs. He walked into his bedroom, unplugged his clock radio, brought it into Leah's room, and crouched by the outlet at the edge of the dresser, plugging it in and tuning it to a country station. His knees ached, and when he straightened, his quads burned.

"Just turn off the overhead. And that . . . noise."

Even above the music, he could hear the oven timer, relentless. "Leah, it's Tuesday night. It's eight o'clock. I need you to get up and get in the shower and be downstairs for dinner by 8:15." He was using his best professional voice. Just the facts, unemotional, unmovable.

"Okay, Daddy," she said, her voice watery.

Malcolm set the table and listened as Leah shuffled to the bathroom. He heard the shower and pulled out lettuce and cucumber for a salad. He hadn't wanted to call the Dean of Students at Leah's college until he'd talked with her, so he called Health Services instead and reported that he thought Leah might have mono. He would let them know the outcome of the tests, but in the interim could they please notify her professors that she was back at home because she was ill.

Malcolm filled two tall glasses with water and set a place for Leah opposite his usual lone one, grateful for the task. During the month that she wouldn't talk to him, he'd been able to maintain the belief that her life was unfolding, even as his was without her. But in the hours she'd gone missing, when he couldn't conjure an image of her in any of the locales mentally ripped from the college brochure, he'd felt his own edges begin to fade. Her existence was an essential corroborating fact of his. He'd barely been able to suppress the urge to tell Cara all this in her session with Noah today, her stinginess a reminder of his own. More than once, he worried that he might grab Cara and shake her and scream "Love him, just love him."

He'd left the house only once yesterday, taking Merlin with him. He'd driven to Spring Street and walked with the dog to the entrance of what had been the Smithport Baptist Church and was now a yoga studio. He knew Cara took a Monday class there, and he knew it started at 5:30. He sat down on the steps and Merlin stretched out one step beneath him. He didn't know how long a yoga class lasted, but he suspected less than two hours. The dog was a cheap trick.

Just as the cold of the stone steps became truly uncomfortable, the first woman pushed out of the church doors, purple mat protruding from under her arm like a battering ram. Malcolm stood, leaned against the budding magnolia on the apron of grass in front of the church, and faced the doors. Merlin's tail, the most solid part of his elongated body, began beating wildly against Malcolm's calf.

Even after she spotted them, Cara continued to smile, her skin polished to a high sheen from exertion and enlightenment. She squatted in front of Merlin, dropped her mat and her bag, took both his long ears in her hands, and stroked them again and again. "You're such a lamb, aren't you?" She kissed the dog on the snout. "A regular little chop."

Just for a second, Malcolm caught a glimpse of something elemental and unstudied. Cara could forget herself and spend it all, generously, lavishly. He tried to take a breath, but only managed a shallow one.

She stood and slid one arm through the straps of her woven bag while Merlin sniffed at the mat still on the ground.

"I've missed you," he said.

She nodded, looked down at the dog. "I know about Noah, that he's been talking to you."

"That's what I was wondering, but I obviously couldn't ask."

"Confidentiality, I know." She was still looking down at Merlin. "Good boy, such a good dog."

"So—"

"Lot to take in."

"For sure," he said.

"I'm glad he's been seeing you. He needs to talk to someone. And I know you're very good at what you do." She was standing with one Lycra-covered leg crossed in front of the other, her thigh within easy reach of his hand. "It's actually kind of a relief."

"He's a great kid, your kid."

She nodded and wobbled slightly in her clogs. "I should get going."

"This has to be hard for him," Malcolm said.

"Lots of things are hard for him." She knelt down to say good-bye to the dog.

"I'm wondering if some things might feel less hard if—"

She stood abruptly.

"I have one of my own kids at home right now, and I'm worried—"

"What's this about, Malcolm?"

"I'm not sure, really."

"Yes, you are." Her mat was under her arm, her body ready to turn away.

"He needs you, Cara."

She stopped and looked at him.

"That's all," he said.

Her shoulders softened and her eyes filled.

"That's all I came to say."

She nodded. "I know."

He watched as she walked down the street to her car, Merlin's tail wagging from the sheer pleasure of having been in her presence, no matter how briefly.

⟣⟣

Leah inched down the stairs in a pair of slippers he'd received for Christmas years before and had never worn. Dressed in layers of castoff turtlenecks topped with an old moth-eaten sweater of his, she was a barely animated version of the stack of blankets on the bed upstairs. He watched as she pulled her chair away from the table just far enough to slide herself and all her clothing into the allotted space. Retracting her hands into her sleeves, she grabbed at her water glass with cloth-covered fingers. He bent slightly at the waist and kissed the top of her damp head. She smelled good again. "Let me get the food," he said as if he needed direction, one minute to the next.

She looked up at him just as he was turning away, her wet hair covering all but a slice of her face. That thick layer of certitude, her signature trait during early adolescence, was gone, and in its place was a kind of blurriness.

"It's eggplant parmesan, the one with all the different cheeses," he said, returning from the kitchen, oven mitts clamped around the casserole. He served her too large a portion and extended the plate in her direction.

"Why do you think you were so tired?" he asked after serving himself, retossing the salad and sitting down.

She shrugged, sipped her water, then looked up at him. "I wasn't sleeping the whole time. Sometimes in the middle of the night, I'd just lay there, completely awake."

"I wish I'd known. I was awake a lot too. We might have talked."

"Before I got here, I hadn't slept much for a while." Her fork hovered above her food.

"I'm really glad you're talking now," he said.

She looked across the table directly at him. "You won't be," she said. Then she drew her knees to her chest, causing her chair to tip backward slightly.

"There's nothing you could tell me that would make me love you less. *Nothing.* Do you understand that?"

She pushed against the edge of the table to slide her chair back, but the chair began to tip again and she caught herself by slamming her slippers against the underside of the table. Above, the glasses and the silverware rattled.

"Why do people say that? Mom told you something that changed how you felt about her. Then you told us something that changed how we felt about you. And now I'm going to tell you something, and it will, Daddy, it will absolutely and irrevocably change how you feel about me."

"I want to know what's been going on."

She picked up her head and looked across the table at him. "You only think you do."

"No," he said more angrily than he'd intended. "No," he softened. "I really want to know."

"You have to promise not to freak out, okay?"

He nodded.

He listened as Leah explained that the class was a year-long one, and she'd been in this teaching assistant's section since September. She'd heard students discussing how intense Casey could be, but Leah said that's what she liked about her. They'd slowly become friends.

"Casey. That's the girl you told me about before, the one doing the search for her birth mother."

"Right. The section meets right before lunch, so since November we'd been going to lunch together after class. She's a good teacher, really good, maybe better than Jennings. Anyway, Super Bowl

Sunday we ended up at the same party, and then we went back to her apartment."

Malcolm forced himself. "Was that your first time with a woman?"

She looked straight at him for a moment, all dark shining eyes and pale skin, and he registered one more relinquishing. He'd spent so much time attempting to acquaint himself with who his children really were, and just as it seemed he might get a handle on it, each girl began to withdraw certain parts of herself, parts they thought he wouldn't miss. But now, in this moment, the purloining was happening before his eyes. *No*, she was saying, *you will not know this about me.* Perhaps he'd encouraged her secrecy. Maybe he wasn't ready to form a picture in his mind of his Leah and another woman together. He thought back to what Noah had said to his mother this morning: *Sometimes I think you're scared of me.*

"It was fine for like almost a month. Everything was good, you know." She stretched a gob of melted mozzarella at the edge of her plate. "But then she just wants to define it, nail it all down, nail me down. And she starts texting me all the time, like constantly, middle of the night when we're not together, leaving gifts outside my door. So I decide I have to put a stop to what's starting to feel totally creepy— like, kids don't do this."

"But she's not a kid, is she?"

"She's like twenty-seven or something. She's writing her dissertation. Anyway, so we meet up one night to talk, and I try to explain to her that the timing is really bad for me. I told her what you'd told us about Mom. I said I just needed to do my schoolwork and get through the semester without having a nervous breakdown."

"Is that really how you felt?"

She shrugged. "She said I was afraid, afraid you'd reject me if I was in a relationship with a woman. And, the thing is, Dad, she's very smart. When she was done talking, she made me feel like I didn't know anything, like I couldn't even trust my own instincts, at all. That's what happens when I'm around her, I just get so . . . lost.

And so, I went back to her apartment again, even though like ninety percent of me felt like it was the wrong thing to do."

They left the plates on the table and moved to the couch, Leah tucking herself into one end, hugging a pillow to her chest. "Last week, each time I walked out of a class she was waiting for me. Saturday morning as my bus was pulling out of the station, I looked across the street, and there she was, sitting in her car. Susannah was the first person I told, really. Su-su-straight-Zannah, of all people."

Malcolm wrapped her in his arms, and she began to cry. He could feel the weight of her wet face on his chest. The sharp intake of her breath, the only sound in the room. For three days he'd stood over her as she'd slept in her childhood bed, silently pouring out his thoughts and feelings with a desperation that convinced him he'd been heard, his message received. But sitting with Cara and Noah today was proof that what you thought and felt mattered not one whit compared to what you said and did. Or what you didn't say and didn't do. "I'm not going to let anything happen to you," he told her now.

"Before . . . before you told us everything," she began slowly, her mouth pressed against his shirt, "I felt like I was disappointing Mom."

"Maybe this isn't really about what Mom would have thought. Maybe—"

The phone rang in the kitchen and the front hall.

"It's her! It's her! I know it!" Leah shouted.

Malcolm leapt off the couch.

"Don't, Daddy. I don't want to know!"

Malcolm ran toward the telephone table in the hall. The machine recorded a loud click followed by a droning dial tone.

"I think . . . I need to withdraw for the semester. I'll pay you back. I mean, I know the money. . . ."

He walked back to the couch where she was kneeling, squeezing the life out of a throw pillow. "Let's talk about how we're going to keep you safe." He'd counseled enough students who'd been harassed or stalked on campus to be certain, at least, of how to handle the practicalities: a no-contact statement, a safety plan, a stalking log. "First, you have to get switched out of her section."

"That would only make her angrier. Why can't I just withdraw?"

"Then I'm going to write a letter—"

"You can't do that. If you threaten her—"

"I'm going to write a note to her explaining that if she contacts you in any way, I will call the dean, and after that I will call her thesis adviser, and then the chairman of the Art History department."

"I think . . . I feel like . . . I'm going to throw up," Leah said, making no attempt to move.

Malcolm looked at her. She was pale. He reached out and stroked her hair, which had dried into drooping broad curls around her neck and shoulders. On her forehead were little pinpoints of acne he hadn't seen since ninth grade. "This girl sounds very ambitious. If she feels that her academic career, teaching fellowship, etc., is at all in jeopardy. . . . Have you saved all her notes, e-mails?"

"How's that going to help when she breaks into my room with a machete and carves me into cubes and stuffs me in a series of Cornell boxes?"

He'd been leaning against the back of the sofa, and now he lowered the great weight that was his body so that he was half-seated on top of the couch. "What would make you feel safe?"

Leah stretched her sweater over her knees and hugged herself. Merlin rolled in his sleep, and his tags clinked against the wood floor in the hall.

"Mom," she whispered from the couch, "that would make me feel safe. And for you not to have lied to us for fourteen years."

Malcolm turned from her to the window. The channel markers were glowing green and red. Reflected in the glass, the lights appeared to be bobbing in the middle of the living room. She was nineteen, and there was no way she could or even should understand what he was about to say.

"There's a tendency to look at what happens in our lives as a deviation from what was *supposed* to happen," he began. "As if life is scripted and unwanted events are an aberration. But what befalls us *is* our life." Malcolm stood up from the sofa and cracked the knuckles of his right hand.

"But in lying to us. . . . How do you know you didn't cause me to . . . make the choices I made because you withheld the truth? Maybe you even knew or sensed something about me, right? And you tried to shift the outcome by manipulating the truth."

In the midst of this conflict, what he wanted most was not resolution but narcotic slumber. "Don't you know how much I love you? Why would I *manipulate* you? Haven't I always encouraged you to be yourself?"

"How could we be ourselves if we didn't know the truth about our own family?"

The pressure in his head was stunning, as if a valve might give way and blow. "It wasn't your story to know. It had nothing to do with you." He vigorously rubbed his temples with his knuckles.

"That wasn't your decision to make."

"But being gay *is* your decision to make, and you're acting like it's my fault."

She looked at him, nodding as if this was just what she'd been waiting for. "You can't even hear yourself. You said that I acted as if it was your *fault* that I was gay. I don't see lesbianism as a flaw, but apparently you do."

Malcolm walked toward the window, staring out at the channel markers in the bay. Red, right, return. Leah had come home to have her fears about him validated, and she'd orchestrated this scene to bring that about. He pressed his nose against the cold glass and cupped his hands around his eyes, blocking out the light in the room behind him. Dealing with other people's pain all day was nothing compared to dealing with your own. When did this life ever get easier?

He forced himself to look out at the water until he could reconcile the girl on the couch with the daughter he loved.

"You've always been homophobic." Leah was perched on the arm of the couch now. "I just never put it all together until you told us about Mom."

He turned and walked to the dining-room table to begin clearing their plates, shiny with congealed cheese and sauce. "How come you never told me in high school? About your feelings for girls?"

"I must have known you wouldn't approve."

"And this is what disapproval looks like? It's fine to be confused. But don't confuse your disapproval with mine. Really, just like I said when we sat down to eat, there is nothing you could do or say that's going to change how I feel about you. That's the sad, disempowering fact of being my daughter."

17

D o you want to have kids?" Alex shouted at Noah. "I mean,
someday, do you want to be a parent?" She was competing
with the roar of the Maine Turnpike through the open sunroof
of her father's car. They were on their way back from an interview for
summer jobs. The arts camp in the Berkshires had been Alex's idea. If it
all panned out, she would be working in the kitchen and Noah would
be teaching voice and drama. Noah's original plan, that they get jobs
on a cruise ship, had fizzled. But the camp seemed like a good enough
alternative. The director was a bearded guy in Birkenstocks who lived
in a big chaotic Tudor in Weston, Massachusetts. How bad could it be?

The important thing was that they were sticking to their vow to get out of Smithport for the summer. That, and to spend a semester abroad before they graduated. The goals had been Noah's idea, as a way of bolstering his friend. Well, that wasn't entirely true. Getting away for the summer, even possibly transferring in a year—that had been Dowd's suggestion. "It's a big world, Noah." The kids they went to school with thought nothing of hopping on a plane for a long weekend. Everybody had been to Europe—multiple times. They skied out West, sailed in the Caribbean, gambled in Vegas. Neither he nor Alex had ever been away from home for more than a week. And even when they'd left for college, they'd traveled no farther than the high school bus had taken them every day. It was time to get out. Noah and Alex had started looking for apartments off campus for the fall.

"I want to have kids, definitely. And I don't want to wait until I'm too old, either." She continued the conversation by herself—half-hearted, he thought, in her attachment to the steering wheel.

The car's wind tunnel had sent her into another dimension from him. Why was she even talking about kids? "This summer might make you change your mind. What if we hate the little bastards?"

"No. You won't hate every one of them. That's the way it is with kids. You'll definitely like some."

"When are you going to tell your dad?" he asked.

"What?"

"That you won't be working for him."

"First, I'll tell him—you know, I'll come out to them, and then when I say that I won't be working for him this summer—I mean, that will slip right by compared with the other."

"Was that Dr. Evil's idea?" Noah asked. Alex had started seeing a counselor at Behavioral Health, who she seemed to make less and less fun of as time went by.

"No. I came up with that on my own." She glanced in the rearview mirror, something she didn't do nearly often enough.

"I think my mother will be thrilled that I'll be away. And making money." He looked in the passenger's-side mirror.

"Well, do you? Want kids?"

"With you? Now?"

She pinched him just above his knee.

"First I want to bust out. Having kids is the opposite of busting out. Come on, Al, we've got to go everywhere first, and do everything before that."

"But what if it never happens?" She was looking at him way too intently for safety's sake, and he sensed a sudden surge of highway anxiety. He could feel his body breaking free of the restraints of the seat belt, his whole freakishly ambivalent self being catapulted through the sunroof and across three lanes of heavy traffic.

"What if you die alone?" she said. "Childless and friendless."

"I'm more worried about dying this minute, the way you're driving."

"I'm serious," she said, craning her neck to look at the exit sign they'd just passed. "Shit, I think that was Scarborough. Didn't you want us to get off in Kennebunk?"

⟨∽⟩

Noah chose a table in the corner, with a view of the Kennebunk River. He'd seen the men sitting at the bar as they walked in, and he'd crossed the entire room without feeling watched or judged. He glanced back at them now. They might be staring at him, but he wasn't back there with them watching himself. He was, for once, inside his body, taking up all the room his not-so-sorry carcass allowed. This is what being alive felt like. You had plans, and the plans were weightier than the fears. You and your friend decided to apply for jobs at an artsy sleep-away camp. On the way back from the job interview, you didn't drive straight home, but decided on a whim, sort of, to take an overnight detour. You paid for the only slightly sketchy motel room with money you'd earned shoveling snow during the last freak April storm. Your life seemed almost as three-dimensional as other people's. And even if those guys were talking about you right now, the you

199

they were talking about wasn't really you, so you didn't need to be on the defensive.

"What is that?"

Alex placed two bowl-shaped glasses on the table.

"Margaritas." She walked back to the bar and returned with a plastic basket of chips and salsa. "I told you she wouldn't card me, and these are free." She lowered the tortilla chips to the table. "I love this place. You can wipe the salt off the rim if you want. I didn't know—"

"Tequila," he said, slightly annoyed. He didn't want to be drunk for what they'd begun referring to these past weeks as "the lab." If Alex was attracted to women, and he was, in spirit, a feminine presence, why couldn't she be attracted to him? He'd posed this hypothesis to her while they were shoveling the steps of the Baxter College Library, an outsized neoclassical structure with a ridiculous number of stairs. They'd begun at the top and worked their way down, starting in the center of each step and pushing the snow outward in the directions of the columns. The multi-leveled bases of the columns were impossible, and when they'd gotten through clearing the steps, Alex returned to the columns on his side and set about improving on his shovel work.

"What about attraction, sexual attraction?" She slid the shovel down along the rectangular base as if cutting into a cake pan.

"I'm working on that."

"I wasn't talking about yours for me." The metal shovel scraped the granite again and again.

"Oh." His face was already flushed with the exertion of hefting the wet spring snow. It couldn't redden any more. According to Dowd, this was one of his issues. He was so focused on himself, on what he deemed his flawed self, that he didn't allow or register feelings of attraction. At the mere flicker of desire, his self-consciousness kicked in. He could desire female attire, because it couldn't reject him and couldn't hurt him. But to want somebody instead of something would be to open himself to what seemed unbearable vulnerability. That openness was called living, Dowd said, and he needed to practice it, in some small way, every day. "What's the worst thing that could happen?" Noah thought this a particularly idiotic entreaty.

"It's not that I'm *not* attracted to you." She paused while some students trudged past.

He looked at her in dismay as she motioned for him to follow her to the steps leading down to the service entrance. "When the sun hits this, it'll be fine," he said.

"But I don't look at you and think, you know, *let's do it,*" she said. "Here, we have to start at the bottom and work up."

"You're shitting me." He looked at the drain at the bottom of the stairs and wondered if they could uncap it and just shove the snow in.

"Some people are attracted to everyone. I mean, not indiscriminately, but sex is just kind of, you know, top of mind. Maybe we're just not like that. I mean, maybe if we were, we already would have."

"Maybe if we put ourselves in that situation, where we saw each other that way. . . ."

"Why?" She stopped and watched him try to heave a shovelful over his shoulder and out of the cement bunker that was the service ramp.

"As an experiment. To see if my theory is right."

"What's your theory again?"

⁂

"Don't worry, I watched the pour. It's like almost all mix, very little liquor."

"You have it then. I'm getting a beer." He reached into his front pocket and pulled out a five.

"I'll get it for you." This was their pattern. She protected him from being noticed in places where notoriety was unwanted.

"No. I'll get it." He flashed his fake ID at her. "You want anything else to eat?" This was something he often did for her, when she was embarrassed to order more food.

"Nope."

While he stood at the bar waiting for his beer, he looked back at her. She had dressed up for the interview that afternoon, trading her usual black sweatshirt over black sweats for a navy tunic over jeans.

"That she-he belong to you?"

Noah slid a single across the bar for a tip.

"Leave it alone." The bartender, a woman with tightly curled salt-and-pepper hair, addressed the group of men who seemed to be in their assigned seats at the far end of the bar.

"She have one of those sex changes? Like Sonny Bono's kid?"

Noah wasn't sure how many men were sitting there. He didn't look up to see who was talking, who was guffawing, who, if any among the group, might be frowning. He kept his chin tucked, circled his beer bottle with his fist, and began to walk toward the table where Alex was looking out the window.

"Big enough to eat hay, that's for damn sure."

"Excuse me." Noah was just about equidistant from Alex and the men. He was in the middle of a room with very few people and a lot of wooden furniture, the only light a reflection of the setting sun on a tidal river and the yellow-green flicker of soundless sports on a big screen. He settled his gaze on a man wearing a cheap dress shirt, a car salesman among plumbers and sheetrockers.

"What's the attraction? We're just wondering—got a little wager going on the deal between you two."

Noah didn't move. He could feel the cold beer bottle in his hand.

"Stuart," the bartender's voice cut through the snorting and the coughing, "give it a rest, already."

"What, what? I'm just making conversation."

Noah sensed the heat of his flushed face. Always what was on the inside was on the outside for him. He turned and walked with his beer over to the table where Alex was watching.

She leaned across to him as he pulled out his chair. "Maybe we should leave."

There would be no salvaging this trip if they left now. He knew enough about sex to know that humiliation wasn't an aphrodisiac.

Only minutes before, he'd been congratulating himself on having transcended some old erroneous sense of self. He willed himself to look over at the men. The bartender was leaning across the bar and the salesman was standing, hitching up his pants.

"Shit," Alex said. She was rubbing her hands up and down her thighs, jostling the table. "Is he walking over here?"

Noah kept his gaze fixed on the men. The one with the Bruins cap was exclaiming now about something on the TV. Everyone but the salesman shifted his attention toward the television. As the man moved closer, Noah saw that he was younger than his thinning hair had indicated. Not more than thirty, already with a potbelly. He was walking so deliberately that Noah wondered if he was drunk. Noah stood from his chair and slid his right hand into his pants pocket. His mother had clipped a Chinese token to his keychain when he got his license. Several times a day he cursed the jagged edge it had developed, a little metal spur. He fingered the flaw now and wondered if it would work as a weapon.

"What is it you'd like to know?" Noah said with the man still a few tables away.

The man started laughing a slurry, derisive laugh. "You're standing there, like you're gonna fight me." He motioned with his long thin hands at his own chest. "Me, now, I'm a lover, not a fighter. You, on the other hand, are a . . . you are a. . . ." He stopped and exaggeratedly scratched his chin.

"Annoyed. I'm annoyed." Noah forced himself to take a sip of his beer. Act. That's what Dowd had told him. You're an actor: adopt a role, play a part, fashion yourself after the person you need to be in whatever the situation calls for. It's what this other guy was doing. He'd turned the empty bar into a stage for his star turn.

"Am I pissing you off?" The man made a pouty face and aped surprise as he continued to move closer to Noah and Alex.

"Yeah." Noah forced out the word.

"So sensitive."

"Jesus, Stu, come on," the bartender said from across the room.

"Yeah, Stu," Noah said, "you're annoying your friends too." The man was a body's length away from their table now.

The guy smiled, a weird Jack Nicholson kind of smile, and nodded slowly. "What's its name?" he said, taking one more step toward Alex and running his index finger down her arm, as if he were inspecting for dust.

Noah clenched the coin in his pocket and leaned in toward the man. "Leave her the fuck alone!" he howled. He screamed so loudly and so suddenly that even he was shaken by the violence of his voice exploding into the empty room.

Only Noah had seen the man's face when he screamed. His back was to his compatriots. Only Noah had seen him startle, had seen him suck in air, his features go soft and slack.

"Come on, Stu, the kid's like a head case or something," the guy in the Bruins cap said.

"Or something." He turned as soon as his friends gave him an excuse to let it go.

Noah leaned over the table and gulped down a sizable portion of his abandoned margarita. His legs were trembling inside his jeans; and between that quaking and Alex's obsessive rubbing of her palms on her thighs, their little table was rocking with anxiety.

"What's he doing now?" Alex moved one hand from her thigh and began to break chips in the basket.

"He's putting on his varsity jacket."

"He's leaving?"

"Seems to be." Noah had injured his throat, scratched it in his rage.

"It's like a half a mile walk back to the motel. What if he parks and waits outside?"

It was just getting dark. Noah turned and looked at the river behind him. "Nothing else is going to happen. It's over." Like everything else that had transpired in the past few days, saying it seemed to make it so. *Think it, say it, do it.* Dowd had tried to pawn off some maxim like that on him.

"How about the other ones? What are they doing?"

"Turn around and look," Noah said, reaching for one of the few intact chips in the basket. But she didn't. Instead, she lowered her shoulders a bit more and looked past him out toward the water. He reached under the table and placed his calmer hand on top of her frenetic one. "Can you go up and get us a couple of waters?"

"What? Now?" she asked.

"I'm thirsty."

"Fuck you, have a beer and a margarita."

"I'm thirsty for water," he said.

"Noah, I really just want to go. Home."

"Home, or to the motel?" He could hear the slight note of desperation in his question. Before she could answer, he said "We're going to the motel. That was our plan. Nothing's going to happen."

"What if he follows us and beats down the door? Can't you just see the links flying off that chain on the door?"

Of course he could. It was maybe the fourth thing he'd thought of after they'd checked in—how unsecure the room was. It was as if someone had paved a parking lot, set up a bunch of beds, and then—oh, yeah, as an afterthought—thrown up some shitty fiberboard walls to separate them from one another and the outdoors. You couldn't look at that place and not think three little pigs. "Get the water," he said.

"Why?"

"Because it will be good for you."

"I'm scared."

"No shit."

"She-he. What the fuck? Do you think I look like an it?"

"I think you're beautiful, especially with your hair like that. You could do something about those sneakers, but aside from that. . . . Get the water. Now."

"What's the incentive?"

"You mean, your motivation? I'm thirsty."

The pizza was between them on the bed. There were two slices left and about twenty minutes to go in *The Office*. Whenever Noah felt a wave of anxiety, he reminded himself that it was impossible for this situation to be more frightening than the one he'd endured earlier. What was the worst thing that could happen? He'd told Dowd about their proposed "lab experiment," shamefully aware as he paraded the prospect before his therapist that there was something untrue about it—either about what he was saying or about what he planned to do. He caught himself anticipating Dowd's approval for being active and social and, even if only for ten minutes, heterosexual. Oh, what a good boy am I. But it wasn't just Dowd's approval he was after, it was his own. And it was utterly suspect. He thought about it now as he looked at the orange grease on the wax paper under the last two slices. No matter what anyone said, the temptation to occasionally be counted among the majority was powerful. It wasn't just what other people thought, either. That divide existed within himself as well. Maybe he'd proposed having sex with Alex as his own personal hazing ritual? Everyone loved to talk about being true to yourself—as if it were the key to the universe. But what if it were simply the key to marginalization and isolation? You're alone, you'll always be alone, but, hey, at least you've been true to yourself.

"You've got to watch for overexposure, you know?" Alex lifted the remote and shut off the television. The only light was coming from the bathroom.

"Huh?"

"Steve Carell."

He nodded.

"What's the matter?"

Noah realized he'd had a piece of pizza crust taking up space in his mouth for a while. Somehow thinking and chewing had been mutually exclusive. He held up a finger and began working his jaw.

"You promised you wouldn't get weird. You swore to me."

"Not weird," he said, his mouth still partly full.

"We don't have to, you know. Just because—"

"We do. No more talking about it, either. That'll wreck it. That's like all we do."

"No, it's not." She turned to face him on the bed.

"I think we should take off our clothes." He reached for a napkin and closed the lid of the pizza box. *You've tried the rest, now try the best.* Jesus.

"See, right there. We shouldn't have to talk about taking off our clothes, you know?"

"Well, we do." He stood up and started to unzip his jeans.

"Is there a way to hook up your iPod to the back of the TV?"

He reached over and grabbed what he thought was a bra strap beneath her blouse.

"Hey." She turned and hit her hip against the dresser.

"Just keeping you focused."

"I think you should use two."

"Two what?" He pulled off one sock at a time and rolled them into a ball and tossed them in the direction of the rest of his clothes piled on the one aqua chair. He was only in his underwear now, red and blue striped, knit boxers that looked like an abbreviated version of an old-time bathing suit. He moved the pizza box to the floor and got under the covers.

"I really don't want to get pregnant . . . or anything else."

"You're not going to *get* anything." After they'd left the bar they'd decided not to drink anymore, and now Noah thought that had been a mistake. He was sure the whole endeavor was not supposed to be so conscious or conscientious. Wasn't it supposed to flow seamlessly, like a musical in which the singing numbers segue unnoticed from the dialogue?

He listened to Alex brushing her teeth in the bathroom and realized he'd better do the same. She opened the bathroom door and a crack of light wedged its way across the bottom of the bedspread. He waited until she had walked around her side before he got up to go brush his teeth. The carpet was cold, but the yellow tile in the bathroom was even colder. He wasn't really worried about performance.

He could always get an erection, and he wasn't going to come in five seconds like some hysterical teenager. No, he'd been working on that. He was pretty sure it was just a matter of mind control. What he was less sure of was the geography, that's where there were all kinds of possibilities for making mistakes. He knew she'd be comparing him to her only other experiences—with women, with people who had her same setup, knew all the trapdoors and secret handshakes. If he ended up sticking it somewhere as pleasing as her ear or her armpit, how long would it take for that memory to recede—a week, a year, a lifetime?

"Honnnney! I'm waiting!" Alex called in what he knew she thought was a convincing Bronx accent. He couldn't think of a comeback. He wasn't feeling very funny. Maybe that was good. He looked at himself in the mirror. Delicate, that's how he looked. But it wasn't how he'd acted, not earlier today, anyway.

"Oh, good, your hands aren't cold," she whispered when he slid in beside her and began some tentative exploring. He really didn't want her to talk, so he turned on his side and pressed his lips against hers. Her lips were plump, like the rest of her, and he tried to let his brush hers a few times, to see if lips could really feel other lips without the whole mouth being involved. He sensed that kissing was a kind of relief for her, something easily accomplished, something at the top of the list, and she set about doing it in a very systematic middle-school way, lots of unnecessary tongue. Big and soft as she was, Noah could feel a webbed tension in her shins, her back, even her facial muscles. He kneaded the tops of her arms, but he certainly did not want to get into a back-rub thing.

He'd been worried that she might just lie there impassively and make him do all the work, thereby highlighting his every misstep. What he hadn't counted on was her turning the whole thing into a kind of competition, a headlong rush to getting it over with. He ran his fingers down the front of her chest, up along her neck, around and then under each breast, lifting them one at a time, seeing what it felt like to hide his fingers, even part of a hand, under there. A marvel of engineering to have a balcony on your body.

She was growing increasingly intent on pulling him into her, but he resisted, moving himself a bit to the side, twisting the big hank of hair that dominated the pillow and tucking it under her head. Christ, hadn't she ever seen a sex scene? He ran his mouth across her closed lids and then her freckled nose and cheeks. His body was stretched alongside hers on the bed, his hands around her head and face. She had stopped trying to tug at his hips or pull down his underwear. He began to suck on her earlobe. Then he noticed she'd stopped moving altogether. She'd seized up. He continued to kiss her earlobe and only slowly removed his mouth, then his arms. He propped himself up on one elbow and looked down at her in the dark.

"It's just not for me," she said, using an expression he remembered his grandmother invoking when his mother would hold up a blouse while out shopping together.

"What part?"

"Doing this, with you. The pizza, the movie—even sleeping here—that's all great. But I'm your buddy, and I can't see myself in any other way when I'm with you. Just buddy."

He nodded and pulled the sheet and then the slippery bedspread up toward his chin. "I guess it was a stupid idea, my stupid idea."

"Yeah. Actually, it was a stupid idea, but you're very good at this, you know. I mean, I think you'll make someone a very good lover—"

"Yeah, right."

"Don't do that." She sat up abruptly, causing the headboard to slam against the wall. "Don't cut me off, and don't make my words sound false. That's not fair."

"The body doesn't lie."

"You're such an ass sometimes, you know that," she said. "This has nothing to do with you. God, you can't make everything be about you and your gender shit."

"Fuck you! Oh, no, wait, I can't."

"If you're sexy, sexual, all that stuff—which you are, for fuck's sake—why can't you see that—you only need to meet the right person.

And I'm not the right person. And we knew that before, and if you fucking sulk now, I swear to God—"

"Then why did you agree to this if *WE* knew that before?"

"I don't know."

Noah was thankful his underwear was still on. He turned his back to her and stared at the wallpaper no more than six inches from his nose, a beige Colonial girl carrying a beige candle again and again and again. He wished he were home, no, in the dorm, in his own bed, by himself.

"Noah, you were really awesome tonight, before, at that bar and just now. You have to believe me. You saved us back there. But this, this isn't—"

"I swear to God, if you say it wasn't meant to be—"

She grabbed his clenched fist. "It just wasn't meant to be."

18

The girls said they'd kayak out to the mooring, and now every once in a while as Malcolm moved about the boat adjusting the stays, he looked back toward his house, the orange kayak still visible in the yard. He'd only just taken the boat off the trailer that morning. Before heading home, Matt, Susannah's boyfriend, had helped him step the mast. The task, challenging for three men, was punishing for two.

Malcolm knew before the boy told him, knew even as they were straining to secure twenty-seven feet of metal, the sun heating up the pong of low tide around them. But the kid had waited, waited until the inlet had filled with water again, the sailboat brought around to the cove and clipped to the mooring, the two of them sweaty and motionless on the bobbing boat.

"I bought a ring," Matt said. He stepped down into the hull from the bow, and Malcolm thought momentarily about standing on one of the benches so as not to be towered over.

"A diamond. I'm planning on proposing, on Friday, the solstice. I thought—well, I wanted to tell you first." He leaned against the bulkhead, took a breath and looked Malcolm in the eye. "I wanted to ask, you know, for your blessing."

Malcolm embraced the boy and told him he knew how much Susannah loved him. "It's hard work, marriage."

"I know," Matt said.

Malcolm smiled at that. "Make her as happy as she's made me," Malcolm said.

"I can do that." Matt nodded, lowering his head so intently, he almost seemed to be bowing. "Oh, and by the way, Happy Father's Day."

⁊◌⁊

Malcolm crouched on the deck now, screwing down a cleat that had come loose over the winter. He'd found the card, in the shape of a putter, propped up this morning against a brand-new coffee maker, the coffee already brewing. Inside they'd written only "Love, Susannah and Leah."

"Every holiday has its elfin aspect," Noah had told him in their last session together. They were sitting in Malcolm's office in Watson's Mill, where Noah had come three times since the semester had ended.

"At Christmas there's Santa, Easter's got the Bunny, St. Patrick's Day—leprechauns. I just figured Father's Day required some test of faith too, you know? So if I left out a card and a wrapped gift for my father, like the way you hang stockings on the mantel or stick the bloody tooth under your pillow, maybe he'd be there in the morning." Noah had laughed, twisting the turquoise beads at his neck. Toward the end of the term, Noah's wardrobe had vacillated wildly between the genders, but in the last couple of weeks he seemed to have found some balance. Today he was wearing khaki cargo shorts and a black tank top.

"What was the gift?" Malcolm asked.

"A tie. I'd steal ties from my Uncle Billy, which was tough because he owned so few."

"How would you feel, then, after all that work and all that wishing, when no father was there in the morning?"

"Disappointed, I guess." Noah looked down at the ice-blue nail polish on his toes. "But not devastated."

∞

Malcolm heard the girls before he saw them, their laughter carried on the wind and the water. Matt had trusted him with his secret, dumb to the fact that a father's stricken look or watery eyes might be enough to give it all away. He was in no hurry now to be in the presence of his firstborn daughter with the full-on knowledge that she'd be leaving him.

Malcolm wanted Leah to take the tiller, but she deferred to her sister and instead leaned out over the bow and unhooked them from the mooring as Malcolm raised the mainsail. Once under way, Malcolm watched as Leah tied blue telltales to the mainstays, a ritual he'd started with the girls to mark the first sail of every summer.

"I need you up, both of you," Susannah shouted as they came into a gust and the boat heeled, spraying them with salt water.

"What, Dad, no *yeehaw*?" Leah said, her long bare legs braced against the centerboard housing, her hair whipping about her face.

"Lee," Susannah pulled the barrette from the back of her own head and passed it to Malcolm to pass to Leah.

"Nope, the skipper needs clean sightlines." He handed it back to Susannah, and she made a face. In the past couple of weeks, Malcolm had noticed that Susannah had become not so much her sister's keeper as her sister's emotional trainbearer.

"You want to sail, Dad?" Susannah asked.

"What, so you can give your sister the hair thing?"

"No, because it's Father's Day and I'm trying to be nice."

Last week, Susannah had told him that her decision to come home for the summer and waitress at the Bayberry Inn was solely to protect Leah. She thought Malcolm was pushing her too hard, too quickly. "Do you have any idea what she's been through?"

An arrangement had been worked out with the dean and Leah's professors. Lecture notes for the last two weeks of classes had been e-mailed to her. Art History was her only in-class final. The night before the exam, Malcolm drove her to Providence, and they rented a hotel room. In the morning, he walked her to the door of the classroom where the test was to be administered. Three hours later, he was waiting there to pick her up. Every few days, he worked the conversation around to her pressing charges against Casey. Susannah inserted herself at each mention of such action.

"Jesus, Zannah, take it easy." Leah looked up at the mast, which was looser in the footing than Malcolm would have liked.

"Think you'll rejoin the club team at school this fall?" Malcolm asked, bringing up one of the subjects Susannah had deemed off-limits.

"If I go back?" she asked tentatively.

"What do you mean?"

"She's thinking about transferring to Baxter," Susannah said.

"I can tell Dad this stuff myself."

Malcolm turned slightly from Susannah to Leah. "A little late to transfer now for September."

"I don't know what I'm going to do next semester." She stopped and looked over at her sister.

"What?" Malcolm asked.

"There's this gallery. I kind of got offered a job, in Boston."

"Fall off," Malcolm said, motioning to the tiller.

"You could let out the sail, too, you know." Susannah reached over for the mainsheet.

"When did all this happen?" Malcolm asked.

Leah looked up at her sister again and then at him. "Susannah's been e-mailing with Elizabeth Lang. And when I went to Boston over Memorial Day weekend, I met her."

Malcolm listened to the water drum steadily against the hull, watched the life vests slide inside the open cabin, felt the salt already dry and tight on his face.

"She's really nice, Dad. I mean, she'd have to be, right, if Mom. . . . She's got a son. Luke. He's ten. She's going to be opening a gallery in London this year."

"Does she have a partner?" Malcolm asked.

"I don't think so. Maybe she did, for a while. I'm not sure. She told me lots of stuff, though, about Mom." Leah loosened the windbreaker that had been tied around her waist and put it on, waiting for her head to emerge before she continued. "I mean, she told us that she really loved Mom, was in love with her; and that for a long time after, she couldn't even feel sad because she felt guilty."

Malcolm had never considered Elizabeth's grief. He was as ashamed of that particular failure as he was of his irritation at hearing about her single-parent status now, the competition moving once again to stranger ground.

"Elizabeth's been good about trying to explain you to us." Leah tucked her knees up into her windbreaker.

"That would be my job," Malcolm said.

"No, Dad." Susannah looked out at the water. "That would have been Mom's job, probably. And then, our job. You don't get to control that."

"She said I look like Mom, that I kind of reminded her of Mom."

"You're way taller," Susannah said.

"She asked about you. I mean she had a lot of questions about your life now and how you were doing. She asked me if I thought you'd be open to seeing her."

∞

In their last session together, Malcolm had asked Noah why he thought it'd become easier to dress the way he wanted in public.

"It hasn't. I just make myself do it, you know. Every morning I tell myself to sac up. When you think about it, if I'm so illuminated about gender, then I'd better stop acting like my own personal skinhead, you know?"

Noah had stood to leave, extending his hand to Malcolm before turning toward the door.

"Nice shoes," Malcolm had said, looking down at the canvas sandals that were tied with black ribbon at the ankle.

"You don't always get me." A rare smile broke across Noah's face. "But you never make me pick and choose the parts to show you."

⟨∞⟩

"You should come about." Malcolm shaded his eyes with his hands. "We're almost to Enoch's Rock."

"No, let's keep going," Leah said. "Peck's Island."

"We've got to make dinner." Susannah looked back in the direction from where they'd come.

"Fuck that," Leah said.

"Easy for you to say, I already bought everything and made the marinade."

Malcolm placed his palm on the tiller and motioned for Susannah to trade places with him. The girls went up to the bow. Trying to keep warm, they lay down in the path of the lowering sun, uninterested in where he might be taking them.

⟨∞⟩

Malcolm had run into Cara on the last day of the "Origins" exhibit at the Baxter College Museum. He'd been studying a wispy drawing by Edward Hopper when she approached. A very young Hopper had penned the scene on the back of his own report card:

a little boy with hands clasped behind him, standing at the edge of the ocean.

"All his themes, the solitary figure, the stillness, the sea. All right there at nine," she said. Malcolm hadn't seen her since her joint session with Noah two months before. She was wearing a white beach dress, the straps of a black bathing suit tied behind her neck, and she was standing close enough for him to smell her sunscreen.

"How've you been?" He stepped back from the sketch and turned toward her.

"This is my fourth time here," she said. "What really stuns me about this is the perspective."

Malcolm looked once more at the drawing. The picture was heartbreakingly sad. The soft back of the boy all that was known of him. The clasped hands strangely adult behind the round child body.

"He's the subject," Cara said, grazing Malcolm's arm as she pulled her glasses from her face. "But he's not doing the looking. There's a larger camera than his eye, something bigger than him. He was so young to have figured that out."

Malcolm could feel her staring at him now, and not the drawing. "How've you been?" she asked.

"Solitary," he said.

"Me too." She looked down at her tanned legs

"If this is your fourth time here, maybe you can show me what not to miss."

⚭

The waterfront was empty as they approached the shore in front of his grandparents' house, not even a dinghy or a rowboat tied up, as there always had been. The docks looked brand-new, made of some composite material that wouldn't splinter or weather. Three white Adirondack chairs had been arranged in a semicircle halfway up the hill, near the flagpole, where an American flag drooped at half-mast, either intentionally or, Malcolm hoped, simply because it had been carelessly hoisted. The house and the barns were too far away for him to discern much. But the boathouse had been reshingled, pale virgin shingles still smelling of the mill.

"Jesus, Dad, can you get any closer? Christ, what if they're home?" Susannah propped herself on one elbow.

Leah ducked beneath the jib. "Let's tie up and walk around."

Malcolm shook his head. There was very little wind within the cove, and he was worried they might get stuck there.

"Bougie bastards," Leah said.

"You ever wish you hadn't sold it?" Susannah turned from the bow and looked at him.

"I miss the boathouse," he said.

"I remember when you first brought us over here and told us it was where you'd lived as a boy. It was right after we'd moved from Belmont. You said sometimes houses could make you sad, too sad, because of the things that had happened there." Leah stepped down into the cockpit.

"You were trying to explain, again, why we had to move," Susannah said.

"You probably thought you were being reassuring." Leah looked up at him. "But, really, what I remember thinking was that sad things had happened to you in every house you'd lived in, and I wondered why you didn't realize that."

As they headed back home, Leah took the tiller and Susannah leaned against him in the cockpit. He wrapped his arm around her, and for the first time in months she didn't resist his touch. He doubted that this young man who wanted to marry her understood what she had lost. If she were fortunate, he would learn to love her the way she needed to be loved, which was all anyone could ever hope for.

"Do you ever wish we'd stayed in the house you lived in when you were little, the house you lived in with Mom?" he asked after a while.

Susannah lifted her head from his shoulder. "We'd have been good with you no matter where."

"Sometimes I think you confuse your childhood with ours," Leah said.

As the boat headed out beyond the protection of the cove, the wind picked up. Leah shouted for Malcolm and Susannah to hike out. "Way out," she yelled half screaming, half laughing, salt water spraying into her open mouth. Malcolm hooked his hands under the gunnel and leaned back beside Susannah, the two of them stretched over the rail, the sails clipping the water, his grandparents' boathouse receding in the distance as they headed home.

Acknowledgments

I am most indebted to The MacDowell Colony for the incomparable gift of the place and the artists I met there. My gratitude extends as well to the Collegeville Institute for Ecumenical and Cultural Research, and to Debra Leigh Scott and Hidden River Arts.

There have been many iterations of this novel and many readers I need to thank: Sue Glenn, Joan G. Kelley, Dr. Fay T. Greenwald, Bill Patrick, Baron Wormser, Bonnie Friedman, Hannah Basch-Gould, and Logan Garrison. A special thank you to David L. Gould, who read this first one long, hot, summer day without stopping and whose support made all the difference. And my never-ending gratitude to Dr. Jeff Von Kohorn, not only for reading, but for ceaselessly reminding me that what matters is to keep writing.

Thanks to Susan Weinberg for her sage publishing counsel. My deep gratitude to Nalini Jones for her generosity in introducing me to my agent, Sarah Burnes. Sarah invested tremendous amounts of time and energy in making this novel into what it could be. I am beyond grateful for her determination to get this story into the hands of readers. Finally, I would like to thank my editor at Pegasus Books, Iris Blasi, for her abiding enthusiasm, critical insight, and narrative acumen.